HELLSBANE

Paige Cuccaro

i.

HELLSBANE

PAIGE CUCCARO

Entangled Publishing, LLC
2614 South Timberline Road
Suite 109
Fort Collins, CO 80525
Visit our website at www.entangledpublishing.com.

Edited by Stacy Abrams
Cover design by Karen Phillips, Phillips Covers

Ebook ISBN   978-1-62061-235-4
Print ISBN   978-1-62061-233-0

Manufactured in the United States of America

First Edition December 2011

The author acknowledges the copyrighted or trademarked status and trademark owners of the following wordmarks mentioned in this work of fiction: Jeep Wrangler, Styrofoam, TGI Friday's, Coke, Primanti Brothers, Sherwani, Ripley's Believe it or Not, Rice Krispies, Converse, Doritos, Walmart, Mack Trucks, Golf, Plexiglas

To Eric, Bailey, Zoey, and Rowan for being who they are and for allowing me to do the same.

CHAPTER ONE

I couldn't breathe. My heart slammed in my chest like a caged animal and sweat chilled down my back. Muscles all over my body tensed, and instinct screamed through my mind, telling me to run. *Run. RUN!*

I shook my head, unclenched my fists, and forced a slow, steadying breath. The instinct wasn't mine. *It's not mine.* I had to focus. I blinked at the older woman's smiling, pudgy face across the table from me and centered myself in reality again.

"Yes. Of course, Mrs. Bellmen. I'm…I'm sorry. I'm just getting some…outside psychic interference and it's, um, clouding my concentration."

Either that or my *gift* was finally giving me that aneurysm I always figured it would. Some gift.

God, I hated when other people's emotions swamped over me like that. It was like drowning on dry land—drowning in someone else's emotions with no life raft in sight. After twenty-three years of living with my gift, at least I'd gotten a handle on it. Gained control.

Feeling other people's emotions—happy, sad, angry, horny…

whatever—as though they were my own could seriously suck. If someone was close enough when the mood struck them, their emotions kind of splashed onto me, overwhelmed me until I couldn't tell which were mine and which weren't. My high school years, surrounded by raging hormones—mine and everyone else's—were all kinds of torture. Thanks to the control I'd worked hard to establish, it hardly ever happened anymore. And luckily, when it did, I'd learned how to push away the false emotions and keep my head above the surface.

I'd also figured out a way to parlay my annoying talent into a marketable skill. A girl's gotta eat.

I straightened, pushing the confusing clamor of angry, panicked emotions from my brain. I'd worry about where, and who, the emotions came from later.

"That's all right, sweetheart," Mrs. Bellmen said, nervously smoothing the giant gypsy-style scarf that doubled as my tablecloth. "You were saying something about my Dicky. That he wasn't…"

Hope raised her brows, tugged at the corners of her age-thinned lips. I didn't need my gift to know the answer she wanted from her psychic.

I smiled. "He wasn't cheating before he died. Mr. Bellmen loved you very much. That's not to say he didn't notice his secretary, mind you, but you're the one he loved."

I was making it all up, of course. But I could feel by the rush of relief flooding through me—hers, not mine—that it's what she wanted to hear.

Mrs. Bellmen sighed, her smile going full wattage. She snagged her enormous purse from the floor and stood. "Forty-three years. They weren't all a walk in the park, but he was a good man. You're a wonder, Madame Hellsbane."

"Thank you, Mrs. Bellmen." I waited while she slung her purse over her shoulder, and then followed her through the pocket doors to the entry.

"You take cash, don't you, dear?" She crossed the hall into my dining room, which I'd converted into a waiting-room-slash-mystic-boutique.

"I love cash."

After picking up a smudge-stick bundle and some cleansing candles, Mrs. Bellmen settled her bill. With a happy wave, she left, and I closed the door behind her, my mood light and happy…or maybe it was her mood. Either way…

I liked using my oddity to help people. Made me feel like there was a reason I was the way I was, rather than just random bad luck.

"God, I'm hungry." I hadn't had anything to eat since breakfast, and it was coming around dinnertime already. Business was good, which meant I found little time for pesky things like eating. A nice problem to have.

With a smile stretching my cheeks, I pattered down the hall, the flat leather soles of my sandals slapping against the hardwood floor. The peanut butter and jelly sandwich I had pictured in my head beckoned me toward the kitchen.

I hooked my thumbs on the elastic waistband of my peasant skirt and shimmied it down over my hips as I walked. Couldn't wait to get out of the thing. I absolutely hate skirts, or dresses of any kind, but the look played great for customers. I had shorts on underneath, so it felt a little less commando. The maroon, bell-sleeved top was actually kind of comfy.

I made it as far as the half-bath under the steps before someone started pounding on my front door. After a second or two debate as to whether I should pretend I wasn't home or hike the skirt back on and answer the door, I tugged my skirt up, turned, and headed for the front entry.

It might be a client. I don't take walk-ins, but some of my regulars drop by when they've got something big brewing. They pay extra for the convenience so…that helps.

The knocks came again—harder—rattling the inlaid fan window in the top half of the door. I could see the crown of someone's head through the glass as I neared. I was still four steps away when the person pounded the door again. The sound was urgent. I hesitated.

"Hello?" I pushed up to my tiptoes, but at five feet, I'm just too short to see through the window. The instant I leaned my body against the door though, my gut sank.

It was like the sensation you get on a rollercoaster or when your car goes over a hill at just the right speed. I dropped flat on my feet again, head down, my hand on the knob for stability.

"Yeah. Hi. Uh, Emma Jane?" The voice was vaguely familiar, but I couldn't place it. And no one called me Emma Jane anymore. I licked my lips, concentrating on slow even breaths, letting the sensation in my stomach pass.

"Can I help you?" I asked.

"It's me, Tommy. Tommy Saint James. From high school."

The sound of his voice above made me look up. He must've pushed onto his toes. Now, I could see the top of his face to his nose. He was trying his hardest to peer down at me with the same pretty blue eyes I remembered.

No way. Of all the people I knew in high school, Tommy Saint James was the last person I'd expect to show up on my doorstep. I hadn't seen him since he'd blown off the last half of our senior year. I unlocked the door and opened it. "Tommy? Hi. What are you doing here?"

"Hey, Emma Jane." He glanced over his shoulder, then back to me. "Long time no see. I was…I was in the neighborhood. Thought I'd stop by, say hi."

He glanced over his shoulder again, fidgeting on his feet. He hadn't changed much in the eight years since I'd seen him. I took a second to do the mental math—I was twenty-three and, even though we'd been in the same grade, he was two years older than me in high school. How could he be twenty-five and look exactly the same? He still had curly light hair, the kind that goes sun-bleached blond in the summer and creamy butterscotch in the winter. It was early summer, so his hair was nearly the color of corn silk…and it looked damn good.

He kept it short. The curls used to relax a little when he let it grow, but not much. He was tall, six foot three or four with a sinewy, athletic build. Tommy had the kind of body that at a glance might be considered thin, but he was all muscle.

He'd been our star pitcher in high school, the typical jock who'd made all the girls melt with his perfect smile, smoky DJ voice, and pretty pale blue eyes—a blue made more intense by a dark circle around the irises. Everyone had loved him or wanted to be loved by him, which had made his sudden withdrawal during senior year all the more strange.

"I can't believe it's you. How'd you know I was living here?" I was pretty sure he hadn't even known my name in high school—I wasn't exactly Miss Popularity. I was a couple of years younger than the other kids in my grade because I tested well, and Mom agreed with the school to let me skip ahead. No one had asked me. I know she'd only wanted what was best for me. But she just hadn't understood the social ramifications I'd had to deal with because of it. A mom who didn't understand teenage angst? Go figure.

Tommy shifted his weight, and suddenly, he was the suave jock-star all over again. One hand against the doorjamb, the other curiously hidden behind his back, he smiled. My awkward high school years swamped over me—Tommy had always had a sort of embarrassing effect on me. I'd lost IQ points when he was near and my stomach had rolled and flopped like I'd hatched a flock of butterflies in my belly. Not that he'd ever noticed.

He raised a brow. "I remembered your gram lived here. Can I, uh, come in?"

The house was my gram's. She'd left it all to me two years ago when she died. Still didn't feel like any of it was mine. But it was free and fully furnished, so I called it home.

He'd used the *hey-there-sexy* voice I'd heard him employ a hundred times in high school. Not with me, of course, but the effect was just as potent, eight years later.

"Sure, come in." I stepped back, opening the door wider, and he slipped through. His hand dropped to his left ribs, clutching himself over a tear in his T-shirt. I hadn't even noticed his shirt was ripped until then.

I glanced behind him as I went to close the door, my thoughts ping-ponging with questions when something caught my eye. I stopped the door. It looked like a bag of garbage was smoldering in the street. Smoke twined up from the melted black plastic, but there was no flame, just bubbling black goo.

"What is that?" Before I could open the door wider, Tommy reached over my head and shoved it closed.

"Lock it," he said, then reached past me to throw the lock himself.

"Hey! Rude much?"

Something changed behind his pretty blue eyes. He switched

back to charming Tommy, flashed his smile. "Sorry. I just…didn't want to let out the air-conditioning."

"Right. I always lock the door to help seal in the cool air." Sure, he was cute, and he still made my body feel like a bowl of Jell-O in an earthquake, but I wasn't sixteen anymore. I'd learned a long time ago how to keep my head around cute guys. "What's going on, Tommy?"

He shrugged and took a few steps down the hall. "Nothing. Just stopped by to see what my old friend Emma Jane was up to."

He couldn't hide his other hand anymore, or he didn't bother to—he must've figured the sword he held was too big to go unnoticed. He held it at his side, hand fisted around the hilt, the point of the blade almost nicking my hardwood floor.

"It's just Emma now, and we were never really friends. What's with the sword?" Years of dirty limericks incorporating Emma Jane Hellsbane had long ago made me drop the middle name.

He glanced at me as he walked into the waiting room. "Sorry. I had a lot of issues in high school."

Who didn't?

He smiled, but it was just a smile, not the heart-melting one he'd always used. This was his natural smile, warm and easy. It lit his eyes and just barely dimpled his cheeks. He was all the more attractive for it.

"Forget it," I said. It was ancient history. "What about the sword?"

His free hand holding his side, Tommy grimaced as he eased himself onto one of my gram's old Victorian sofas, using his sword—hand on the hilt, point stabbing my floor—to steady himself. He settled back, sighing, and propped the long weapon against the front of the couch. Something thick and black edged the blade and covered the lower half to the tip. When he finally pulled his hand from his side, it was covered in blood and more of the black goo.

"Ohmygod, what happened?" I rushed over to him. I couldn't believe I'd been so caught up in the surprise of seeing him, in my own girly brain-freeze, that I hadn't even noticed the blood on his T-shirt and jeans.

"I, uh, had an accident." He laughed, clearly weak. "Mom always told me not to play with knives."

But when I knelt beside him and lifted his torn shirt, I doubted any sort of knife would do that kind of damage. "You look like you've been clawed."

"Yeah?" he said, tipping his head, trying to see the wound better. "Weird. Hey, you wouldn't happen to have any holy water lying around, would you?"

"What?"

"Right. Dumb question. Peroxide, then?"

I looked closer. Three long, jagged wounds tore through skin and muscle and wrapped from his belly to his back. Like something big had tried to grab him and he'd slipped away. There wasn't as much blood as I would have expected. It'd already begun to clot, but the black goo was bubbling along the edges and there were meaty parts bulging out.

"God, Tommy, these are deep. You need stitches. We have to get you to a hospital." I pushed to my feet—I had some peroxide in the kitchen. I'm not real graceful with knives myself, so I'd learned it was best to keep the stuff handy.

He let his shirt fall back over the wounds, hissing when the cloth brushed his body. "No hospital. It's not that bad. Trust me, I heal fast."

"Whatever. Just sit still." I ran to the kitchen, grabbed the brand new bottle of peroxide, a bowl, and some gauze, and came back as fast as I could.

"Those aren't cat scratches, Tommy," I said, snagging a pair of scissors from Gram's china cabinet. "You might need surgery. At the very least, you should be worried about infection. What's that black stuff?"

"You wouldn't believe me if I told you."

"Try me."

"It's…it's brimstone."

"Brimstone? Brimstone's black and gooey?" I dumped the medical supplies on the coffee table and sat beside him on the couch, reaching for the sword to move it out of the way.

Tommy lunged, moving so fast he'd grabbed it before I could blink. "Don't touch that."

"Okay, sheesh."

He laid the sword, still dripping goo, across the coffee table I'd personally refinished. But I gritted my teeth and kept my mouth shut. He was a guest and he was oozing guts, or something, so I could let it slide.

"It's not just brimstone," he said. "But that's what's making it bubble and burn."

"Lean over." I pushed up his shirt. "Lift your arm."

He did, and for a guilty half-second I let my gaze drift to the hard ridges of his abs. The man was still solid muscle. I shifted my attention to his wounds. "Whoa. You're healing."

"Told you."

"No, seriously. The skin is closing up." It still had a way to go, but whatever had been bulging out was back beneath the surface, and the edges of the wound were already shrinking closed, the very corners turning the wrinkled pink of new scars.

I wet the pad of gauze over the bowl with the peroxide then dabbed the wound. Blood turned the gauze pale red, but the black ooze wasn't affected. I could see the raw muscle and meat was still coated as the skin healed over it.

"How are you healing so fast?"

Tommy flicked his gaze to me. "It's a long story. But I didn't have anywhere else to go and I knew you were...*Shit*, I shouldn't have come."

Instinct chased a chill down my spine. "You knew I was what? What did this to you, Tommy?"

He shook his head and took the wet gauze from my hand, dabbing his wounds. "Nothing. Don't worry about it. I'll get out of here as soon as I can stand without feeling lightheaded."

He hissed again, gingerly touching the ends that were already healed. "Dammit. I have to get this crap out of me." He looked up. "You have a cross, a Bible...anything like that?"

"Are you kidding? You've obviously never met my family." Religion to my family was like medals to a soldier. It was something you worked at, suffered for, and used as an all-purpose excuse, reward, or threat, depending on the situation. Religion was like this great club they'd joined, and no one else would ever be as worthy as they were.

I left Tommy where he was and headed for the stairs. I'd kept Gram's bedroom suite. It was way better than anything I could afford. She'd always had a Bible in the bedside table, and since I don't clean where people can't see...

I would've gotten my own Bible for him if I had one. I don't. I'm waiting for the sequel to come out.

I'm not an atheist. Actually, I'm not sure what I believe. I just need more to base an opinion on than a bunch of old stories.

I was halfway up the stairs when my doorbell rang. I crouched to see through the window on the door. It was the mailman. If he had something for me to sign and I didn't answer, it could be days before he tried again. I turned and jogged back downstairs, glancing in at Tommy as I passed. He was struggling to stand.

"Who's that?" he asked, then seemed to decide it didn't matter. "Don't answer it."

I wrinkled my brow at him. "Bossy much? It's just the mailman."

"Emma Jane…"

I opened the door.

"Hi. I need you to sign, but I can't find my pen," the beefy mailman said.

"No problem. Come in; I've got one in my office." I left the door open and turned.

"Don't let him in, Emma Jane," Tommy said.

"Relax. He'll be gone in a second." I was halfway down the hall when Tommy yelled, "Emma Jane, look out!"

Tommy charged from the boutique room into the entryway behind me. He swung his arm, bringing his big sword to his shoulder.

Time slowed. Something behind me growled, like no animal I'd ever heard. I spun around and saw—I kid you not—a great, horned demon.

Spittle sprayed out with every breath from his big, red nostrils and from between his white, pointy teeth. The nice, normal-looking mailman had morphed into a red-skinned devil-thing. There were veins bulging up his thick neck and along his forehead, where his horns poked out from his head like a bull. And he was still wearing the tattered remains of his mailman's uniform, shoes shredded by cloven hoofs.

Tommy swung his sword, but he was weak and off-balance.

The big devil-thing dodged him easily, shoving an arm out to send Tommy flying past me and into the wall. Drywall cracked and Tommy slid to the floor, breathless. The beast charged toward him, and like a deer in headlights, I stood in his way.

Barreling at me, he pulled a dagger from his mail pouch and swung it. I hit the floor, reflexes taking over. When he lunged forward, swinging again, I rolled out of the way. He kept coming, stomping my grandmother's hardwood floors with his big, goatlike feet.

I snagged the little table under the mirror in the entryway and shoved it in his path. He stumbled into it, then swept it to the side, slamming it into the wall and knocking the mirror off its nail. The heavy frame hit hard, glass shattering across the floor. I turned and covered my face just as Tommy leapt over me.

Metal clashed against metal. I pushed up, scooting backward on my butt, away from the fight. Sword and dagger were swinging so fast, they were mostly a blur. Tommy lunged and swung, caught meat, then ducked back. The devil-thing parried, then attacked, his fat, three-fingered hands wielding the dagger as though he'd been born holding it.

He caught Tommy's sword arm, slicing flesh, spraying blood, and Tommy yelled, dropping his weapon. He was already injured. It was a wonder he was even standing.

He stumbled back, searching the floor for his sword, eyes wide, panicked.

Where is it? Frantic, I used the bottom of my skirt to grab a big shard of the mirror and jammed it hard into the devil-thing's ankle. He didn't even look down, his yellow gaze on Tommy, stalking toward him, dagger dripping with Tommy's blood.

He reached out, snagged his big hand around Tommy's neck,

and lifted him off his feet.

"Time to die, nephilim," he said in a gruff voice that still sounded creepily like the human mailman I'd welcomed inside.

Tommy fought in the devil's grip, kicking at his body, landing blow after blow. He pounded his fists against the thing's thick red arms, but he just laughed, raising his dagger, ready to plunge it deep into Tommy's gut.

Where was his damn sword? I scanned the entry, spotted the hilt sticking out from under the crumpled rug. Without thinking, I scrambled over on hands and knees, shoving slivers of mirror out of my path. But when I took a second to glance back at Tommy, a glass splinter jammed into the side of my palm. I plucked it out. Tommy was still hanging from the demon's stiff-arm, his face ashen, his lips turning blue. He jerked wildly, his gaze steady on me instead of the devil. He shook his head as best he could, his dark lips mouthing, "No. Don't touch it," in little more than a hoarse croak.

My fingers found the sword, gathered the handle into my palm. I lifted it in one easy motion. The weight of it felt good in my hand, the round grip settling perfectly into my palm. I raised it to my shoulder like a baseball bat just as a searing white heat burned along my inner wrist.

"Ah, shit!" I ignored the stinging pain and swung. In that brief instant, as the blade sailed toward him, the demon turned as though something about me was suddenly worth his notice. The blade sliced cleanly through his neck. His yellow eyes, with creepy, vertical, black-slit pupils, blinked at me.

"Nephilim," he said.

And then his head fell off.

The body collapsed, and Tommy crumpled to the floor with it. He sucked breath into his lungs, then scooted backward a moment before the whole of the demon who was once a mailman melted into a big pile of black, smoldering ooze.

I flicked my gaze to Tommy, who was clutching his neck, staring at the pile of gooey devil. I swallowed around the emotion clogging at the back of my throat. "That was *not* a mailman."

CHAPTER TWO

"I told you not to touch the sword," Tommy said, leaning his back against the wall. His fingers felt over the blotchy imprints the devil left around his neck as he winced through a hard swallow.

"Right. Sorry. Didn't mean to save your life."

"You got lucky. Only way to kill a demon is to take his head," he said. "If you'd done any less, you'd be the one lying there dead."

"Demon. Right. Makes sense," I said casually, as though I wasn't totally freaking out. "Mailmen are demons in disguise. Gives the phrase 'going postal' a whole new meaning."

"Not all mailmen. Just this one," he said.

The house reeked of rotting eggs, the smell wafting up from the pile of melting mailman ooze in the middle of my entryway. My stomach, already roiling with nerves, felt worse because of the smell. Whatever the devil-thing was, he'd been alive when I'd hacked off his head. He had looked human two minutes before that. And I'd killed him.

My hands shook so hard, I had to put the sword aside before I dropped it. I couldn't keep my knees from wobbling, so I slid down the wall and hit the floor with an ungraceful jolt.

"God, I can't believe I killed the mailman."

"Stop saying that. And he wasn't a mailman," Tommy said.

"Stop saying what?"

"God," he said. "Don't take His name in vain."

"Seriously?"

Tommy's eyes met mine, somber as death. "Yes."

"Wow. Um, okay. Sorry." Never had figured him for the Bible-thumping type.

His gaze shifted to my wrist and he sighed, leaning his head back so he could stare at the ceiling. "Dammit, Emma Jane, I told you not to touch the sword."

The burning sensation on the inside of my right wrist had dulled, but the mark left behind looked like I'd been branded with a hot iron.

"What the hell?" I rubbed my thumb over the raised, puckered flesh, careful not to press too hard. The pink blotchy scar was in the shape of an X with a straight line down the center, about two and a half inches long and maybe two inches wide.

And it was healing—fast.

"You're being marked," he said, without raising his head. "It's like a tattoo…from the inside out."

"What? Why? How?"

He shrugged, still not bothering to look at me. "How does God do anything? You're like me now, an illorum, a soldier. Welcome to my life." He didn't make it sound like a good thing.

"God? Ha. No. Wrong," I said, watching the wrinkled flesh heal and smooth. Slowly, an image darkened through my skin. The X sharpened into two keys and the line defined into a sword. "I never agreed to this."

"Free will, sweetheart. You picked up the sword and used it to smite a defamer of God."

"Smite? Seriously?"

"You chose." He opened his eyes now, straightened his head to look at me. "I told you not to touch the sword."

"*You* stop saying *that*. I didn't have a choice. That thing would've killed you."

"You did have a choice," he said. "You could've—*should have*—let me die."

"Right. My bad." I rubbed at the scar, now almost completely healed. "So, that sword did this? What is it, some kind of booby-trap thing? An antitheft device? That's a little over the top, don't you think?"

"Listen to me, Emma Jane. You're a nephilim, like me. You picked up the sword, your actions committed you. It's done. There's no going back."

"Whatever." I pushed to my feet and wiped at something tickling my cheek. The back of my hand came away with a smear of black ooze. "Ew, what is that?"

"Demon blood," he said. "Better go wash it off. It'll start to burn."

"Demon. Right." I laughed, but my heart wasn't in it. After all, what else could it be? The guy had turned into a friggin' devil-thing right in front of me. He'd tried to kill Tommy. And that pile of stinking goo on my floor didn't look like it'd ever been something human.

Shit. I'd killed him…whatever he was, human or not.

Was I a murderer or a hero? I wasn't sure, wouldn't think about it. I tiptoed around broken mirror shards and hurried to the bathroom at the end of the hall, trying hard not to totally wig out.

"So demon blood burns people?" I called back to Tommy. I snagged the washcloth from the set hanging behind the toilet and leaned against the sink for a closer look in the mirror.

Apparently, when I'd sliced off the devil-mailman's head, his gooey black blood had sprayed everywhere. There were gobs all over my blouse, in my hair, on my cheeks, and—grosser still—a hairsbreadth from the corner of my mouth.

With my short hair, the gunk wasn't too hard to get out. I had the same sunny-blonde hair as Tommy, but mine was poker-straight. I kept it in a short bob, off my neck but long enough I'd still look like a girl.

I've never been the girly-girl type, but I like guys, and I've never had much trouble attracting their attention—even the ones I'd rather not attract. My blue eyes helped, and more than enough men like petite, athletic types, so I do okay.

I left the white washcloth, with its little rose appliqué now stained gray, to soak in the sink and noticed the pale smear of blood on the side of my palm. I brushed my finger over the spot and found smooth, undamaged skin. The cut I'd gotten from the broken mirror was already healed. How was that possible? How was I healing so fast?

It was too much. I couldn't think about it, so I pushed the questions from my mind and padded back down the hall to Tommy. The putrid odor of sulfur was like a thick cloud in the air.

Tommy was exactly as I'd left him. I sidestepped around the splatters of steaming demon blood and jagged mirror shards and knelt beside him. "You okay? You didn't answer me."

His eyes fluttered open and he swallowed hard, grimacing. "Sorry. Yeah. What was the question?"

"I asked why demon blood burns people."

"It doesn't. Just nephilim. And it's not the blood that burns, it's the brimstone mixed in it. Brimstone is like acid to us." His head kind of wobbled like it was too heavy. He blinked, scanning the hallway. "Where's my sword?"

I walked around the heap of black ooze to where I'd left the sword and bent to grab it, then stopped. "Is this thing going to tattoo me again? I don't want a barcode on my forehead or something."

His brow wrinkled and he shook his head. "No. It's already done the damage."

I picked up the sword, surprised again at how right it felt to hold. "It looks way heavier than it is. What's it made of?"

Tommy held out his hand and took it from me as soon as I crossed the hall to him. He relaxed a little the instant the hilt was settled in his palm. "Metal forged in the fires of Heaven and the power of my will. Pure humans could use it and nothing happens."

"Oh, yeah?" I was going to laugh, but when I saw how serious he was, I swallowed it. "What're you saying? I'm not human?"

"Half. You're half human."

I knelt beside him. "And half what?"

"Angel. You're a nephilim. The child of a human and angel."

This time I did laugh. Loudly. I couldn't help it—it was like something out of a sci-fi movie. "Listen, I love my parents, but angels they ain't. Plus, my dad died two years ago. As far as I know, angels don't die."

"He wasn't your father," Tommy said, like he knew it for a fact.

"Yes, he was," I said, but a prickle of doubt itched up my spine. I'd always been different. My gift was something I'd instinctively hidden from everyone because I knew it wasn't normal. But I was human, wasn't I?

"Your father was an angel. He seduced your mother and fell

from Grace. Just like mine," Tommy said. "He's one of the Fallen. An affront to God."

"Okay, there you go. Besides the whole sleeping with fallen angels thing, my mom wouldn't cheat on my dad." The certainty eased the tension knotting across my shoulders. "In fact, it's because of the sanctity of wedding vows that I'm sure she wouldn't go back on them. My whole family's crazy religious. She just…wouldn't."

"She didn't have a choice. They're angels, Emma Jane. They can take what they want." He shifted against the doorjamb, pushing up, trying to sit straighter, though judging by the pain twisting his face, it didn't seem worth the effort.

"Rape? You're saying an angel raped my mother?"

"In a way." He leaned forward and raised his sword behind his head, point down, aiming for the sheath I could see peeking from under his shirt at the base of his neck. But just before Tommy slid it into place, the blade vanished, disintegrating into a million sparkling particles that spread out from the center and faded, leaving only the hilt to nestle into place. The handle stuck up behind his head, and he leaned back against it as though it were a kind of comfort.

"No way. My mom would've told me. Someone in the family would've hinted, would've let it slip." My family sucked at keeping secrets. Somebody would've gossiped.

"Not if no one knew, and she didn't remember it happening."

"Right. 'Cause rape is one of those things that slip the mind, like where you left your car keys or losing the TV remote."

"The Fallen wipes the woman's memory," he said. "They're pretty good at doing whatever it takes to avoid punishment. The woman never remembers that it happened."

"Until her kid picks up a sword."

"Right."

It sounded crazy, but something about it struck a chord deep inside me. It was nuts to believe any of it, but denying it was almost as hard.

The scar on my wrist itched the way newly healed wounds do sometimes. I turned my hand to look. The two keys crossed over the long sword were so clear it was like they'd been drawn with a pen. It was real, if nothing else. That mark, the memory of it burning into my skin, was real.

"If I wasn't half angel, a nephilim thing like you said, would the sword have burned me like this?"

"No," he said. "To a full human, it's just a sword."

I flexed my hand, watching the veins and tendons play under the scarred flesh. "So when you told me not to touch the sword, you already knew I was like you?"

"I've known you were nephilim since high school."

"High school? I wasn't even on your radar back then." *Was I?* Hope fluttered through my chest, and for a second, I was that insecure sixteen-year-old again.

"You were, but not in a way I wanted anyone else to know about. I could sense you. Wasn't sure what it was at first, but after I walked in on Coach Clark killing a demon in the showers during a ball game, I found out everything pretty fast."

"Coach Clark? He died of a heart attack."

Tommy closed his eyes, tried to shake his head, though it didn't move much. "A demon ripped his heart out of his chest. I picked up his sword to help him, and the next thing I know, I'm an illorum, too."

"Damn sword."

"Right?" He tried to smile, but it faded fast. "An angel, most likely a seraphim, cleaned everything up afterward. Made it look like a regular heart attack. Can't have the masses finding out how deadly their kind can really be."

"Seraphim?"

"Yeah. They're angels, but they don't talk much." He hissed out a breath, grimacing, then relaxed. "Actually, they don't communicate with us at all. You'll see. They just stand around, watching. Too pure to dirty themselves by conversing with us illorum."

"Wait, illorum? I thought we were nephilim."

"A nephilim is the child of an angel and a human. An illorum is a nephilim who's been marked to hunt the Fallen. Most nephilim go their whole lives never knowing what they are, never being marked."

"Lucky them," I said.

"Yeah. It'll make you wonder what your life could've been like if not for one stupid impulse to pick up a sword." He gave a half smile that didn't have the oomph to reach his eyes.

"So Coach Clark was an illorum?"

"Yeah. It was totally messed up, seeing him fight that pizza delivery guy," Tommy said, his gaze drifting as though remembering the scene.

"The pizza guy wasn't a demon?" It sounded weird to say.

Tommy's gaze flicked to me, his eyes a little too wide. "No. I mean, yeah. He was a demon. They don't always shift into their natural form. They're stronger when they do, but lucky for us, they're cocky, too."

"So you've been doing this, hunting demons, since high school?"

"Demons and the fallen angels who called them up to do their bidding." He exhaled, as though suddenly feeling the weight of the past eight years. "I tried to forget. Tried to pretend it didn't happen. But they wouldn't let me. They kept hounding me, bugging me to fight."

"Demons?"

"No. Angels," he said. "The ones who will talk to us…incessantly. They're called magisters. They wanted me to train, to pick up the fight where Coach Clark left off. I didn't want to. I didn't know what it meant. So I ran. It was six years before I saw my parents again. They'd thought I was dead. Wanted me to move back home, but I couldn't. I couldn't expose them to the kind of life I had."

"They don't know?"

He shook his head. "They'd never believe me if I tried to explain. They're safer this way."

"Must be nice." He couldn't have given me the same protection?

Tommy looked away. "If there'd been anywhere else safe I could've gone today, I swear…"

He looked at me, and I could see in his eyes he meant it. He hated what he'd gotten me mixed up in. Even more troubling, I still wasn't sure exactly what that was.

"What do they want, the demons? Why are they trying to kill you?"

"Us." He winced, hugging his arm around his belly. "They'll be after you now, too. And they want us dead. They want to kill us before we kill them and send their fallen masters to the abyss."

I laughed. Not because I thought anything was particularly funny, but because my brain had finally reached its capacity to accept the unacceptable and no other reaction occurred to me. "You know how insane this all sounds, right? This can't be for real. It can't be. I mean, I don't even believe in this God and angel junk."

"Yeah?" He sucked in a sharp breath and used the doorjamb to leverage himself up to his feet. He exhaled, holding his side. After a second or two, he straightened. "Well, you're about to become a believer, real quick."

"You can't make me." Geez, I sounded like an eight-year-old.

"That's what I thought. And then the demons came, and came, and came. And Eli kept dogging me, saying I had to train." He stepped around me on his way to the door, limping, moving slower than he had when he'd come in. "The demons can find you anywhere, Emma Jane. They feel you the way you and I can feel each other when we first come together. You know, the way your stomach rolls?"

"The roller-coaster thing? You feel that too?"

He smiled his star-jock smile. "Yeah. I feel it, too. That's how I knew you were nephilim in high school. I felt it. Felt it around Coach Clark, too. 'Course, I didn't know what it was until Eli explained it. Before that it was kind of…confusing."

"That explains a lot," I said. "Who's Eli?"

He turned and opened the door. "Eli will keep you alive. Unfortunately, if I don't get to some holy water soon, I won't survive to introduce you."

Tommy took a step and his legs gave out. I lunged to catch him, but I was too late. His body sprawled across the threshold, his legs on one side, his upper body on the other. I was at his side just as he pushed up to sit. I caught a glimpse of his wounds.

"Jesus, Tommy." I shoved his torn T-shirt out of the way so I could get a better look.

"Emma Jane. It's not just a rule, it's a commandment," he said, even as he tried to wrestle his shirt out of my grip.

I couldn't stop staring. The claw marks had healed…sort of. The edges of the wounds had closed, but the flesh was bulged and misshapen, like he'd somehow trapped a line of cauliflower underneath his skin. And a fine line of black goo oozed at the seal.

"Why's it like that?"

Tommy finally gave a hard yank to his shirt and got it free of my grip. He shoved it down, covering himself. "Brimstone. It's boiling my insides. Holy water will neutralize it. Holy objects slow it down, but—"

"Wait here." I ran up to my room. The rosary was right where I remembered seeing it in the drawer of the bedside table. I brought it down to Tommy and hung it around his neck. Pain eased from his expression almost instantly—if only a little.

"Thanks," he said. "It helps, but I still need holy water."

"I think I've got some mineral water in the fridge. Do they even sell holy water somewhere?" I was seriously drawing a blank.

He leaned his back against the open front door. His throat worked hard to swallow, and he finally managed to say, "I have to get to a church, Emma Jane. A church, holy ground, priests, get it?"

"Oh. Right."

Duh.

CHAPTER THREE

There was a church down the street from my house, but that one wasn't good enough for Tommy. Apparently, the holy water was holier at St. Anthony's Chapel, all the way on the other side of Pittsburgh, in Troy Hill. So I loaded him into my Jeep and we took off.

St. Anthony's is a nice little church, with Gothic, old-world-style architecture. I'd heard about the ton of religious relics housed in the tiny chapel. I'd also heard most of them were bone fragments from saints. Kind of creepy, but a part of me was always curious to see them. Careful what you wish for.

On the way, Tommy mumbled something about the power of those bones being concentrated in one place, and how it made their holy water potent. Whatever worked. He wasn't looking too good.

I turned off the engine and ducked a little so I could see the top of the church turrets through the passenger window. It was smaller than I'd thought it would be. My gaze dropped to Tommy, sleeping in his seat. He'd passed out twice on the drive over, though potholes jolted him back to consciousness a few times. I tried to avoid them, but Pennsylvania potholes don't just lie in wait, they attack.

I got out and came around to the passenger's side of my Jeep, opening the door enough to stick my hand in. I braced Tommy by the shoulder while I opened the door the rest of the way. The movement revived him enough that he helped keep himself upright as he turned in the bucket seat, swung his feet around, and slipped out.

His legs buckled the second they were asked to hold his weight. I lunged fast enough to get my arms under his, and he grabbed for the Jeep. Together, we kept him from going to his knees. He didn't argue when I tugged his arm over my shoulder and slipped my other hand around his back. He needed the help. It was why he'd come to me.

We hobbled across the parking lot like losers in a three-legged race. It was a warm day, even for July in Pennsylvania, but as we walked, the air seemed to cool. Apple trees and lilac blossoms scented the breeze.

The smell reminded me of lazy summer days at Gram's house as a kid, playing with my sister and our cousins. The same secure comfort washed over me, like coming home.

I stopped and looked to the chapel at the end of the parking lot. "You sure it's cool that we go in? I mean, we're the result of a pretty hefty no-no. Right? I don't want to be struck by lightning or something."

"You've never been to church?"

"Well, yeah. Of course, but…"

"You were born nephilim, Emma Jane. It's what you are," he said. "The only thing that's changed is now the other side knows it. Besides, you think God needs a church to take you out?"

"Right." We started walking again.

St. Anthony's was like the Little Engine That Could, a tiny chapel that strived to be so much more than a one-room church. I could almost sense the power some people might expect inside the Vatican itself thrumming within its walls.

There was no real vestibule, so when we walked through the doors we stepped into the chapel. Stunning stained-glass windows ringed the top of the wall beneath the cathedral ceiling, illuminating the small chapel with a hazy, unreal color. Each window depicted a different Apostle, plus three more for Mary, Joseph, and St. Anthony himself.

Beneath the windows, tucked into the side walls, were life-size wooden figures depicting the Stations of the Cross. Each one was housed in its own gilded nook, framed with Roman columns and scrolling filigree. Banks of prayer candles glowed midway in the chapel, but it was what lay beyond that drew my attention.

A shaft of soft, white light, like an otherworldly spotlight, beamed through the high cupola at the far end of the church. An ethereal haze drifted over the altar and the ornate, golden reliquaries behind it.

I knew from the articles I'd read that some of the holy artifacts those reliquaries housed supposedly included slivers of the crucifixion cross, small pieces of the table from the Last Supper, and thorns from the actual crown of thorns.

But the moment my gaze settled on the gilded cases, a breath-stealing wall of energy slammed into me. I wasn't sure if it was an innate power those objects possessed or some other unseen force within this church, but the wave of heat that rolled over my body staggered me. I clutched at Tommy, leveraging myself against him to keep us both on our feet.

My skin tingled in the wake of the power burst. "Holy crap.

What was that?"

I'd no sooner caught my breath from the last slam than another wave hit. This time, I managed to keep my footing.

"Faith. Belief in the relics," Tommy said. "Now you understand why I wanted to come here?"

I nodded, unable to form words. The power radiating through the church made the air thick, tightened my chest. It was hard to breathe, hard to think. It was like nothing I'd ever felt.

"Over there," Tommy said, tipping his chin toward the brass bowl on the wall by the door. "Holy water."

We stumbled up to it, and Tommy reached for the ornately carved wooden chair next to the bowl. I helped lower him, found him a position that wouldn't let him crumble onto the floor. The table behind the last pew held a fan of promotional flyers, a few collection plates, and a tray of plastic cups with a pitcher of water.

I snagged a cup and went to the bowl. Despite my flimsy belief, dipping a plastic cup into a holy font felt wrong. Tommy's hiss of pain pushed me through the hesitation.

"Lift your shirt," I said, ready to pour the sanctified water over the wound.

Tommy shook his head, reaching for the cup. "It's inside me. The wound's already healed." He chugged the water, then asked for more. He'd barely emptied the second cup before his hand dropped to his lap, exhausted. Tommy leaned his head back, his eyes fluttering closed.

Was it working? Who knew? It was all I could do to stand there, waiting to find out. The power washing over and around me itched and tingled along my skin, like my flesh was trying to crawl off my bones. I held my breath to withstand the sensation, gulping air in before the next wave hit. It was like standing chest-deep in an ocean with the water rolling over my head, keeping me down. I could never quite fill my lungs.

My gaze drifted back to the enormous reliquaries at the far end of the chapel. Was this maddening sensation really coming from them? It was crazy. How could any of this be real?

I tensed just before another wave hit. I sucked in a breath, held it until the energy wave passed. I couldn't stand it. I had to get out.

"Relax," Tommy said, and I flicked my gaze to him, realizing he'd been watching me. "It's worse if you fight it."

"I'm not fighting anything. I'm just standing here." I crossed my arms over my belly, held my breath an instant before another invisible wave slammed into me.

"It's smothering because you're fighting it. You don't have to." He pushed straight up in his chair, obviously feeling better. "Nephilim are more sensitive to the feel of faith than most humans. Instead of making it push around you, relax and let the power flow through you."

"It makes my skin crawl. Don't really want that going through me," I said. My skin itched and squirmed like millions of tiny bugs were gnawing at my flesh. I rubbed my arms, trying to ease the sensation. It didn't help.

"Faith is like a house in a tornado. There's air all around, inside and out, but if you keep the windows up, pressure builds and the place will blow. Open the windows and nature finds a balance."

"Or it rips the friggin' roof off." I said it harsher than I'd meant to, but I couldn't help it. I wanted to crawl out of my skin.

"Trust me, Emma Jane," he said. "Relax. Let down your guard."

"I can't." My feet were already backing me toward the door. I rubbed my arms, my neck, everywhere my skin tingled. "It's too much. I can't breathe. I have to go."

"Emma Jane, wait." He reached out to me, but stopped short of getting to his feet. He was still weak, still unwilling to trust his legs would hold. "You have to talk to Eli. You don't know what you're walking into. I mean it; I can't let you be alone. Not yet. I'm sorry, but you have to wait until he comes."

"You're meeting him here? What is he, a priest or something?" *Crap.* Made sense. But the last thing I needed was to talk to someone even more fanatical than Tommy. I didn't remember him being such a religious freak in high school. "No. I can't. I'm done. Sorry. Your friend's coming; you'll be fine. But I...I have to go."

I turned and practically ran out the thick double doors, taking the front steps two at a time. The second my feet hit the blacktop, I could breathe again. I doubled over, hands to my knees, sucking in breaths.

It took me a few minutes, but my skin stopped trying to run away without me, and I stopped thinking about breathing and just did it. I'd be okay.

After a quick glance back at the church, I walked across the long parking lot toward my Jeep. Worry for Tommy tugged through my belly. I hated leaving him hurt and alone, but that priest guy, Eli, would take care of him. That's what they do, right?

Besides, downing those shots of holy water seemed to have perked him up.

I scanned the parking lot and the buildings surrounding it. There were at least two more churches and a smaller building in the same gothic style as Saint Anthony's Chapel. The smaller building had a tarnished brass sign next to the door that read *Saint Anthony's Rectory* and I wondered if the priest Tommy was waiting for was inside. There were a few houses surrounding the parking lot as well, including one that had been remodeled and, judging by the canvas banner hanging on the front porch banister, now served as a kind of museum and gift shop for the quasi-famous chapel. But my attention ultimately focused on the woman getting into a blue SUV parked across the row from my Jeep. We were the only two in the lot.

Just as I reached the back of my car, she came around the end of hers, pushing an empty stroller. I watched her open her tailgate, then struggle to fold the cumbersome stroller.

I'd almost made it to the driver's side of my Jeep when I heard her call.

"Excuse me," she said. "Miss. Could you help me? Please?"

I looked. Was she really talking to me? What did I know about folding those things? "I'm sorry?"

She was pretty, thin, a few inches taller than I was, with long blonde hair and a pink headband to match the cardigan tied over her shoulders. Her white, buttoned blouse was practically perfect, tucked into her khaki culottes. The woman was wearing loafers with actual pennies in them.

She flashed a perfect, white smile. "My husband usually helps me with this. I can never figure it out. Do you mind?"

I smiled politely and crossed the parking lot to her. "Okay. I mean, I can try. Not sure how much help I'll be. I've never even pushed one of these things."

She waved the comment away. "You're probably better than I am. I can't even get the parts back together on our espresso machine without looking at the manual."

I laughed. "You have the manual for this? We might need it."

"No. Unfortunately."

Reflex made me glance into the SUV. I saw the back of the baby carrier peeking above the bench seat. I assumed her kid was in there, but the back was so high, I couldn't see a head. Judging by the weird odor drifting from the car, I figured Junior had made a nice little thank-you gift for Mom in his pants. *Ah, kids.*

I stood, leaning over the stroller to search the other side for a lever, or hinges, or a big honkin' sign that read, "Pull here, nimrod."

"How old?" I asked.

That's what you ask people with babies, right? Standard questions, age, name, and—if they're wearing yellow—sex.

"What?" she said.

I looked at her. "The baby. How old is he?"

"Oh." She seemed thrown for a minute, and then recovered. "Eight weeks."

Well, that didn't track. My sister had three rug rats, and she'd have a hissy if anyone tried to latch them into a forward-facing car seat before they were six months.

Instinct itched across my shoulders. I opened my psychic gift to the seemingly perfect mom and nearly choked on a nauseating wave of hate. It burned through me, tensing every muscle, making my heart race and my teeth clench. Holy crap, the woman wanted me ten feet under. I slammed a mental door in my head. And then that weird smell hit me again, stronger this time, like whatever was making it had suddenly stepped closer.

"So my deliverer might live, you must die," she said in a voice that belonged to a three-pack-a-day smoker instead of an all-American soccer mom.

I did one of those slow-motion turns over my shoulder. Like in a horror movie when the heroine knows the monster is right behind her, but doesn't want to look.

Yeah. The monster was right behind me…sort of. Mom, turned psycho bitch, was close enough that her rotten egg breath left my neck hot and sticky wet.

"You're not really a soccer mom, are you?"

She still looked like she should be on her way to a playdate, except she wasn't smiling anymore. Her pretty face was red with rage—lips curled back, snarling—her putrid breaths coming in quick pants.

I leaned away, but not fast enough. A sharp pain stabbed through my gut. I stumbled back, my hand going to the spot. My blouse was wet to the touch. Something hot and gooey trickled over my fingers and I glanced at my hand. My brain had trouble reconciling what I knew had happened and the speed at which she'd done it.

"You stabbed me." I looked back at her, then to her hand and the bloody dagger she held.

That was my blood. *My blood!*

"Damn you to the abyss, nephilim," she said in a raw hiss. She lunged at me, thrusting the dagger at my chest. It was all I could do to backpedal beyond her reach, falling on my butt two steps past just-far-enough. I rolled before she could re-center her balance and come at me again.

My skirt was ruined. Demon blood, my blood, and now scraps of asphalt will do that to cotton. The problem wasn't the stains; it was all that fabric twisting around my legs and catching under my feet. *I hate dresses, I hate dresses, I hate dresses.*

I managed to get to my feet and scurried around the next closest car—a red something. I'd lost one of my sandals and kicked the other off.

"What's wrong with you, lady?"

"You threaten my deliverer." She tucked some of her pretty blonde hair behind her ear. Very dainty—and so bizarrely normal. We played a slow game of Ring Around the Car for a few seconds while I caught my breath. My hand held my side as much to stem the pain as to slow the blood loss.

My heart pounded against my rib cage, each beat jarring torn flesh, reminding me of the hole that shouldn't be there. My gut was bleeding like I had tons to spare. I didn't. The lightheaded spin to my vision told me that.

I leaned against the car for a minute, steadying myself. "I didn't threaten anyone, lady. You've got the wrong person."

"You're nephilim. You live. That's threat enough," she said in that creepy, ghoulish voice. The next instant, she lunged at me, coming across the hood of the car, snarling, with tiny sprays of spittle flying from the corners of her mouth.

I threw myself backward, and her knife jammed into the shiny red hood, making a clean hole. She yanked it out, metal screeching against metal, then bolted over the car to the other side in a blur. I turned and ran, but she was too fast. Her blade sliced down my back.

The pain jolted through my brain, tightening muscles, stealing my breath. But I kept running. I had to get away, find help.

Her penny loafers echoed the slaps of my bare feet as we ran—so surreal. Her fingers scratched my shoulder once, twice, grasping for a good hold. My skin tore right along with my blouse, her fingernails like claws. She fisted my blouse and the sudden yank staggered me, slowing me down so I had to run sideways. But I kept running.

Another slice with the knife, this time across the back of my neck and down my shoulder blade, ignited a searing jolt of pain. The swing cost her. She lost her grip on my blouse, and I darted around the end of a pickup truck. The tailgate was open, and on the second turn, I cut it close enough that the rusted metal snagged my blouse at the waist, tore the fabric, scraped my skin. Soccer Mom wasn't so lucky.

The sharp corner got her across the gut, folding her in half. It stopped her cold, at least for a few seconds. She grunted from the impact and then gave a very human-sounding howl of pain. I almost glanced back, but resisted the urge. This was my chance…slim as it was.

I kept going, heading for the church at the other end of the lot, opposite St. Anthony's. Each stride punched a yelp from my throat, muscles stretching and pinching, tearing skin, ripping meat. I kept running. I had to.

I was still fifteen feet from the front door when a man, dressed all in black except for a tiny square of white at his collar, came around the side of the building.

"What's going on out here?"

"Thank God." I ran for him.

Without an ounce of pride, I threw myself into the priest's arms. The impact nearly sent us both to the ground. He huffed, shuffled back two steps, but kept us both on our feet.

My arms around his neck, I hugged my ear against his chest. He was at least a foot taller than me, and strong. He'd protect me. He had to. Right?

"She's trying to kill me. She's trying to kill me," I mumbled into the lapel of his suit jacket.

"Yes, dear," he said, and the too-calm sound of his voice turned my spine to ice. "Our deliverer commands it."

My side pinched suddenly, and then burned. I straightened and looked down to see the priest's hand clutching the hilt of a knife, the blade buried deep inside me.

Shit. I shoved him hard—harder than I knew I could. He fell back a few steps, taking the knife with him. I hadn't really felt it go in, but I sure as hell felt every inch of that scary-long blade slide back out. I'd never forget the gross, wet sucking sound it made.

I was suddenly on my knees, though I didn't remember falling. There was a hissing sound, like wind escaping, and I couldn't catch a good breath.

My gaze flicked to the priest who'd stabbed me, his black hair, his dark brown eyes, his pretty pink lips. He looked like such a nice man…except for the blood splattered over his hand and the enormous, red, goo-covered knife he held.

None of it seemed real, not the pain, not the strangely sweet-looking priest smiling down at me as I slowly bled to death. Weirder still, what hurt the most were the scratches on my shoulder from Psycho Soccer Mom. They burned like acid.

Numbly, I cupped my hand over the newest wound on my side, but it wasn't my side I felt under my palm. I looked. There was a hand there, holding me, stemming the blood flow. It wasn't mine.

Sublime warmth, comfort unlike anything I'd ever felt, and a profound sense of safety engulfed me. Like being cradled in my mother's lap as a kid, nothing could harm me; all around me was love.

"You can't interfere, Watcher," the priest said in the same kind of heavy smoker voice that Psycho Soccer Mom had.

"Thomas," the man holding me said, his voice serene. "When you have a minute…"

I felt him then, the man comforting me. The heat of his body surrounded mine, his strength kept me safe, and suddenly there was no other place in the world I wanted to be but in his arms. I didn't care about anything else. Nothing mattered but the way I felt in that moment.

"In…one…second," Tommy said from a distance. "This one can't get it through her…head that she's…finished."

I was slipping, my mind struggling to focus, my eyes fluttering closed against my will. I had the vague understanding Tommy was fighting—his stunted speech pattern, the sounds of metal clinking and sliding against metal. But I couldn't make any real sense of it.

"You can't heal that nephilim, Watcher," the priest said. "It's God's will."

"If God objects, I trust He has the means to correct the error," the nice man holding me said.

"No. That's not the agreement." The priest's eyes narrowed. His hand fisted, the other adjusting its bloody grip on the knife. "My deliverer was promised."

"Shut up, demon," Tommy said, appearing out of nowhere beside him. "You're dead."

Tommy's shoulders rolled, a flash of silvery metal swung, and the priest's pretty, dark-haired, brown-eyed head was…gone.

And then the world faded to black.

CHAPTER FOUR

"Yeah? Well, I told her not to touch the sword. You see how well she listened that time."

I knew Tommy was talking about me. And I didn't even have to use my gift. Someone was holding my hand. I opened my eyes a slit, not ready to interrupt the conversation.

Tommy was at my feet, standing at the end of the bed I was lying on. I couldn't see who was holding my hand without turning my head, but I knew he was male by the brush of hair on his forearm, the muscle, the strength.

"She'll learn," my handholder said. "If she wants to live."

That did it. I opened my eyes.

"Hello, Emma Jane."

The man was…stunning. Beautiful, even. Flawless skin, pale blue eyes, and silky black hair. And he was staring straight at me, as though he knew I'd been faking sleep for a while. I took my hand back.

"Hey." I swallowed. My throat felt like Hell's drainage pipe, dry as baked dirt. I licked my lips, my sluggish brain making a leap in logic. "Are you…are you Father Eli?"

"Eli. Please," he said, and blinked lashes so long and black, they had no business being on a man.

I couldn't stop staring, so I did my best not to look mentally impaired while I gawked. This priest was tall, maybe six-seven, six-eight. His blue-black hair hung in waves, brushing across his forehead, little swirls curling around his ear and over his collar.

His face was oval with a sharp, smooth-shaven jaw, high cheekbones, and a delicate, straight nose that gave him a kind of feminine prettiness—but he was solid male.

He lowered his head and smiled up at me through those impossibly long lashes. The expression crinkled the corners of glacial blue eyes. Figures he'd be a priest.

I exhaled against the wishful shudder rippling through me, and I put the naughty thoughts from my head. "This a hospital?"

I sat up slowly, holding my breath, bracing for the stab of pain I was sure would come from my injuries. Nothing happened. I rolled my head, stretching my neck. My muscles were a little tight, kind of tender, but nothing I couldn't ignore. How was that possible?

"You're in the rectory," Eli said. "How do you feel?"

I glanced around the sparsely furnished bedroom, testing my body with careful stretches this way and that. "I'm okay."

The room was small with only a single bed, a nightstand, a bookshelf, and a chest of drawers. I touched my fingers to the wound on my side, then my gut, and winced, the skin still tender. But it was nearly healed. New, puckered flesh already closed the stab wounds. "How long have I been out?"

"Twenty minutes," Tommy said.

I laughed, panic stirring—not humor. "That's impossible. I should be in surgery. But I feel…I feel like I've had weeks to heal."

I touched my shoulder, which sent a quick jolt of pain slicing along my nerves. I hissed. "Except there."

"Ah. That's the brimstone," Eli said, pushing to his feet. He leaned over me, lifting the collar of my blouse off my shoulder.

The touch, the gesture, sent a quick flood of heat swamping through my body. I couldn't help it. My chest warmed, the flush rising into my cheeks.

I stretched my neck to see the long scars, bubbled pink flesh, running from my shoulder to my back. They looked the same way Tommy's had, like cauliflower had gotten trapped under the skin. It wasn't pretty. Bathing suit season was going to suck.

I tried to keep my mind on my disgusting scars, but the sweet smell swirling from Eli filled my every breath. Like spring air and cotton blossoms, like warm summer sun with a hint of sweet male cologne, his scent was so captivating, I closed my eyes and took another deep breath. He shifted back just as I inhaled. *Busted.*

"You're healing," he said, his voice soft and soothing. "Brimstone from under the demon's nails must have gotten into the wound. It slows the healing process. But you'll feel better in a few hours."

He let go of my blouse and braced his hands on the mattress, one on each side of my hips. Our eyes met, and awareness tingled through my veins, made things low inside me warm. I swallowed hard. "Thanks."

"You ever have one of these? A female illorum?" Tommy's voice squelched the electric charge sizzling in the air, and Eli straightened.

"Yes. Once," Eli said.

"This going to be a problem?" The two men exchanged a look. "No."

"Uh, hello?" I waved a hand. "Newly conscious girl here.

Anyone care to share the info?"

Tommy's gaze shifted to me, and he flashed his all-star smile, though it melted a little around the edges after a quick second. "You can thank Eli for your feeling good enough to sit up like that."

"What do you mean?" I asked.

"He broke the rules for you," Tommy said, plopping his tall, muscled body at the end of the bed. "He's not supposed to get involved. At least not *that* involved. He healed you."

"Healed me how? He's a priest." *What, with the power of prayer?*

"I sustained her. She healed on her own," Eli said. He slipped his hands into the pockets of his black slacks, his knee-length priest-like black jacket held back at his wrists.

Tommy shrugged. "Maybe. But not this fast."

"The holy water healed her, Thomas. I only kept her from slipping away until you could give it to her." Eli walked slowly across the room to the wall. He leaned a shoulder against the tall bookcase, the setting sun casting a soft glow through the window beside him.

"Which is still more than you're supposed to do. But okay, whatever. I'm not complaining." Tommy smiled, his attention shifting back to me. "Anyway, without Eli *sustaining* you, I doubt you would've made it. By the time I took that demon scum's head and dragged you back into the church—where I *told* you to stay— you'd have been dead."

"I'm not a puppy."

"No, worse," he said. "You're a headstrong pain in the butt."

"But I'm house-trained." The sarcasm made my tone sharp. I took a breath. "Never mind that. You're right. I should be dead. So why aren't I?"

"Because you're illorum," Eli said. "You've been chosen. And with that comes certain…advantages."

"What, like random attacks from psychotic yuppie moms and sadistic priests?"

"Demons," Eli said. "They weren't human. They only held the form to draw close enough to strike without discovery. And…yes. Demon attacks are common for illorum."

"Lucky me."

"Indeed," Eli said, totally serious.

I was starting to think he didn't really get sarcasm.

"What Eli means is that the second you were marked, your angelic half kind of…kicked into gear," Tommy said. "We can't do the things Eli can do, but what we can do—heal and move faster than humans, fight, read emotions, sense the Fallen—it comes in handy."

"And Eli has extra special abilities because he's an illorum *and* a priest?"

"Eli's not a priest."

Oh? Things were looking up.

"He's an angel."

Never mind. "An angel? Right." He looked like a rock-and-roll priest in his slacks and shoes and long black jacket. His white shirt had one of those stiff banded collars. I'd just assumed…

"Where are his wings?" I asked, only half-joking.

"They're mostly for show," Eli said.

"Of course they are," I said.

And then he disappeared. *Shit.* My heart jumped to my throat and my brain locked.

"Who needs wings?" he said, suddenly on the other side of me.

"Ack!" I snapped my head around.

"Teleporting—folding time and space—doesn't require wings." His breath warmed against my ear.

"*Holy hell*, you scared me. Nice trick. Houdini's got nothin' on you."

Eli straightened, his hands cupped in front of him. He flashed a smile to stop my heart, then vanished again. The next instant he was back where he'd started, leaning against the bookshelf as though he'd never moved.

"I can also read the thoughts at the front of your mind," he said. "Those thoughts you might otherwise say if not for decorum and self-consciousness. Deeper thoughts, however, are *verboten*."

Thank Heaven for small restraints.

"Indeed," he said.

Crap. I'd have to get a handle on that. I looked to Tommy. "So, when you were saying he healed me, you really meant *he*, Eli, healed me. Not with prayers, but with, what, angelic power?"

"Yeah," Tommy said. "Your body can heal most superficial wounds on its own now. The nastier ones need holy water to help them along, especially ones infected with brimstone. But you still have to be able to get to the holy water. Keep that in mind next time, 'kay? You're not invulnerable, Emma Jane. You're just a little harder to kill."

"I pray," Eli said, as though he was just catching up with the conversation, "but as an angel I have been blessed with gifts… abilities. The power to heal is one of those abilities."

"Speaking of gifts," Tommy said, getting to his feet, "don't you have something for her?"

"I do." Eli straightened. He held out his hands, palms up, and produced a long sword out of thin air. "Keep it with you, always."

I swung my feet to the floor and went to get a closer look. "That's huge. It's not like I can hide it in my purse. People are gonna notice."

"Once you take possession, the blade exists by your will alone," Eli said. "Without your desire focused on a single thought, the blade returns to the ether and to the intangible edges of your aura."

From tip to hilt, the thing was almost three feet long. The blade itself was etched with a semi-circle at the hilt and the same crossed keys as the mark on my wrist. The grip was simple, leather wrapped, with a silver teardrop pommel and, at the end where it met the blade, a thick guard of metal stretched nearly straight across, the ends curving toward the grip with my name engraved in capital letters — HELLSBANE.

"Sweet." My hands itched to hold it. I rubbed my palms against my thighs, resisting the urge.

"It was made for you, Emma Jane," Eli said. "Forged in the fires of Heaven. An illorum's sword is the only thing on earth with the power to dispatch the Fallen to the abyss."

"What about demons?" I asked.

"That's kind of complicated," Tommy said.

I didn't look at him. I couldn't stop staring at that sword. I finally reached for it, and the instant the grip settled into my hand, I realized the hilt on Tommy's sword had been a little too thick, a little too long. This one fit in my palm like a part of me, an extension of my hand, my arm, my body.

I turned and swung the sword. Nothing had ever felt so natural. "Complicated, huh? How about you explain it to me?"

Tommy crossed his arms over his battle-worn T-shirt and leaned his butt against the bedpost. "Demons *are* fallen angels."

That stopped me. "Come again?"

"Which of those words was too big for you?" He flashed his charming all-star smile and winked.

Ass. He was too cute for his own good.

"Thomas," Eli said, "you're not helping. Demons were once angels, Emma Jane."

"They were sent to the abyss but were then freed by the Fallen to serve them," Tommy said. "But what comes out isn't the same as what went in. They're twisted. And they're so grateful to be free of the abyss they'll do anything, even die, for the one who freed them."

"The abyss. You mean Hell, don't you?" I plopped onto the edge of the bed, sword between my knees, tip to the floor.

"Yes," Eli said. "Even angels can sin."

"Rape."

He met my eyes. "Yes. And they are punished for their sins."

"When we can catch them."

Eli shifted his gaze to Tommy. "Exactly. Now, however, there is a means in place to deal with their betrayal."

"Oh yeah?" I said. "What's that?"

"You, and others like you," Eli said. "The chosen. The illorum. Your sword was forged in the fires of Heaven for your hand alone, for a single purpose. To exact God's will and banish the condemned to the abyss."

"And for that we get attacked by demons on a daily basis and possibly killed?" I asked. Calling it a raw deal hardly scratched the surface. "Why us?"

"Penance," Eli said.

"For what?"

"For the sins of your fathers."

"That's not fair."

Eli slipped his hands into the pockets of his jacket. "The Lord is slow to anger and abounding in steadfast love, forgiving iniquity and transgression, but He will by no means clear the guilty, visiting the iniquity of the fathers on the children, to the third and the fourth generation."

"Old Testament. The book of Numbers, verses fourteen through eighteen," Tommy said.

Right. The Bible. What'd I know? "But you guys help, right? The angels help us."

Tommy snorted. "Can you say, hell no?"

"I am here only as your teacher, your magister," Eli said. "I will train you to fight and share what knowledge I am permitted. But the rest will be up to you."

"And by 'the rest' you mean…?"

He looked confused. "Dispatching the Fallen."

"All of them?"

"Until you find and dispatch the angel who spawned you. Then your penance is paid."

"You mean our fathers? *My* father, specifically? Perfect. How hard could that be, when no one even remembers he existed?" I got up and headed for the door.

"Where are you going?" Tommy asked.

"Where do you think? I'm calling my mom. See if she remembers talking to any angels."

CHAPTER FIVE

I love my mom. And from outside the family, she seems almost…
sane.

I checked my watch. She and my sister were only twenty minutes
late, which meant I still had another fifteen or so minutes to wait—
according to Hellsbane time. My family takes being fashionably late
to a whole new level—myself included. It's one of our long-running
jokes.

"You done?"

I glanced up at the potbellied guy standing next to my table,
white paper-wrapped sandwich and matching Styrofoam cup in
hand. "No," I said. "Plus I've got people coming to join me. So…
sorry."

The big guy huffed, angry, and waddled off mumbling, "This
ain't no TGI-friggin-Friday's, lady. Eat and get out."

I don't have a problem sitting alone in restaurants or going
to movies by myself. Sometimes I actually prefer it. But I'd been
getting dagger stares from the other customers since I'd dared to
sit down at one of the busy restaurant tables with just a Coke and

order of fries.

The Primanti Brothers restaurant, in Pittsburgh's Strip District, had started life as a lunch cart, then moved to the brick-and-mortar location still holding to a kind of lunch counter mentality. Over the past seventy-eight years it hadn't changed much. They'd added a wait staff, but locals knew for the fastest service it was best to place their order at the counter—using as few words as possible—get their food, and, with any luck, find an open table or seat at the bar on their own. It's not that the wait staff wasn't good, but trying to get a server to notice you in the busy place could leave one…frustrated.

You were supposed to eat your food and get out. People were constantly moving, tables filling and emptying. That's the way the regulars liked it. And today was no different. The place was busy, seating was at a premium, and I was taking up space. *Oh well.*

I wasn't sure if it was the hater vibe being focused on me or something else, but the longer I sat there, the more my stomach felt like it was trying to make the US gymnastics team all on its own. When my belly gave a particularly strong roll that made me feel like it was in my throat, I decided to take a quick trip to the bathroom before I gave Primanti Brothers back their fries.

I zigzagged through tables and customers to the back hallway and pushed the door on the right marked *ladies.*

"You always make a target of yourself, lass? Or do ya just have a death wish today?" A weird little guy was beside me, when he hadn't been an instant before. He leaned against the wall by the door.

I'd backed away too fast and slammed against the other side of the hall. My stomach roiled, my heart thumping in my throat. "Where'd….How—Who are you? What do you want?"

"Relax," he said, folding his arms and crossing one ankle over the other. "If I was here to take your head, I'd have it by now. Believe me."

"That's not what I asked."

"Aye, but it's what you were thinkin'. At least for a wee bit there in between the 'How'd he do that?' and the 'Should I make a run for it or just scream?' thoughts." He leaned toward me and winked. "I don't recommend either."

His accent made me think Irish, maybe Scottish. Couldn't tell which. He was only two or three inches taller than I was, which made him pathetically short for a man, and his cockiness totally unjustified. He had the kind of red hair that's more brassy, almost orange, and he wore it long to his chin, with kinky wild curls and enough freckles to make me think boy rather than man.

But his mannerisms, the way he held himself, moved, and smiled, with a wise glint in his green eyes, belied the first-glance impression, adding years to his age. I figured he was a year older than I was, maybe two. And judging by his rumpled clothes, a brown leather vest, T-shirt, loose jeans, and battered work boots with broken shoestrings, he wasn't a nine-to-five kinda guy.

"You read my mind?"

"Aye. Wasn't hard. You've got no shielding a'tall. Bess to work on that. Been reading you since you walked in the door there. Couldn't help it if I'd tried. You're like a bloody bullhorn."

"What are you?" Crap, two days as an illorum, and I was already about to be hacked to ribbons for a second time.

His hand dropped to the hilt of a sword at his side. I hadn't noticed it until he touched the silver pommel. "What do you think, lassie? Right now, I'm what's standing between you and certain death, I am. Where's your sword?"

His gaze dropped to my side and my hands flexed. There was

nothing to grab. I'd left my sword in the Jeep. *Sue me.* The thing kept poking me in the ribs or the small of my back when I sat. There was no good place on my belt to keep it.

"Near enough," I said.

"Is it now?" He pushed off the wall, closing the distance between us. My stomach's reaction to another illorum had calmed, but the invasion of my comfort zone had it clenching all over again. "Take a whiff, lassie. A deep one. Smell anythin' rancid, do you?"

I inhaled. "Rotten eggs. A demon," I said, scrunching my face at the smell. I'd breathed too deeply; the taste coated the back of my tongue, filled my lungs, and churned through my stomach. I turned and went back to the end of the hall, scanned the restaurant.

Everyone looked normal. "Where is it?"

The illorum shrugged. "I'd say that's somethin' you should be knowin'. Should be spottin' them on yer own if you mean to live past the day."

"See, that's just not helpful. Why are you bugging me if you're not going to help?"

He smiled. It was a nice smile, with straight white teeth and dimpled cheeks that gave him an odd appeal.

"It's been a while since I've come across someone so new to the ranks. And…" He shrugged, almost bashful. "You're not so harsh on an old man's eyes to be lookin' at."

"You're hitting on me?" *Puh-leeze.*

"And warning ya," he hurried to say. "Don't be forgettin' that. I saw ya sittin' there, not a scrap of metal to defend yourself. You were demon bait if I ever saw it. What kind of eejit goes around unarmed?"

Okay, so fighting demons I couldn't even pick out of a crowd had me a little panicked. But shutting down horny guys? That I could do in my sleep. "Listen. Normally I'd find being called an eejit *such* a turn-on. But I've recently been quite thoroughly bitch-slapped by life, and I'm really not looking to date." *And I don't do leprechauns.*

"No leprechauns? Ya sure 'bout that?" His smile turned lecherous. "Not even if I promise to show you me pot of gold after ya stroke me rainbow?"

Um…ew. It took me a moment to overcome the gross-out and realize he'd said "leprechaun" when I'd only thought it. "Hey. You're not allowed to do that."

"Do what? Read your thoughts?" He snorted. "Who told you that rot? Your magister?"

"As a matter of fact." Technically, he'd said only a person's deeper thoughts were verboten, but I didn't want this guy anywhere inside my head.

"Figures." He leaned a shoulder against the wall, crossing his arms and ankle again. "They don't want us to realize our full potential. To know we're the best of both worlds. Jealous bastards. They'll get us all snuffed."

"Who, the angels? You think angels are jealous of us?"

"That's right. Don't you know what you can do?" He shook his head. "The prick didn't show you bollocks, did he? 'Course not."

"Who *are* you?"

He straightened, held up a finger telling me to wait, and then vanished. A gust of wind tousled my hair, and a blur of movement too fast for my eyes to track rushed by me. A second later, the same rush of movement blew past in reverse, and the leprechaun dude was standing by the ladies' room again. Only now, he was holding a Styrofoam cup.

"The name's Liam McGregor, and I've been an illorum for thirty-one years. This be yours." He handed me my soda. "Now, I've gotten the fiend's attention. Where's your sword?"

"In my Jeep," I said. "Around the corner."

"Perfect. I'll meet you there," he said. "If we both go, he'll follow, and we can send him off to Hell without worry for the mortals."

"Wait." I glanced at my cup. "What'd you just do?"

"What I did, lassie, is the very least of our hidden talents," he said. "You've got gobs to learn and no time a'tall to do it. Now get moving."

He walked away at human speed and I watched him zigzag through the tables to the front door. It took a second to snap out of my stupor, but a strong whiff of sulfur pushed me into action. Whatever the crazy leprechaun was, he was right about the demon nearby. I practically choked on the stench.

The lull between lunch and dinner kept the place from being so packed it'd be standing room only, but there were still too many people to single out which one stunk like three-week-old eggs. I made my way to my table and realized halfway there I'd already lost it to another customer. So I sat my half-empty cup on the counter, taking the opportunity to scan faces all around me. I was looking for that special kind of eye contact that wasn't an accidental glance but an intentional stare. No one stood out.

I caught the attention of one of the guys behind the counter and mouthed, "I'll be right back," while pointing in the direction of my car. He nodded, then shrugged and turned away. I had a feeling I wouldn't find my cup when I came back. *Crap.* I slung my purse over one shoulder and headed out.

The second I pushed through the door, the tiny hairs on the back of my neck stood on end, skin tingling. I went left toward Smallman Street, where I'd parked.

The sun was low in the sky, but nightfall was still hours off. I glanced in Primanti's wall of windows as I passed, trying to see if that pressing sensation creeping up my back was real or my imagination. I couldn't see if anyone was following and I didn't want to tip my hand by actually turning around. Besides, if I moved now, I might spook the demon off before Liam could jump him.

So I strolled along like good little demon bait and turned the corner from Eighteenth Street to Smallman. Liam was nowhere to be seen. *Lying little leprechaun.*

My heart rate ratcheted up a notch, but I kept a grip. I was born to fight these things. Right? My Jeep was exactly where I'd left it, two spots down. And under the backseat was my nifty new sword. I was already focusing my thoughts, imagining the blade at the end of the hilt. Now, all I had to do was convince the demon shuffling his feet behind me to wait while I fished it out. *Damn, I hope this works.*

With nothing to lose, I glanced over my shoulder.

Hey, I know that guy.

He'd come into Primanti's after me. We'd even shared a quick glance, though I'd put him out of my thoughts the next second. Sheesh, I sucked at this illorum-detecting-demons thing.

He wasn't an overly big guy, though next to me, fifth graders look adult-size. He was average, probably five-eight, five-nine, with a thick build. He was wearing a checkered, buttoned shirt and a black windbreaker that molded over his arms and chest with the breeze.

He dragged his feet. I hate that. Not like Quasimodo or anything, just the normal lazy gait that drove me absolutely insane. It was worse when the person wore dress shoes, or boots, but even in sneakers like this guy, it was all I could do not to turn around and scream, "Pick up your feet!"

Oh. And he had that nasty, week-old, rotten-eggs-in-the-summertime smell. Downwind from the guy, I couldn't avoid the stench. Didn't anyone else smell that? Must just be a nephilim thing. Lucky us. *Ick.*

His gait quickened the second I turned back around, *scrape-clomp, scrape-clomp, scrape-clomp.* Resisting the urge to run, I snagged my keys from the side pocket of my purse and made it to the Jeep. The key was in the back hatch's lock just as he stepped between the cars. A flash of a dagger glinted in his hand.

"Nephilim scourge," the guy hissed.

I had an instant to duck before he sliced at me. He missed by a fraction of an inch, but my back window paid the price.

"Try that shit with *me*, ya demon filth," Liam said, appearing behind him. What the hell had taken him so long?

He swung his sword, but the demon brought his dagger up in time to block. The blow was hard enough to drive him back, and the two clashed weapons again and again, Liam striking hard while the demon fought to defend. I watched like a rubbernecker at a car wreck, mouth gaping.

By the time they reached the warehouse wall, Liam's attacks were slowing, his swings less precise. He was growing tired. The demon was simply waiting him out.

Liam threw me a quick glance before he struck at the demon again. "Get your bloody sword, woman. You're not at the flippin' pictures."

"Oh." I snapped out of it and turned back to my ruined Jeep window. *Hell, no point unlocking the thing now.* I shoved my hand through the ripped plastic and reached farther by climbing up on the back hitch. By the tips of my fingers, I touched the hilt of my sword, and the whole of it seemed to slide toward my hand, into my grip. Maybe I imagined it. Maybe not.

Throwing my body back out of the Jeep, I pulled the sword free. Relief washed over me at seeing the blade, real and solid, just as I'd willed it. *Yes.*

I turned, triumphant, just in time to see the demon launching his attack on the now-exhausted Liam. Triumph dimmed and a moment of panic froze me to the spot. I really didn't have a clue how to sword-fight. I'd get us both killed.

"Now, woman!" Liam yelled, swinging his sword up in defense. Metal clashed, sparks lit from the edges, and the redheaded nephilim stumbled back. "Now!"

I had to help. The decision crystallized in my brain, banishing everything else. Worry, doubt, fear, it was all just suddenly gone. Instinct took over, I dropped my purse, and my feet moved me forward. I raised my weapon, swung. Easy. Natural. But not enough.

The demon turned, blocked, and the reverberation of metal striking metal shook through my sword. Like biting a fork, the jarring sensation shot through me, quaked along my arms and rattled me to the bone. I staggered back, and the demon advanced. He swung for my neck, and instinct took over once more.

I spun. The dagger sliced down my back, ripping my T-shirt but missing my skin. The momentum of my turn carried me around, and with me, my sword. The upswing caught him across the chest, opening a line of black ooze from hip to shoulder across his checkered shirt.

Arms open, the demon spared a surprised glance at his chest. I didn't think, I just acted and drove my sword deep into his gut. He doubled over, his hand grabbing the blade, eyes wide.

An instant of regret tightened across my shoulders, knotted my stomach. He looked so human, so pained, and I'd caused it. Dammit, this wasn't me. I couldn't do this; I couldn't hurt people.

And then the demon's sorrowful eyes turned cold, his lips

snarled back. He grabbed the bottom hilt of my sword, just below my hands, holding it so I couldn't pull it free from his body. He raised his dagger and swung. I let go of my sword and stumbled out of reach.

The next thing I saw was Liam's blade slicing through the demon-man's neck from behind. His head wobbled for an instant, a ring of black ooze growing just above the folded collar of his shirt. Then suddenly, the head tumbled off his shoulders and the body collapsed, quickly disintegrating into a smoldering pile of goo.

"Took your sweet bloody time getting your sword," Liam's words huffed between labored breaths. "Keep that feckin' thing on ya from now on. Damn near met me end waitin' on ya."

"Me? The thing practically got in the car with me. Look what he did to the back window. Where the hell were you when I came out?"

"I was waitin' ta see if you had any natural fight in ya," he said. "Seein' if you could take the bastard on your own."

"Really? You could've just asked. Sheesh." I sighed. The guy *had* saved my butt. "Thanks, though. Y'know, for stepping in."

Liam gave me a wink and a nod. "No trouble a'tall, lass."

I grabbed my sword from the pile of melting demon goo and turned back to my Jeep. Liam was right about one thing. I'd have to keep the sword on me from now on. Apparently, demons weren't apt to schedule their attacks at my convenience. *Rude*.

I unlocked the back—pretending hard that the plastic window wasn't ripped to shreds. *Crap*. It was gonna cost me a fortune to fix.

The special sheath was shoved in the corner, under the backseat. I assumed Eli put it there; I don't know how or when. I grabbed my jean jacket from the backseat, shoved it on to hide the rip in my shirt, then grabbed the sheath. It was more of a plain leather pocket than a sheath, wide enough to hold the hilt with its cross of metal where the blade would form, deep enough so only the top, rounded pommel and an inch of handle would stick out to grab.

With a simple thought the blade disintegrated, dissolving into a million sparkling particles that expanded outward, fading to nothing until only the hilt remained in my hand. The leather sheath pocket had loops on it and I slid my belt through so it sat at the small of my back.

With my belt fastened again and my hilt attached, I propped my hands on my hips. "Okay, leprechaun. Spill it."

Liam leaned against the car next to mine and smiled. A breeze ruffled the wild, kinky strands of his hair. "Spill what, lass?"

"Well, let's start with how you were able to move so fast in the restaurant. You were a blur," I said.

"Aye. Pretty awesome, wasn't it?" he said.

"Yeah. It was. How'd you do it?"

"I told ya, we're the best of both worlds. Whatever they can do, we can do." He shrugged. "Or damn near it, anyway."

"What's that mean?"

"Isn't this something your magister should be answerin' for ya?" he said. "Or better still, he should've told you from the start. Why do you think he didn't?"

"I didn't ask him. I'm asking you." My gut told me I could trust Eli and Tommy. But hearing Liam imply my gut might be wrong bugged the crap out of me.

"Fair enough. I'll do for you what no one saw fit to do for me." He stretched his arms out to the sides. "You have the knowledge of thirty-one years of battle at your disposal. For exactly ten minutes."

"Thirty-one years. How old are you?"

"I was twenty-five when I was marked," he said. "Been looking for the fiend that seduced me blessed mother for thirty-one years since then."

I did the math. "Fifty-six? You're joking."

"Naw. Why would I?"

"How? You look my age." My stomach knotted. I wasn't sure I wanted to know the answer.

"We don't age, lass," he said. "Bloody hell, he didn't even tell ya that much?"

I shook my head. It required too much brainpower to form words.

"From the moment we're marked our lives stop," he said. "From that instant on, we live only to send the Fallen to the abyss. The last one we send will be the one that spawned us, and then our lives will be our own again."

My throat closed. I swallowed hard. "No matter how long it takes?"

"Aye," he said. "But don't look so gobsmacked. It's not all bad. It's not bad a'tall."

"Not bad?" I laughed, bitter…and maybe a little manic. "I was marked yesterday. Yesterday! Since then I've fought four demons. And one of them actually grew horns and cloven feet. What's not bad about that?"

"True. The demon attacks can be a wee troublesome."

"Troublesome? Right. And the Enron scandal was just a bad day at the office."

"But there's a silver lining in that cloud you've anchored over your head," he said. "The things we can do. We're no longer bound by human weakness and the laws designed to make all men equal. We're outside the human world now. We're in *their* world, the world of angels."

"Uh-huh. And that means what, exactly?" I was starting to

think he might be more than just a few fries short of a Happy Meal.

"We don't age, for one," he said. "But I told you that. We can read thoughts, understand any language, and travel at the speed of light."

"I can't do any of those things."

"It takes time to fine-tune your abilities, but I'll wager you've had inklings."

I shrugged, thinking. For as long as I could remember, I'd been able to read people's emotions. Sometimes, if I tried hard enough, those emotions could be pretty specific. Had I always known it was more than just a special gift?

"So what? All those abilities only make us stand out," I said. "I have a life, a family, friends, a business. I've never had to hide who I am before, and I don't want to start now. How am I going to explain why I'm not growing older? How can I explain any of it?"

"Aw, lassie, don't ya see?" Liam said. "None of that matters anymore. You're one of us now, not one of them. You've got to cut ties with your human life. Walk away from your emotional bonds."

"No. Nobody said anything about cutting ties. No way." I snagged my purse from the ground where I'd dropped it and walked to the front of the Jeep. "Everything that's happened the last few days is hard enough to accept. I'll never get through it without my family, without something normal in my life."

He pushed from the car and followed me, stopping to lean a hip against the hood. "So be it. But know this: every minute you stay with them, every time you're seen with them, you put them at risk. They're cannon fodder, lassie. Demons don't give a damn who gets in their way. And the Fallen? They'll use the ones you love against you. Mark my words."

The truth itched through my subconscious. I knew Liam was

right—I could feel it—but I wasn't ready to fully accept it. I just couldn't.

"I need my old life. It's not fair. They can't expect us to give up everything. Besides, the logistics of survival demand we keep some semblance of normalcy. I've got bills. I like to eat occasionally. What're we supposed to do about the basics?"

"Bills?" He laughed. "You're nephilim, woman. The child of angels. The world is ours. There's no such thing as bills."

I gave him the once-over. He clearly wasn't a slave to the latest fashions, so his wardrobe probably didn't drain his finances. But he still had the everyday expenses of survival. "So what do you do for food, shelter?"

He puffed his lean chest. "I take what I want, eat what I like, and sleep wherever my head falls to rest."

"You're a thief," I said.

Liam straightened, his hand dropping to the hilt of his sword, his orange brows tightening over the flash of green fire in his eyes. "I'm an illorum, warrior of God, executioner of His Word. I rid the world of those judged and sentenced so their wickedness no longer pollutes His Creation. And for that, humans should be grateful."

"Ya think?" I shrugged, refusing to be intimidated by a prideful leprechaun. "From what I heard, God didn't give us this assignment because we're His go-to guys."

Liam's offense seemed to ease a bit. He shook his head. "Speak English, woman. You're makin' no sense."

"It's Emma," I said, because if he called me "woman" or "lassie" one more time, I was gonna slap him.

"Emma."

I nodded my approval. "I mean, this gig isn't so much a reward as a punishment. He gives us this crappy job that forces us to abandon everything that matters to us. The power we get is only enough to keep us from being creamed. Everything else we care about is stripped away. Call me crazy, but I don't think acting like the angelic assholes we're hunting is going to get us off His divine shit-list."

For three solid heartbeats Liam stared at me, his brow tight, his expression unchanging, and then he suddenly shook with an explosion of laughter. "Aye, lass—sorry, Emma. You are a crazy bird, I'll give ya that. But you're a woman, so I suppose that's explanation enough."

Ugh.

"Think what ye likes, missy. But mark me words. If you don't break ties with what you hold dearest in your heart, they'll all pay the price." He walked past me, then stopped and looked back over his shoulder.

"We're chosen, Emma. There's no question on that. If you want to live out the year, you'd do well to see it as a blessing." And then he was gone, a blur of movement, a gust of wind. Pretty impressive for a man who looked like a leprechaun.

I turned, heading back to the restaurant. Too bad he wasn't really one of the magical green men—I could've made him grant me a wish. I'd have given anything not to be the one to have to tell my mother she'd cheated on my dad without knowing it.

And I was the proof.

CHAPTER SIX

Mom and Lacey, my older sister, were already sitting at a table when I came back into Primanti's. I checked my watch. They were a half hour late—right on time for my family. They're not perfect, but they love me.

My mother was a petite beauty in her day. Now she was just Mom. Her hair, once a thick coco-brown, was thinner now, but the same color, although it came from a bottle to cover the gray. Her bright, greenish-blue eyes were half-hidden by sagging lids and by the bifocals balanced on the end of her nose as she read the menu.

Lacey spotted me first as I made my way to their table. My sister was seven years older than I was, and I don't think she ever really forgave me for ruining her chance to be an only child.

She was the perfect combination of my parents. Lacey had my late dad's height and thick, wavy hair. She'd inherited Mom's curvy shape, her full lips, and her stunning green eyes. At five-foot-six, with naturally straight, white teeth and hair the color of sugar cookies, she'd always been the favorite of both our parents.

"Where have you been?" Mom said. "Your sister has to get

back to pick up Nicki from preschool."

The rest of the world's tardiness is utterly unacceptable to my family. Which is understandable, right? I mean, when you're already running late, anyone else behind schedule can really muck things up.

Nicki is the youngest of my sister's three children. Lacey and her lovely family live in Upper St. Clare—an affluent suburb of Pittsburgh. They have three cars, and an enviable three-thousand-square-foot home. She has the perfect life, and yet still manages to worry our mother senseless every other week with her so-called problems. I think I could probably top her in the problems department now. Not that it's a competition.

"Sorry, Mom." I kissed her cheek, and hooked my purse on the back of my chair. "Sorry, Lacey. I forgot something in the car."

"How ironic, a psychic forgot something," Lacey said, snickering at her own humor.

I threw her a squint-eyed smile, mustering years of sibling discourse in a single expression, and sat. "I told you, I'm not a psychic. I'm an intuitive consciousness explorer. There's a difference."

"What's that?"

"A psychic would've foreseen this conversation and remembered to grab her phone out of her car to avoid it."

"Oh. Well, that clears that up." Her smile brightened, scanning her menu. "You've always marched to your own drum, Emma."

"You hear that pounding too?" I asked and made her smile again. My cell phone clunked against the table when I set my purse down a little too hard, and the hilt of my sword poked me in the back. I winced and resisted the urge to reach around and adjust the sheath.

My mom shook her head, her face wrinkled with frustration

over her sniping daughters despite the fact we were just teasing each other—mostly. I knew Mom loved me, but sometimes I felt like a perpetual disappointment to her. I guess I couldn't really blame her—it wasn't like I hadn't given her good reason. After graduating high school a couple years early, I'd gone to college and gotten a degree in psychology. But instead of continuing on for my doctorate, I'd used it and my gift to land a job as a telephone intuitive consciousness explorer—okay, psychic. Although as a consciousness explorer I could charge more for in-person readings from my home. Mom thought I'd thrown away four years of college and a perfectly good degree to basically sit at home and talk on the phone. Which I kind of did, but at least they paid me to do it.

I mulled over how best to get the answers I needed from her. What could I ask? Whatever angel had done this to her wouldn't have left the memory of it. But if she couldn't remember the affair, maybe she'd remember the events leading up to it.

My mom and Lacey already had their sandwiches, busily tweaking them with mustard, salt and pepper. I scanned the crowd for our waitress despite having no idea what she looked liked. Two seconds later I decided I'd never find her, and I pushed to my feet. "I'm just going to go order something at the counter. Be right back."

I needed time to think, anyway, to get things straight in my head before I could figure out how to broach the subject to my mom without making her worry I'd completely lost it. Liam had me on edge, wondering if I was taking stupid risks. But what choice did I have? I had to figure out who my real father was, so I could put a stop to all this craziness.

My mother and sister both nodded without looking up. So I got in line at the counter and ordered a new Coke and one of Primanti Brothers' famous all-on-the-sandwich sandwiches—roast beef topped with coleslaw, fries, and tomatoes. My mouth watered just placing the order.

By the time I sat back at the table I had it all worked out. "Mom, do you…believe in angels?" It was as good a place as any to start. "I mean, I know you believe in God and the Bible and all that. But what about angels? Do you believe they exist, that they talk to people, interact with us?" I glanced at her across the table, then dropped my gaze to my soda, took a casual sip.

"Yes," she said. "I believe in angels, but no, I don't think they hang around, talking to everyday people."

"Why not? I mean, they did in the Bible. Why not now?"

"What are you getting at, Emma?" my sister asked.

What was I getting at? What did I want them to say? *Yes, angels exist. We've seen them, talked to them, had sex with them. Let me tell you where to find your real father.* I turned my wrist over, and stared at the illorum mark. *If only.*

"What if God sent an angel to Earth, and that angel said he was here to seduce you? What then?"

"Who, me?" Mom said.

I didn't look. I just nodded and said, "Yeah."

"That wouldn't happen," she said, confident. "God wouldn't send an angel to seduce a human."

"Okay, what if the angel did it on his own?" I looked at her, tried to read her expression. She looked like she thought I was joking.

"It still wouldn't happen. God forbids angels from…" She leaned close and whispered, "Having *sex* with humans."

"But what about nephilim? I mean, do you know about them, what they are?"

"Of course. I've read the Bible, dear," she said. "As well as the wild interpretations some people have come up with. The myth is nephilim were children of angels and humans. But angels are…well, they're angels. I can't imagine them doing something so…" Again, she leaned close to whisper. "So deviant."

"What if they did it, anyway?"

She blinked, and something flashed behind her eyes, some emotion she banished nearly as fast as it had occurred. I opened my gift to her. Maybe I could sense it—some buried truth she didn't realize was there.

The virtual doors opened in my mind and a wave of confusion crashed into me. My heart raced and my throat went dry, my emotions swirling, trying to fight, to deny a shadowy ghost of feeling. What was it? *Guilt?*

The thin wisp of emotion was so faint I couldn't connect with it, couldn't bring it to the surface to examine it. Every time I tried to focus on it, the emotion slipped away like smoke on the wind.

An instant later, doubt tingled across my shoulders, pinched through my gut. There was something there, something she couldn't or didn't want to deal with. My question had sparked something deep inside her, and despite her confident tone and expression, my mother wasn't sure.

"What's this all about, Emma?" she asked.

This was pointless; there was nothing she could tell me. Whether she was blocking the memories and emotions herself or the angel who'd seduced her had done it, she wasn't willing to push to remember.

"Nothing. Forget it," I said. "I had a client today who insisted she'd been seduced by an angel. She said he got her pregnant, and then tried to make her forget the whole thing. It just got me thinking. Wondering if it was possible."

Lacey snorted. "That's some clientele you've got there, Emma.

Why don't you just use your little trick to figure out what she really wants you to say, and say it?"

My sister's always given me grief over my gift, except when she wanted me to use it for her own benefit. When she was in high school, she'd ask me to meet her boyfriends so I could read them to see if they really loved her or just wanted sex. Most had just wanted sex. Teenage boys. Go figure.

When I'd called her on the contradiction between making me feel like a freak and making me feel useful, she'd punched me in the arm and told me to shut up. *Ahh, sisters...*

"I think she's telling the truth," I said. Mom didn't know about my ability. The few times I'd tried to mention it, she'd smile like I was telling her about some crazy dream. She'd rub my back or give me a hug, and then tell me not to think about it and it'd go away. After a while, I'd stopped trying to clue her in.

Mom leaned toward me. "You think she's really been with someone and suppressed the memory? Why? Is it possible she was raped?"

"Yeah, actually, I think it might be," I said, realizing my fake client might actually be helpful. "But she doesn't remember much, and she doesn't really want to."

"Well, you have to help her, Emma," Mom said. "You have to help her remember. What if it was someone she's still associating with? He could try again."

"Right. But how?" I said. "She doesn't remember anything. It's just a feeling she has. How do I figure out who it was?"

"Maybe you should tell the police," she said.

"Tell them what? There's no proof except her daughter. She had a boyfriend at the time, but they tested him, and he's not the father."

A busboy hurried to clean the table next to us, scooping

sandwich paper, cups, and napkins into his big plastic bin, then wiped the table with lightning-fast grace, lifting to clean under the napkin and condiment holder. Before the kid could lift the bucket from the chair, customers were already sitting in the empty seats, another waiting for the busboy to move.

The three of us watched in hypnotized silence, our mouths full. Lacey was the first to swallow. "You should talk to people who knew her around the time she would've conceived. See if anyone remembers a guy hanging around. Maybe someone who seemed overly interested in her."

"Yeah, okay," I said. It was a good idea, but who was close enough to my mother twenty-three years ago who might've known she was with someone other than my dad?

Mom had been married for eight years when I was conceived. Lacey would've been six. I'd seen pictures. There was one of my parents sitting on a glider at Grammy's house with Lacey climbing up on their laps. Mom's sister, Aunt Sara, and her husband, Uncle Greg, were standing behind them.

Maybe Aunt Sara knew who my father was and didn't realize it. It was worth a shot. Hell, it was the only shot I had. At the very least, she could clue me in on who else I might ask.

"So, how'd the boyfriend take it?" Lacey asked.

"Huh?"

"Your client's boyfriend. How'd he take finding out the daughter wasn't his?"

"Oh. Not well," I said, then I realized this could be another chance to use the fake client to my advantage. "In fact, he was pretty freaked. Yeah, she, um, had to take out a restraining order on him. And, uh, so did I."

"What?" Mom and Lacey said in unison. They both stared at

me, their faces mirror images, both creased with worry.

"Yeah, he blames me for not figuring out who she cheated on him with," I said, taking a quick swig of soda, giving me time to form a plausible story. "He thinks I'm holding out on him to protect her and the other guy."

"Well, that's nonsense," Mom said. "How could you possibly know? You're not psych—"

Awkward pause.

"Did he threaten you?" She used her mother lion voice, like she'd tear anyone to pieces if they dared touch her baby.

My mom's awesome.

"Not just me. He threatened my family, too, unless I told him what I knew," I said. The lie was beginning to sour in my belly. I had to protect them on the chance Liam was right about demons trying to get to me through my family. But I couldn't remember a time I'd lied to my mother and it had turned out well.

"You told him you faked it, right?" Lacey said. "I mean, you told him it was all for fun. That you can't really tell people's futures or explain the problems in their love lives or any of that junk. You told him you couldn't possibly know if she cheated on him except for what the DNA test proved, and that wasn't your fault."

"Uh…no."

"Emma," Lacey said, like she was about to punch me in the arm.

"Lacey, I can't ever say anything like that and then expect to be taken seriously in this business." Never mind that it was a moot point.

"Whatever," she said. Lacey knew the truth. I just weirded her out sometimes.

"Besides," I said, "I don't think he's that much of a threat. The only reason I'm telling you guys is so you can keep an eye out. Just in case. I doubt he'll bother you, but if you see someone hanging around that seems kind of…off, male or female, don't let yourself be alone with them."

"Why female?" Lacey asked.

Because demons can take any form. And I like you with a head. "Because he might…he might use a friend to get around the restraining order. I'm covering all the bases. Okay?"

"We'll be fine. Lacey has a different last name, and I live an hour away," Mom said, always the voice of reason. "He'd never find us, even if he bothered to try. Don't worry about it."

Maybe she was taking this a little too casually. I didn't want them to be afraid to leave their homes, but they'd have to be on guard when they did.

"Right." I sighed. There was nothing I could say that wouldn't tip the balance too far one way or the other. So I just took a bite of my ginormous sandwich.

"So, Emma Jane," Mom said, and I felt my gut tighten at the familiar tone. "Are you dating anyone new?"

Angels, illorum, and demons be damned, some things never change.

CHAPTER SEVEN

"You're late."

I checked my watch. "Only a half hour."

Tommy opened his arms, his sword loose in his hand. "Yeah?"

My brain shifted. *Oh, crap*. The Hellsbane family time issue strikes again. I'd become my mother. "Right. Sorry. I overslept."

"You were sleeping?" Tommy said, crestfallen. "It's three am, and I've been standing on this overlook for almost an hour. You think I don't need sleep?"

"I said sorry."

"Sure. Whatever." He sliced the air with his sword, obviously still angry.

"Hey, this was your idea. Mount Washington isn't my neighborhood," I said.

"Yeah, I know. You're right." He looked dutifully pitiful. "I'm so whipped. Just got off work. I wanted to get some training in with you before I hit the sack. My apartment's like two blocks away, but I don't have a backyard. This was the first place I thought of. After this, I'm hitting the sack."

I shrugged. "It's okay. I love it here. This place is kind of visually epic, you know?"

With the Appalachian foothills as an observation stage to the city, the view from the Mount Washington overlook was fantastic. On a clear day you can see for miles, beyond the city and off into the nearby suburbs.

But at night, the scenery is even better. It's like a postcard, buildings twinkling like Christmas trees, stoplights blinking color, neon signs adding a rainbow of hues and the lights tracing over the bridges shimmering along the dark rivers. Epic.

I kicked off my flip-flops, the cement cool against my feet, and drew the hilt of my sword from its sheath, willing the blade to gather and form. Knees bent, feet wide, I assumed a fighting stance, hands double-fisting the hilt.

"I'd like the place better after a few hours sleep," he said.

I straightened. "Me too. I had five live readings today and four phone readings. *Plus*, I had lunch with my mother and sister. Tired is an understatement."

"You should keep your distance from them," Tommy said. "From anyone you care about. Never know when a demon's gonna show up."

"I didn't think about that," I said, trying to keep the guilt from showing on my face. "I mean, I'm used to talking to them all the time. Damn, this sucks."

"Tell me about it." He sighed. "Okay, enough complaining from both of us. You need the training, and if this is the only time we can get together, so be it."

"Yeah, except when we're done, you'll be home in bed two minutes later. I'll still be on the road."

"Ah, grasshopper, the road to true wisdom is long and full of potholes," he said in his best Master Po voice.

"Ah, Master Tommy, you spew much bullshit." My Master Po wasn't so hot. But he got the point.

"Right." He raised his sword and I mirrored him. "Remember, you have an instinct for using your sword. Just relax and trust your gut."

"Absolutely. Wait—no. We're not actually going to hit each other with these things, are we? I mean, 'cause...that'd hurt." My side gave a quick little twitch of phantom pain from where I'd been stabbed by the demon.

He shook his head. "Don't worry. You won't get through my blocks and I'm just going to push you hard enough for you to feel your power take over. It's just practice. No going for the kill. Besides, we heal fast, right?"

"Riiight." I'd worn sparring clothes just for the occasion: khaki shorts, loose on my hips, and two ribbed tank tops—pink over white. I'd even scooped my too-short hair into a spastic ponytail...mostly. A lot of the pieces had already slipped free from the elastic ring. Not sure why I bothered.

We circled each other. Tommy swung and I blocked. I swung and he blocked. He swung again, faster, and I blocked. I sliced down fast enough that the blade was a blur, spinning as I advanced. Tommy blocked and then sliced straight out toward my gut. I jumped back and he lunged, stabbing forward. I blocked. Somewhere between the first couple attacks and parries, I stopped thinking about any of it and just did it.

The clanks and metal hisses of our swords hitting and sliding against each other echoed off the nearby townhouses and over the cliffside.

The upside to innate ability is that it doesn't take much mental concentration. I realized conversation was surprisingly easy.

"I met a guy today."

"Should we celebrate?" Tommy said, driving me back three steps with a volley of blows. After the third strike, I found an opening and drove him back.

"Har-har, cute and funny. I'm all a-twitter. I didn't mean I met a *guy* guy. I meant I met a person who happened to *be* a guy," I said. "He was an illorum."

"Hold it." Tommy took several quick steps back then lowered his sword, rested it point down against the cement, effectively stopping our sparring. "Are you sure? How do you know?"

"He told me." I shrugged. "After he got done bitching about me not having my sword on me, that is."

"Did he tell you his name?"

"Liam." I rocked on my feet, knees bent, waiting for Tommy to raise his sword again. "He told me a lot of stuff. Stuff you and Eli conveniently forgot to mention."

"Emma, you have to be careful," he said. "There are some illorum who've been at this so long their view on things is kind of…"

"Twisted?" I said.

"Yeah."

"I got that." I straightened. "He's kind of developed a God complex. Actually, I guess it's more of an angel complex. He's convinced human laws don't apply to us because of the stuff we can do. Some of which, by the way, would've been nice to know. Why didn't you tell me we don't age?"

It dawned on me then that Tommy didn't just look like he hadn't aged since high school. He actually hadn't. He'd put on some weight and changed the cut of his hair, but he was still an eighteen-year-old kid.

"You weren't exactly taking the whole 'nephilim, illorum, killing fallen angels and demons' thing well to begin with," he said. "I figured it was best to hold off on the sticky details until you'd accepted your situation."

"Eternal life is not a sticky detail," I said. "It's pretty much the whole enchilada."

"Not eternal life," Tommy said. "More like…extended life. Just until you find the angel who fathered you."

"Yeah, so I've heard. How's that working out for you?"

Tommy shrugged, his lips sweeping up to a brilliant natural smile. My heart skipped a little at the sight of it. When he wasn't trying to be cute, he was positively stunning. It was almost like he glowed from the inside, his whole face lifted, his eyes brightened, and his dimples made his expression irresistible.

"I think I found him," he said.

"Your sperm donor? Seriously?"

Tommy nodded, excitement stretching his smile. "I'm not sure. I mean, I saw him on TV the other day and then in person in New York, but from a distance. It looks like him. I haven't been able to get close enough, though. He's got an army of people around him twenty-four-seven and most of them are demons. Not that the humans he's seduced are any easier to get around. A lot of them were nephilim."

"What do you mean, humans he seduced?"

"He's an angel, Emma," Tommy said. "Even though he's Fallen, he still has an angel's magnetizing qualities. Just being in the presence of a Fallen can be seductive if he doesn't do anything to temper the effect."

"And why would he?" I said.

"Exactly."

"So, once we get past the besotted humans and the ever fanatically faithful demon army, we still have to be on guard that the creep doesn't seduce us?"

"Basically," he said. "Being half-angel, we aren't as susceptible as humans, but we're not completely immune."

"Perfect," I said, dejected. I took a deep breath and pushed past it. "So who is he?"

"Richard Hubert. He's a televangelist." Tommy said it like he'd had something to do with the fact and was weirdly proud of it. I knew it was all from being tickled stupid at finally being so close to getting his life back.

"Congratulations."

"Thanks. Yeah, it'll be sweet to get into the swing of things again," he said. "Y'know, after it's all over. Hey, can you believe my little sister's graduating high school next year? Until a few days ago, I figured there was no way I could risk going to watch without exposing her."

He laughed to himself. "Eight years ago she was a whiny little pain in the ass, now…I miss her, y'know? And Jill, my older sister, she had a baby, a son. He's two and I've never met him. He's too young, too vulnerable. The demons could take him and use him against me. I can't let that happen."

I nodded so Tommy would know I understood. I didn't know Tommy's family well; I hadn't even known he had an older sister. But I could imagine what he was feeling, wanting so much to be with his family, but needing to protect them more.

His eyes met mine for an instant, glistening. Then he sniffled and looked away. "Man, I've missed so much. Nothing turned out the way I thought. Figured I'd be a pro ballplayer by now, rolling in money. That I'd have a big house, cars, women. Now, I'd be happy just to have my family back."

My chest pinched. In high school, and even over the last few days since he'd turned my life upside down, Tommy had been so cheery, so strong. It hadn't occurred to me that he'd lost his future too, when he picked up that sword. Just like me, but worse, because he'd only been eighteen. His life hadn't even gotten started before fate had snatched it out of his hands.

I cleared my throat, swallowed the knot of emotion. "So, your angelic fertilizer is a cult leader? That's different," I said, turning the conversation to a less tear-jerking topic.

"Well, he's not a bigwig or anything…I don't think. At least not yet," he said. "I had the TV on the other day for the news, and there he was. They were reporting on some religious conference in New York. I went to check him out—his seminar was packed. Standing room only. That reminds me, I have to ask Eli about some of the nephilim I sensed in the audience. There was something weird about them. I could feel their power, but I know they weren't marked."

"Ah, unfair," I whined.

"I know, right? Anyway, I couldn't get close enough to the Fallen to feel him."

"I'm sorry—what? Feel him?" All sorts of odd images flickered through my head.

"When we're near enough to a Fallen, the scar on our wrist burns," he said.

"Burns how? Like pins and needles? Or a tingly warmth kind of thing?" *I hope—I hope.*

"Naw, kind of feels like it did when you first got it," he said.

Crap. "See, this is the sort of thing you should tell a person straight up at the beginning."

Tommy shrugged. "Sorry. You have to be pretty close—like

striking distance close. I figure it's so we don't hack the head off the wrong dude."

"Clever."

"They think of everything."

"Castration's an idea."

"That plan never goes over well with guys," he said. "Don't worry about it. Most of this stuff just comes to you. It's hardwired. You don't know it's there until you need it."

"Oh. Well then, by all means I'll put my full faith in that theory." *Not.* "So, what happens to everyone else? I mean, I assume raping human women is kinda like eating potato chips—you can't stop at one. A Fallen could have hundreds of kids. What happens to them once Dear Old Dad is sent to the abyss? Are they just, y'know, off the hook? Do they automatically get their lives back?" Hope bubbled up from my belly like a hot spring.

"Yeah," he said.

"Sweet. How will we know? I mean, what happens? Do we get an email, certified letter, winged messenger, a strategic bolt of lightning?"

Tommy shook his head. "I don't know. I guess Eli would tell us."

"Eli. Right," I said. Why didn't I trust that plan? *Liam.* Despite my effort to ignore his mistrust, some of it had seeped into my brain anyway. I pushed the doubt from my mind. "So this guy, this televangelist, what makes you think he's your…guy?"

"I saw a picture once," he said. "But my dad…I mean, my mom's husband, burned it. I only caught a glimpse. He said he just felt like getting rid of the picture. He didn't even know who it was."

"That's it?" I said. "You got a glimpse at a picture, how many years ago, that you think might have been your angelic father who might, kind of, look like this famous televangelist? That's what you're going on?"

His brow tightened. "Well, after I sat in on his seminar in New York, the demon attacks started picking up. So he must've sensed me. I know he's a Fallen. I just…know it. I'm going after him, either way. I'll know for sure if he's Fallen when I get close enough. I'll know if he's *the one* after I take his head."

"Then what?" I asked. "If he's your mom's baby-daddy, what happens? How will you know he was the one?"

"I fall off the radar. I'll be able to stand face-to-face with a demon and they won't even raise a brow," he said. "'Course I won't notice them anymore either. I won't see or sense any of the messed-up stuff we do now."

"You lose your power, your sword?"

"Yeah. All of it. Eli says the blade will just stop forming." He laughed to himself. "Honestly? I don't care. I'll be normal again."

I hoped it worked out for him and wished I had his confidence and experience already. "How many Fallen have you killed?"

He looked away. "Two."

"Two? You've been an illorum for eight years now, and you've only killed two fallen angels?" The weight of our duty pressed against my chest. I'd never get my life back.

"I had to get past their demons first," he said.

"How many demons have you taken out?"

He seemed to think about that for a second. "I don't know. I stopped counting two years ago."

"What was the last count?"

"One hundred and fifty," he said, and for a second the hardship of every one of those battles and all the battles yet to be fought shadowed across his boyish face.

"This sucks."

"Little bit," he said. "But it's God's will. Our penance for what our fathers have done."

"How much do you trust Eli?" I asked. "I mean, how can you be so sure this 'kill the father and the kids go free' stuff is true?"

"I trust him. I have to." Tommy shook his head and turned away, closing the small distance to the railing.

A cool breeze kicked up from the dark valley below and shifted through his sun-bleached curls. I willed the blade of my sword to disperse, then sheathed the hilt and went to lean against the metal railing beside him. "I didn't mean anything against Eli. I know you guys are tight."

"You don't know anything, Emma. You're so new." He leaned on his forearms against the railing, gazing out at the city below. "We're alone in this, Emma. Except for our magisters, we can't trust anyone. The demons…they're not all stupid. Some — a lot of them — are smart. Really smart. They know how to blend in, how to stay calm, so you can't smell them until it's too late."

"What do you mean, stay calm?" I asked. "How does that help them?"

"The more excited or emotional they get, the more the brimstone smell comes out of them." He glanced at me, then away. "It's like b.o. If they can stay calm and don't overthink what they want to do or let their lust for killing us get the best of them, they can stand right next to you and you'd never know it."

"Well, that's not fair."

"Not even close." He rolled his sword in his hand, from one to the other, his eyes fixed on the flash of streetlight off the long, silver blade. "I had one lead me on for two days once. We talked for hours, had drinks, told jokes, just like normal people and then…then she clawed out my femoral artery and tried to suck the blood right from my thigh. I cut off her head while she was still kneeling between my legs."

"How very vampire-esque." I didn't ask what she was doing, kneeling between his legs.

"No. She was a straight-up demon," he said. "She was just trying to make me bleed out faster. I was an idiot to trust her, to let my guard down like that."

"Why did you?"

"I don't know," he said, purposely avoiding my gaze. "I'd been on my own for a while. I had Eli, but it's not the same, you know? I just didn't want to be alone anymore. I needed to feel human again. To connect with someone. That was three years ago, and I haven't… *been* with anyone since. It's hard going through life being suspicious of everyone."

"And now?" I said.

He looked at me, his clear blue eyes so intense, so full of emotion, of memories. "I know I said I didn't mean to drag you into this, and I didn't. I swear. But…I've got to admit, it's hard to regret the day I stumbled onto your doorstep."

A trickle of heat sizzled over my skin. My belly fluttered. I leaned closer, felt my brow go high with a coy smile. "Yeah? I guess opening my door to you wasn't the worst thing that's happened to me."

I licked my lips and his gaze tracked my tongue like he wanted to do it for me. Muscles low in my body tightened. He was going to kiss me, I could feel it. His gaze flicked from my mouth to my eyes and back again. His lips parted. He leaned closer.

I lifted my face toward him, closed my eyes just as his breath warmed over my lips. He smelled like cinnamon Fireballs, hot and sweet. And then he kissed me, and the taste was just as sweet, just as hot. His tongue traced over my lips, and I opened my mouth, felt the firm sweep of his tongue over my teeth, brushing my tongue.

Too soon he leaned back, breaking the warm seal of our lips. I exhaled. My schoolgirl fantasy finally realized.

"Good luck, Emma," he whispered, and my overheated brain couldn't care what he meant.

"You see? That's all we want," a raspy male voice said.

I opened my eyes and turned my chin to my shoulder.

"A little slap and tickle. A little swapping spit and…other bodily fluids," the man said. He was about as tall as Tommy, six-four maybe, but thicker, more like a football player, though he was dressed like a stockbroker.

He wore a blueberry-colored knee-length jacket with a stiff banded collar that reminded me of an Indian style Sherwani suit. Very stylish. His honey-colored hair was neatly combed, parted to the side, and cut conservatively to his collar and over his ears.

Lavender eyes smiled at me, bringing my notice to his goat-like pupils, slit vertically. He titled his head to the side, knowing I was taking his measure. His narrow, pointed nose and matching chin gave him a look of class and sophistication that went perfectly with his outfit, though his larger body type ruined the effect.

The stench of brimstone tickled my nose and a rush of goose bumps shivered over my body. He was both weirdly attractive and creepy.

"It's just the two of us then?" he said. "Perfect. I do so enjoy these intimate affairs. And in such a lovely setting."

I snapped my head to Tommy, or at least to where he should've been. He was gone. *Perfect.*

"Who are you?" I asked the demon.

"I am, or I once was, Bariel." He tugged the cuff of his sleeve with the opposite hand. "You may call me Bob."

Bob? Seriously? "What do you want, *Bob*?"

After he coolly tugged the other cuff, he reached across to his hip. At the exact instant his hand wrapped around the hilt of his sword, it materialized. He pulled out the weapon in one fluid movement, the gleaming metal sliding free of its sheath with a soft hiss.

I drew my sword, willing the sparkling particles to gather, forming into the gleaming long blade. My gut balled into a fast knot. Nervous perspiration beaded at the small of my back and above my lip. This probably wouldn't end well. *Crap.*

"Dear, sweet, ungrateful child," he said, his voice growling out the sugary words. "I want you to respect your fathers."

"Fine. Done. You bet," I said, my voice going higher with each word. Practicing with Tommy was one thing, but taking on a demon…I wasn't ready to test how much I'd learned.

"Were it only so easy," he said, soft laughter making his raspy voice waver. The demon lowered the tip of his sword to the overlook floor, the shiny metal scraping cement as he strolled in a slow circle around me.

"Why is it you children bite the hand that gave you life? Would your anger not be better served directed at those who shun you? Those who would see your souls cast to oblivion rather than take you into the warmth of their holy bosom?"

"Yeah, I know we're just a bunch of suck-ups. But hey, He's God." I shrugged. "Whatcha gonna do?"

"A God that does not love you," Bob said. "Not like your father. Wouldn't you rather know what it's like to be loved unconditionally, the way He loves the humans? Put down your sword, child. Be thankful for the gift of life your angelic father has bestowed on you, and I shall take you to him."

That made my brain hiccup. "You know who my biological father is?"

"Of course," Bob said. "We are every bit as connected with each other as we once were with our former brothers. We did not break our bonds with our holy brothers. They broke with us."

"So at any given time you know where every Fallen is, every demon, what they're doing, who they're with?" I asked. If that were true, he had everything Tommy and I needed to get our lives back. If he wasn't lying.

"Indeed," Bob said, sounding like a smoker's version of Eli. "You need only show your good faith by laying down your weapon."

Faith. There was that word again. At some point I'd have to get me some of that, and time seemed to be running out.

Bob opened his arms to welcome me into his embrace, his sword still loose in his grip. "Come, child. What's your name?"

I tightened my hold on the hilt of my sword. "The name's Hellsbane, demon. And sorry to tell you, it ain't a coincidence." It was—but he didn't need to know that.

He dropped his hands to his sides, tilted his head like a puppy listening to a new sound. "Look around you, nephilim. I have existed longer than anything your eyes behold—longer than the trees, the grass, the very land on which your hovels stand. I am older than the waters in your rivers and the ancient sediment beneath. I am… eternal."

"Color me impressed," I said. "You look like a pile of stinking black goo to me. At least you will in about ten seconds."

His purple, goat-slit eyes flicked to my sword at my shoulder, then back to me, his lips pressing tight. "I've been free from the abyss low these past one hundred years. You believe you can best me, child? Very well. Let's have at it."

Bob moved so fast I felt, more than saw, him advance on me. I don't know how my sword blocked his attack, but the impact staggered me backward. He was behind me suddenly, and then he wasn't. Wind blew past me, and my shoulder burned. Blood trickled from a fine line and Bob appeared several steps away on my right.

Just my luck, I got one who wasn't only smart, but skilled, too. *Crap*.

He smiled, flashing his teeth and the whites of his lavender eyes. His sword in hand, low at his waist, he charged, raising his blade the instant he was near enough to strike. I tracked him this time — barely — and blocked his swing, twisting my sword the way Tommy had, circling my blade so my momentum carried my sword up his back.

Bob roared, arching away, spinning to strike again. I got my sword out to block before his slammed down at my head. The blow was more powerful than anything I'd ever felt and drove me hard to the ground, buckling my legs. In the corner of my mind I saw his weight shift, his feet opening to brace his legs and give him leverage for another swing.

Horror-movie-slow, he swung his sword like a baseball bat. He kept his shoulders back, knees bent, weight on his hind leg, aiming for the strike zone — a.k.a. my neck.

I raised my sword to block the strike, knowing his sheer power might drive my sword into my shoulder anyway. I closed my eyes and braced for impact. It never came.

A loud clash of metal echoed, snapped my eyes open. I looked up in time to see Tommy was suddenly there, engaging the demon, driving him back with a blur of sword strikes.

Bob was good, really good, their attacks and parries so fast and hard, sparks showered around them like tiny fireworks. Their speed and strength made the edges of their blades heat up, glowing against the night sky. They moved so fast, my eyes only caught a glimpse of black ooze, a flash of red blood, though neither fighter showed evidence of slowing from the injuries.

Without warning, a hard wind gusted up from the valley, swirling a fine rain of debris around my body, stinging my eyes. For several terrifying seconds I couldn't see, couldn't breathe in the vacuum. Then just like that the wind was gone.

And so were Tommy and Bob.

CHAPTER EIGHT

"You're wounded." The instant Eli spoke, I exhaled, tension draining from my body. I could breathe again; I could think. I closed my eyes.

Eli knelt beside me. His hand brushed along my shoulder to the back of my neck, his hard chest warming against my arm. I could feel him there, next to me, smell the sweet, comforting scent of his body. His presence seeped over me like I'd lowered myself into a warm, soothing bath.

I let the calming sensation wash away the sting of my wounded shoulder, let him calm my panicked heart. It felt like cheating, like I should be able to handle the fallout from a fight on my own. But I couldn't refuse the relief he offered any more than I could push water away when I was sitting in it. The feel of him engulfed me.

"What are you doing?"

My eyes snapped open and I lifted my head to see Tommy glaring down at me. No. Not at me. At Eli.

"Did you end him, Thomas?" Eli asked, his voice sliding through me like liquid silk.

"No." Tommy's gaze flicked to me then back to Eli. "I lost him."

"Then the Fallen who sent him will know of Emma Jane," Eli said.

"You don't think I know that?" Tommy looked at me, and the tight knot of his brow smoothed. "You okay?"

I nodded. "My arm hurts a little."

"Doesn't look that bad." He raised his sword over his head just as the blade faded to nothing and he slid the hilt into its sheath on his back. His worried gaze still on me, he worked a thin leather strap around his neck from under his shirt, then pulled it off over his head.

There was a small pouch on the end and he held it out to me. "Here, get up and drink this. It'll make the wound heal faster."

I frowned at him, then at the little pouch. The comfort of Eli's embrace seemed wrong after Tommy's kiss, but I couldn't help wanting to stay in his arms just a little longer. "What is it?"

Tommy shook the necklace at me, anxious. "It's a sip of holy water. I refilled it at Saint Anthony's. C'mon, Emma, get up." His gaze flicked to Eli. His voice turned hard. "Let her go."

I looked over my shoulder at the angel beside me and my chest squeezed. He was…beautiful. His clear, ice blue eyes gazed up at Tommy, his expression serene. His perfect mouth gave nothing away, neither smiling nor frowning, and only a slight lift of his brow beneath the dark wisps of his bangs seemed to indicate his question of Tommy's tone.

Eli took his hand from my back and rose to his feet in one slow fluid movement. "This cannot be allowed, Thomas. She isn't ready. You must find the demon and dispatch him."

"I know," Tommy said, offering me his hand. I took it, and he pulled me to my feet, shoving the soft little pouch into my palm. I willed my blade to disperse, then sheathed the hilt and glanced at the cut on my upper arm.

It was deep—I'd need stitches—but it'd stopped bleeding, and it didn't hurt as much as it should. My attention turned to the tiny little water pouch and the impossibly small cork.

"So, uh, what happened? One second you were there and the next it was just me and demon Bob," I said, finally yanking the itty-bitty stopper out before I downed the stale water in one gulp.

Tommy took the necklace back and looped it over his head without meeting my eyes. "I wanted to see if you could handle a demon on your own. I was close by."

"Oh. Well, I can answer that. *No*," I said.

"It was a foolish risk," Eli said. "Bariel is far too strong for an untrained illorum to defeat."

Tommy shot him a withering glare. "You think I would've left her if I'd known how old the bastard was?"

Eli slipped his hands into the pockets of his slacks, still wearing the priestly suit I'd first seen on him. He lowered his chin and looked up at Tommy. "She shouldn't have been left at all."

Tommy shifted on his feet, shoved a hand through his hair. "What're you even doing here, Eli? You said this wouldn't be a problem. What's going on with you?"

"I am her magister," Eli said, the calm, quiet tone of his voice making Tommy's seem all the less for it. "It's my duty to train her."

"And that's it?" Tommy asked, his hands propped on his hips. "Nothing else? Nothing I should be worried about?"

Eli looked at me, his gaze so intense I felt the weight of his stare all the way to my gut. He looked away, shook his head. "Nothing else."

"You know I love you, Eli," Tommy said. "You're the only friend I've had for years. But if it comes down to it…"

Eli looked at Tommy and something passed between them, an

understanding of some kind, and Eli nodded. "Agreed."

Tommy scrubbed a hand down his face. His gaze flicked from Eli to me and back again, then he sighed. "Yeah. Okay. I'm going to see if I can pick up the demon's trail. I have a good idea who sent him."

"The televangelist?" I asked.

Tommy nodded. "Yeah. He's probably headed back to report. Since I know where he's going, I should be able to cut him off."

"You must," Eli said. "A Fallen wouldn't waste an opportunity to destroy an illorum so new to duty. He'll double his efforts to kill her before she becomes any greater threat."

"I know," Tommy said, then he looked at me. "Listen, Emma. Go home. Lock the doors. Your threshold protects your home. Demons—anything non-human—can't come in without being invited. You'll be fine if you don't give permission. In fact, don't even answer your door until I get back. You understand?"

I started to nod, but Eli spoke first. "Emma Jane will stay with me."

Tommy narrowed his eyes at the angel. "No. She can go home; she'll be safe there. From *everyone*." He said the last as though it had more meaning than the simple words implied. I didn't have a clue what was going on between the two of them, but whatever it was, the fine hairs up and down my arms suddenly stood on end.

A tingling wash of energy rippled in front of me, similar to the power I'd felt in Saint Anthony's Chapel, but different, hotter, more focused. Tommy and Eli were facing each other, with me to the side between them. The power wave hit Tommy head on, blowing his curls from his face, and he gasped. He closed his eyes and swallowed hard, bowing his head.

"Thomas, I care for you deeply, but do not forget to whom

you speak." Eli seemed taller suddenly, grander. "Find Bariel and dispatch him before he reports to his deliverer. Emma Jane must continue her training."

Tommy blinked up at Eli, his chin still down, his tone notably more reverent. "With all due respect, from what you told me about the last one, maybe...Maybe it'd be safer if you didn't spend as much time with her."

"I've trained countless illorum, Thomas," Eli said. "It is my duty."

Tommy stood straighter. "But only one of them was a woman."

"It makes no difference."

"But—"

The angel raised his hand and stopped Tommy's protest. "Enough. Go. Fulfill your duty. Emma Jane will stay with me."

Tommy sighed. "Yeah—yes, magister." Then he turned and in a blur of movement and rush of wind he was gone, leaving Eli and me alone.

I'm not an idiot...mostly. I couldn't be completely sure what Eli and Tommy were talking about with the half-finished sentences and knowing looks, but I knew it had to do with me and the fact I was a woman.

I smiled, nervous, and went to get my flip-flops, slipping my feet in one at a time. Clearly Tommy didn't want me to go with Eli. Why? Did he know how the angel affected me? Was he worried I might jump the guy? *Wise man.*

Or worse, was he worried what Eli's response would be if I did?

"You're a beautiful woman, Emma Jane," Eli said, and I turned to see his gentle smile tugging the corners of his lips. "But I love God more."

"Hey. You're not supposed to read people's thoughts." Especially when they're particularly embarrassing.

He bowed his head in apology, though his smile remained constant. "Forgive me."

I did. *Sigh*.

"How's your arm?" he asked, touching the gash just below my shoulder.

The heat of his fingertips brushed my skin, and I trembled. His gaze flicked to mine. Every time Eli touched me a ribbon of heat rippled through my veins, stirring my body in ways that wouldn't do either of us any good.

After a decisive exhale, I smiled, and he smoothed his fingers over the healing pink skin. The sides of the long cut had already stitched themselves together, the skin now a long, wrinkled scar. At this rate it would heal completely smooth, not a mark left behind.

Despite the distraction of my increased healing abilities, my mind couldn't focus on anything but the feel of Eli's skin on mine. I walked away, putting some distance between us.

A soft breeze shifted my hair, bringing the scents of the city to tickle my nose. I filled my lungs, willing myself to feel better all on my own.

"I think there's been a mistake," I said. "I don't know if I was supposed to be marked. I mean, I can't fight. That innate ability Tommy keeps talking about…I'm not feeling it."

"But you survived the battle with Bariel," Eli said.

"Yeah, thanks to Tommy. I seriously didn't have a clue what I was doing." Memories of blurring swords and blinding movement made a tiny, nervous laugh bubble out of me. "I think my eyes were closed most of the time. I was just hacking at the air, hoping I'd hit something."

Eli stood in my comfort zone again. I hadn't seen him move,

hadn't notice he'd even taken a step. "Thomas aided you because you survived to be aided. If you were not meant to wield that sword, you would not have been marked, and you would not have survived."

"That's kind of backward logic, isn't it?" I stepped away, but the distance between us was still too close.

I could feel him again, that wonderful, addictive ease that settled over my body, warmed me, soothed my muscles, calmed my nerves. I rubbed my hands up and down my arms, trying to keep my mind focused on real sensation instead of what Eli's presence made me feel. I didn't want to like it so much.

"Why do you fight my comfort?" he asked.

"Because it's not real." A press of delicious heat oozed up my spine at the soft sound of his voice, and I shuddered. "Seriously, I thought you weren't supposed to read minds."

"I can read your thoughts, Emma Jane. I choose not to because I value free will," he said. "The thoughts I receive from you are not those you choose to keep private. Your mind broadcasts them. It is an effort, in fact, not to receive them."

I remembered Liam said I was like a bullhorn. *Rude*. But apparently true. So, that sucked.

"For example," he said, shifting to catch my eyes with his, and I couldn't look away. "I know you fight the comfort I offer, but I don't know why."

I shrugged, hoping I seemed more together than I felt. "I don't need it. At least I don't want to need it. I figure I should get used to dealing with the fallout after a fight all on my own."

"There's no need."

"There is for me," I said. "Being near you feels good, yes, but it also feels a little like being high. Like I'm not totally in control of myself. It just kind of freaks me out."

The creases along his brow deepened and he eased back. "Extraordinary."

"Right. Call Ripley's. I'm a friggin' enigma." I stepped around him and went to the overlook's railing. Even that close, the feel of him was making my mind swim and my body too warm and loose.

I braced my hands on the railing, anchoring myself. I cleared my throat. "You, uh, were kind of hard on Tommy. Don't you think?"

"He was laboring under a false assumption." Eli came to stand beside me. I didn't feel that wave of bliss this time, even when his shoulder brushed mine as he leaned his forearms against the railing.

He looked sideways at me and I knew he'd read my thoughts. "I will not caress you again unless you request it of me."

"Thanks." I smiled as my belly tightened. I'd never ask for his fake rapture. My pride wouldn't allow it. "So…what was Tommy's false assumption?"

"He assumed he knew better than I do how and when to train you."

I snorted. "He's a guy. Of course he thought he knew better. *Hello*?"

Eli laughed. "So I've heard. However, that's not the case with Thomas. He believed I was incapable of clear judgment where you are concerned."

"Because I'm a woman?"

"Yes. He assumes that because you're a woman, you're too great of a…temptation to me, and my judgment suffers for it."

"But that's not the case?"

"No." He gazed out at the city below, the skyline turning a soft pink at the edges as dawn approached. "The temptation I feel with you has little to do with you being a woman. In truth, Thomas doesn't realize you're only slightly more of a temptation to me than he is."

Only slightly? I let the twinge of jealousy go. Who knew angels swung both ways? "I'm sure he'll be thrilled."

"Not everything is about sex," Eli said. "However, I'm not so different from the Fallen. I, too, feel the lure of the *daughters* of men, though I have had eons to bridle my passions. Thomas is more likely to fall victim to your beguiling ways than me."

The warm memory of Tommy's lips on mine tingled through my thoughts. Even though I knew Eli might read them, I couldn't help it.

"Ah." Eli looked at me from beneath his dark blue-black bangs. "I see he's already succumbed to your seduction."

"Hey. *He* kissed *me.*"

Eli nodded. "Of course. How could he not?" He turned and leaned his backside against the railing, his hands resting on either side.

"There is something indefinably exquisite about the child of an angel and a human raising a sword to battle in the name of God," he said. "I know of nothing more harrowing, more arduous than the duty of the illorum. And one answering the call is an enticing, infatuating sight. These people, like you and Thomas, are a temptation unlike anything I have ever known."

"But you've got a grip on that…right?"

His smile blossomed across his lips, as breathtaking as a sunrise. "Yes, Emma Jane, and my grip is ironclad. The lessons that made it so are not ones which I would experience again."

"So, you've given in to your feelings before?"

He shook his head, eyes down. "No," he said. "But there were times I opened my heart too much, loved more than was safe, and it cost me…dearly."

"You were punished?"

"By no one other than myself," he said.

"Then…?"

"I've trained hundreds of illorum, and I've watched nearly every one of them perish in battle," he said. "Each death is vividly etched into my mind and seared forever on my heart."

I could read his emotions. I wasn't trying, but I didn't have to. The way he held himself, the tension across the shoulders, the tightening around the eyes, the hesitation in his voice, gave away his feelings. I knew his pain was even more than he could admit.

"But one, at least, hurt more than all the rest," I said. "Didn't it?"

He shrugged—casually pretending the memories were less painful than he'd first let on. "There was one. Jeannette d'Arc. She lived more than five hundred years ago, in a small village in France. She was just a child when I first met her. All of twelve years old, with the light of faith and grace bright as Heaven itself in her eyes."

"She was pretty?" I sounded jealous. Maybe I was.

"What is pretty?" He shook his head. "She was captivating. I'd never met a human so sublimely alluring and so fully connected to earth and spirit. She was the ideal blending of Heaven and earth if ever there was one. And she was mine. That is, she was my… responsibility. Or she soon would be." He looked away.

"Relax, Eli," I said. "You're not the first person to stomp all over good sense and fall for someone y'know damn well you shouldn't."

He smiled and my heart skipped, stupidly pleased that I'd put him at ease. "I enjoyed being near her, talking to her. Strong-willed, fearless in a way I'd never known, she was…addicting. Her wisdom and grace, the ethereal beauty within her was a powerful thing."

"Tommy talked like you'd crossed some kind of line with her. Or at least came close to it."

Eli dropped his gaze, staring at his shoes. "It's not my duty to protect—I am forbidden to interfere. I instruct, advise, *only* those marked for duty. In all respects, my interactions with Jeannette were suspect. She was not marked. She was not yet mine to instruct. I knew it then as I know it now, but I was…powerless to turn away."

"You fell in love with her?" I made it a question but I knew the answer. Everything about his body language let me know his feelings for her cut to the bone.

"I love all those in my charge. But Jeannette…I loved her wholly and completely, with every breath of Heaven in my soul. I loved her…as I love God."

"And that's a bad thing?"

"It is a dangerous thing. It compelled me to act in ways that I shouldn't have. The times in which Jeannette lived were tumultuous. Kingships and successions were argued and fought over. Her country was in turmoil. The simple tasks of life were treacherous. Every day brought the threat of death."

"And you kept her safe."

"Not directly—it's forbidden. But I diverted danger when I could," he said. "Even when her village was sacked time and again, I did what I could to keep her and her family out of harm's way. I tried to stay hidden, to watch from a distance so as not to influence her life…"

He stopped for a moment, his gaze swinging up to the night sky, and then he exhaled. "That's not true. I hid from her sight, but not from her. She felt me as you do now. I made sure of it. I wanted her attention, craved it. I wanted to see her smile for me, to hear her speak. When I wasn't with her, I thought of her constantly. Worried she would come to harm and I wouldn't be there."

"You would've defied God to protect her?"

"No. I..." He looked away again. "I don't know. Once she was marked, everything changed. My conflict between duty and desire both eased and worsened. Now I had cause to be with her always, but this only amplified my infatuation. She was besieged by demons almost instantly. And Jeannette's superior swordsmanship drew the attention of military commanders who were desperate for any kind of edge in their battles."

"They wanted her to fight with them," I said.

"They wanted her to *lead* them," he said. "Seeing her battle against demons disguised as English soldiers and common ruffians, they believed she fought with divine aid. And Jeannette knew with my help she could accomplish more than any mortal man."

"Lead them?" Understanding dawned and pity pressed against my chest like a heavy weight. "Eli, are you talking about Joan of Arc? Is Jeannette d'Arc, Joan of Arc?"

He met my gaze. "Yes."

"Oh, Eli..." It was both amazing and heartbreaking at once. I knew how this story ended. "And she wanted you to interfere in politics, in the evolution of an entire human society...that's huge. But you aren't allowed to do that, right?"

His jaw clenched for a second and his brows knitted tight. "I am well aware of what I can do and what I should do, Emma Jane."

He pushed off the railing, striding to the center of the overlook, then stopped and turned to face me. "I knew what she asked of me was more than I could give, but I swear to you, I could not deny her. Still, I managed to temper my hand in matters. I played the invisible scout, going ahead to spy on the enemy, listening in on critical conversations. It was enough."

"She used the information to help her army win?" I asked.

"Yes. And her army helped her defend against a constant, ever-increasing barrage of demons," he said. "The two fates, hers and her country's, seemed intertwined. The battles they fought brought her closer to the Fallen who sought to kill her."

"You knew who it was," I said. "You knew who the Fallen was and where he was hiding. Didn't you?"

"Yes," he said. "I put her on his path."

"Did she know?"

"No. I couldn't tell her. I shouldn't have done as much as I did, but I wanted the attacks to stop. I wanted her to be safe, and only the Fallen's end would achieve it." His lips tightened. "My feelings for her ruined my reason. It was my fault."

I wanted to go to him, comfort him. But I didn't. The way he could make me feel on purpose worried me for what he might do by accident. What if I couldn't stop? Instead, I leaned against the guardrail and hugged my arms around my belly. "Who was he?"

"The Duke of Bedford," Eli said. "He'd amassed a great deal of power and influence among humans. And when he heard Jeannette and her fellow warriors had been captured near Compiegne, he ordered that she be sent to him."

"You couldn't do anything to stop it?"

"There was no reason," he said. "Their meeting was inevitable. I'd set her on this path myself. But I underestimated the Fallen's will to evade his punishment. She was brought to him bound and helpless. He didn't leave a sliver of opportunity for her to free herself. For nearly a year she was tortured mercilessly."

"Why didn't he just kill her?" Seemed the smart thing to do, to get rid of the threat once and for all.

"He wanted to turn her," Eli said. "He tried to seduce her to turn from her duty, from God. She wouldn't. So he brutalized her every day. I cannot put into words how much I wanted to go to her, to ease her suffering."

"You didn't? You just left her to go through that alone?" My stomach twisted. How could he?

"You think I wouldn't have rained down the fire of Heaven itself if I could have?" he said, anger burning through his tone. "Every wound, every snap of the whip on her tender flesh, cut me to the bone. But I couldn't risk interfering any further. God help me, look what my interference had already brought her. My impatience to see her safe put her on this path too soon. I should've known she wasn't ready. I should have surrendered to her destiny long ago. I should have…"

His knees buckled, and he dropped to a squat, his head falling forward into the cup of his hands. "Dear Father, forgive me. He tortured her for nearly a year and Jeannette never once forsook God or me. She fought to hold onto this world for Him…for me."

Eli lifted his chin, his long fingers still covering his mouth. His cheeks were wet from tears, though none fell as I watched. He stared straight ahead, as though he could see his memories in living color before him.

"The Fallen's desperation pushed his cruelty to unfathomable lengths. He demanded she turn from God. She refused, so he had her tied to a stake and set her ablaze. This time when she cried out in pain my courage crumbled. I couldn't refuse her. Not then. Not anymore. I stood with her, shielding the worst of the pain until she finally let go her mortal coil."

My throat closed, imagining her anguish as the fire ate at her flesh, imagining Eli's as he forced himself to let it happen. I didn't care what his effect on me might be. Eli's memories were swallowing him up. He needed an anchor, and I was the only one around to offer it.

Kneeling in front of him, I held his wrists, his fingers still cupped over his mouth. I wasn't sure he noticed my touch.

"She knew," he said, his eyes wide, glistening and unfocused. "She knew I would finally let her go. Her smile was so exquisite, so beautiful, even as the fire burned the rags they'd given her to wear. She told me she loved me and then she...kissed me." His hands shifted, fingertips touching his lips as though he could still feel hers there. "A moment later she was gone."

His eyes focused, his hand reaching to brush my cheek. "Trust in this, Emma Jane." His voice came on a soft shaky breath. "I would not feel that loss again for anything...or anyone. I swear it."

CHAPTER NINE

"Joan of Arc died, Eli. I don't want to end up the same way," I said, swallowing through the tightness in my throat. "This may come as a shock to you, but I don't want to have my head hacked off or be burned at the stake or have my arms and legs tied to four horses while they run in opposite directions."

"I don't want you to die either, Emma Jane," Eli said, rising from his squat on the overlook.

"Right. That might go over better if I didn't know most illorum die under your watch."

"You're fighting creatures stronger and more cunning than anything on earth. Their desperation makes them driven, not stupid," he said. "Naturally, there's some risk."

"Yeah, I'm picking up on that."

"You were born for this," he said. "I'll practice with you. Help you develop your angelic gifts."

"Why? So I can die with skill? No thanks." Images of heads rolling, fires licking at my feet, and brimstone boiling under my skin filled my brain. This couldn't be my reality. "I want to go home."

"Emma Jane, don't you know how lucky you are? How special?" he said.

Oh, he had to be on drugs. "Right. Lucky me."

"Come." He held a hand to me. "I have something to show you."

I didn't move. Everything inside me ached to reach out and feel his hand in mine, but I was tired, more than a little freaked, and maybe a smidge stubborn.

"I'm outta here." I turned, heading for my car, but only managed five steps before I smacked my nose into Eli's chest. He'd teleported into my path.

"Hey." I rubbed my nose. "That's not cool."

"Perhaps you've mistaken my statement for a request," he said. "It wasn't."

"Ah. So it's like that, is it?"

He snaked an arm around my waist, jerked me to him so our bodies were flush against each other. I gasped, my hands going to his chest on reflex.

"Yes," he said. "It's like that."

A soft wind shifted through my hair, and the world around us blurred as if in motion. But our feet hadn't moved. The overlook, the cars, the townhouses, the sky, everything raced past us.

Then it was gone. Darkness engulfed us, with only the distant stars twinkling in the vast emptiness. My hands leached around Eli's neck, brought us cheek to cheek.

"You're safe in my arms, Emma Jane. Always," he said, his lips brushing my ear. A shudder traveled straight down to my center with the sweet sound of his words. The man had an orgasmic voice. What a waste.

His embrace loosened, and I leaned back enough to see his face. A soft glow lightened the shadows from behind me, just enough to cast a silvery glow over his expression. Time and space suddenly rushed in on me, and my brain spun like I'd been twirling around on my toes for an hour.

I let go of him with one hand, pressing it to my forehead to stop the spin and to keep my brain from coming out of my ears. "What was that?"

"Your mind is struggling to match speed with your body. May I help?"

I'd told him never to use his power to give me false rapture, but I guess it was like asking a fish not to swim. I nodded and he rested his hand over mine, the warmth of his skin heating through me. The nauseating twirling stopped.

"I hoped moving slower would help lessen the shock, but it seems the effect allowed your vision too much time to try and compensate," he said.

"We moved at angelic speed?" I asked, guessing.

"No. I am able to travel at the speed of thought. We moved an increment slower."

"Um, thanks." I tried to see over his shoulder, to get my bearings, but I couldn't push up on my toes. I moved the muscles, and nothing happened. I looked at my feet—there was nothing beneath us. No floor, no ground, no…anything, just more blackness and millions and millions of distant twinkly lights.

An icy bolt of panic shot up my spine and I clutched at Eli. My gut twisted and a scream caught in the back of my throat. Eli hugged me tight.

"Where are we?"

"Look behind you," he said.

It took a few seconds of internal argument, but eventually my courage rallied, and I glanced over my shoulder. "Is that…"

"Earth," he said.

Sheer awe loosened my grip. I shifted my feet to his—I had to stand on something—and turned, holding his hands to my hips to anchor me, my back to his chest.

The world looked exactly the way it does in all the pictures… but so much more. More beautiful, more breathtaking than any picture could capture.

There was a storm swirling over one of the oceans, and night was quickly approaching for half the world. A thick line of darkness crept over land and water as the planet spun. On the other side, brilliant light ate away the darkness at exactly the same pace.

"This can't be real. How?" I asked, my brain fighting reason and everything I knew about space and time and reality.

His hands slipped over my belly, his embrace enveloping me. "In the arms of an angel, Emma Jane, all things are possible."

My eyes closed, and I leaned back into his chest. I tried not to enjoy the feel of him around me, but the heat of his body, the comforting strength of his muscles, and the sweet, summery scent of his skin decimated my willpower.

"Behold what your birthright has brought you, Emma Jane," he said. "No mortal human could claim as much."

I opened my eyes and felt that rush of awe all over again at the view. "It's amazing, Eli. Thank you."

"This is only the beginning. You have been chosen to battle creatures far more powerful than mere mortals. You are not like other humans; you cannot be. Your task requires much of you, and for it, much has been given. Time and space unravel for you to traverse with the same intrinsic understanding as those you hunt. The world is quite literally at your feet."

Before I could take a breath, I found myself staring out over a large valley and an ocean beyond. Gone was the great global marble spinning in the endless black of space. Suddenly, I was blinking at a waking cityscape miles below with large water inlets and busy harbors. There was blue sky above me and green land below. We were back on Earth.

Hard, unrelenting wind whipped my hair, making it difficult to see. But I could make out the white sand-lined shores and the short mountain ranges that blocked sections of the city from the ocean.

"Where are we?" I yelled, but my voice was lost on the roaring wind.

Eli tucked me under his arm, and silence descended over us like he'd closed a door. My hair floated back against my head and I could stand on my own. I shoved at the strands over my face and tried to clue in my brain. "Brazil." Eli pointed at the city. "Rio de Janeiro."

"It's beautiful." My gaze followed the landscape below to the base of the mountain, then to the long winding staircase tracing up the side until they disappeared far below the edge of the outcropping we stood on. It'd been nearly six a.m. in Pittsburgh by the time Eli and I left Earth, which made it nearly seven a.m. in Rio, and the city was already bustling.

What are we standing on? I fisted my hand around Eli's jacket and leaned over for a better look. "No way. Christ the Redeemer? Seriously?" We were on his arm and I looked to the left at the huge, white, carved face of Jesus.

"Remarkable, isn't it?" Eli said. "And yet it pales in comparison to the miracle that is you and those like you."

He smiled wide, so pleased with himself, and I could *almost* forgive him for not warning me one wrong step could send me tumbling over a hundred feet to the very, *very* hard landing below.

I looked to the growing crowds and the endless line of pilgrims still climbing the mountain. "They don't see us?"

Eli shook his head. "As in everything, humans only see what they wish to see, what is easily explainable—what is normal."

With Eli, I was outside everything normal. And I was starting to like it.

"You could reach this spot on your own," he said. "It's within your abilities."

"Really? How?"

"Speed of movement is the key. If not for the physiology of humans, illorum could travel from place to place instantaneously like their fathers," he said. "But even moving faster than light, there are few places in the world you cannot reach."

"Sweet." My mind shifted through the possibilities. "What do I do? Is there a magic word or something?"

"Put the image of where you would like to go in your mind," he said. "Allow your desire to stand in that exact spot fill you. Then take a step."

I really wanted to be off the nearly two-hundred-foot statue. Not that I'm afraid of heights, but I figured it'd be better to aim small for my first run at teleportation.

I'd seen the wide landing at the base of the statue when I leaned over, and the stone railing that circled it. I closed my eyes and brought the image of what I'd been looking at seconds before to mind. Wanting to be at the railing was the easy part. Yeah, I wanted to be there, on the ground, safe, before I fell to a horribly painful death. The desire swelled up in me, like turning on a faucet. I took a step.

My second step stumbled me into the stone railing, cracking my knees, scraping my hands when I reached out to stop myself.

Eli popped in beside me and scooped an arm around my waist, steadying me.

Tourists already milling about the base threw curious glances my way. It took a second, but I realized they weren't freaking out, pointing at me in frightened astonishment because I'd suddenly appeared out of nowhere. It was like they hadn't even noticed.

I forced a smile, nodded, and turned to find a seat on the wall next to Eli. He leaned toward me, bumping shoulders. "Don't aim into solid objects; you'll hit them."

"Thanks for the warning."

"I thought it went without saying."

"You thought wrong."

"Obviously." He rocked forward onto his feet. "Would you like to try again?"

I rubbed my knee then brushed off my hands. "Where to? Some place soft?"

"The choice is yours," Eli said. "I will know it when the image enters your mind."

"Okay. We've been to Christ the Redeemer," I said. "Let's not play favorites. Ready?"

Eli raised a brow and dipped his chin in acquiescence.

This time the trip took a half second or so longer. I wasn't traveling across the globe, but Sri Lanka wasn't exactly a step away…at least not for most people.

The greater distance allowed me to learn more about this lightning-fast mode of travel. This time I felt myself move. Wind rustled through my hair, pressed at my body as I sliced through space and time.

I could see the world blurring by. There were no shapes, nothing I could identify, only a wash of colors gushing from a pinpoint ahead of me, like traveling down a tunnel with a sudden, very abrupt stop at the end. With my next step, I stumbled across the uneven lap of the giant Buddha and into the arms of Eli. My hands latched around his hard biceps, and his hands caught my waist.

"You beat me here," I said, finding my footing before stepping back from him.

His hands slipped from my body and he rubbed them together, nervous and empty. A moment later he cupped them behind his back.

"My angelic speed is faster," he said. "The Fallen travel an increment slower, but still faster than any illorum I've known. Most demons move slower than light, but far faster than anything humans can visibly track."

I nodded, letting him know I understood. My gaze tripped out over the city of Kurunegala. Standing in the folded lap of the eighty-eight-foot Buddha statue atop Elephant Rock was a view worth a moment of awed amazement.

It wasn't as windy here as it'd been in Brazil. At about three thirty, the day was well underway, and the air was warm, the gentle breeze welcome.

"This time," Eli said from behind me, "you follow me."

I turned. "Where are you going?"

"See it in my thoughts."

"Of course. Um, how?"

He clasped his hands in front of him and smiled. "I'm not shielding. Simply find me in your mind and my thoughts will open to you."

"Right." I sighed and closed my eyes, reaching out to him with my mind, the same as I'd done a million times when I performed my readings. I found him, and the invisible door inside me opened.

My heart squeezed; a powerful swell of love and peace stole my breath. Electricity tingled down my arms, all over my body, heating my blood through my veins. Ghostly warmth tingled my palms. I rubbed my hands, trying to ignore the feeling, to forget it. But I wanted to experience it again, the sensation of flesh against flesh.

These were emotions I was feeling, Eli's emotions, same as I'd ever been able to read from anyone. I was in his mind. I focused, pressed beyond the cloud of energy, the aura that surrounded every intelligent mind. I didn't know if I could; another person's emotions swamping through me had always been enough to make me want to pull back. I ignored my recoil this time and punched through.

Follow me to the Shiva. Bangalore. The thought suddenly rippled through my brain as easily as my own.

"India?" I opened my eyes, but Eli was already gone. The image of yet another giant statue flashed through my head. I'd never seen this one before. Not in pictures, not on TV, yet it was clear in my thoughts. I closed my eyes again and imagined my gaze traveling up the statue. Thoughts, buried beneath the image I'd read from Eli, now emerged.

So beautiful. The details, the colors, the marvelous ingenuity of humans.

These were his thoughts. I was seeing the statue through his eyes, through his memories. It was enough. I wanted to go there and I took a step. My next step and the ones after that moved me across the black stone floor to Eli. He leaned an elbow against the guardrail at the base of the statue of the Hindu deity.

It wasn't as big as the Buddha, but it was still scary big. The four-armed man sat with his legs folded, one set of arms resting in his lap, the other set bent upward at his sides. The right hand gripped a giant trident; in the other he held a small drum, shaped like an hourglass.

He wore a cobra around his neck like jewelry and two more on each bicep. His bent knee was at least six feet over my head. *Scary big.*

"Remarkable, isn't it?" Eli said, staring up at the statue's meditating face.

I followed his gaze. "Pretty sweet. A little effeminate. Whatever. Could do without the snakes." I looked back to Eli. "So how'd you like the entrance? No slamming into things or stumbling. Smoooooth as glass. Pretty slick, huh?"

Eli straightened. "Indeed. With each flex of your angelic abilities, your control sharpens." He turned and walked toward a canvas awning, where a crowd of tourists stood in line. "Shall we go again? Follow me, Emma Jane."

I had three strides to open my mind to his, to pluck the words and images I needed from the top of his thoughts. And then he vanished. "Rush much?"

No one noticed us arrive, and I was confident they wouldn't care that we vanished. Eli was simply there, then not. I assumed that when I disappeared, they'd see no more than a gust of wind, like I'd seen when Tommy had disappeared from the overlook on Mount Washington.

My vision tunneled, colors whizzed past me, and I stepped to the edge of the rocky cliff next to Eli.

"Wow. How far down is it?" I asked.

We both leaned forward; the mist from Angel Falls beaded along strands of my hair, moistened my face.

"Over nine hundred meters," Eli said. "More than three thousand feet."

"Cool. Angel Falls. Venezuela, right?"

"Yes."

"Nice they named it after you guys."

"Fitting, I think." The sun was just lighting the sky, pushing at the horizon to break the dawn. The bottom of the falls was hidden in the dark shadows of the early morning, the roar of falling water nearly deafening. The sky was still rich with deep purples and blues, the horizon a breathtaking canvas of reds and yellows from the rising sun. Eli straightened, smiled, and I recognized the look on his face as he pictured another destination in his mind.

I thrust open my thoughts to him and only managed to pluck out the word "Sphinx" before he vanished. *Crap.* I knew enough about the human-headed cat to get me there. But that was about it.

My desire rose and I took a step. With the next, I walked across the wide head of the Sphinx and stopped next to Eli. He stood at the edge, inches from where it rounded down over the forehead. He clasped his hands in front of him, the wind flapping the edges of his black jacket against his knees, fluttering through his dark hair. He blinked up at the sky and the afternoon sun.

My mind was already open to him, feathering over the top of his thoughts, reading whatever he offered. Fool me once, shame on me; fool me three times, and I'm just not trying.

You must move faster, Emma Jane. Reason quicker; open your mind to your prey on reflex. I could hear his thoughts echoing through my head.

"I'm trying," I said.

Eli lowered his head, his gaze fixing on mine. "There's one more thing I wish to show you."

"Lucky me," I said, frustrated he wasn't as blown away by what I'd learned as I was. "What is it?"

"Only this," he said, but his lips didn't move. I blinked. It wasn't like I'd been staring at his mouth, but I was sure it didn't move. And then I heard his voice in my head again. *Capri, Italy. Walk with me in*

Augusto's gardens. He vanished.

A shudder rocked across my shoulders, the sound of his voice smoothing through my body like a physical touch. This was different than me opening my mind to his and listening in on his thoughts. This was closer to what it was like feeling another's emotions. Except I didn't do it.

He'd reached out and placed his thoughts in my head. He'd touched me with his mind, and the sensation left my knees weak. I sucked in a deep breath, trying to center myself again, to cool the flood of heat he'd ignited in my core. *Concentrate.*

My mind raced. I'd never been to Italy, let alone in some garden in Capri. I'd gotten a brochure once from a tour company in Rome. I knew Rome. I could picture the Coliseum. An instant later I was there, the city noisily racing before me. Tiny cars and humming Vespas whizzed by, enormous tour buses rumbled along, the smaller vehicles buzzing around them like gnats on a dog. People pushed past on their way to somewhere else. No one noticed me.

"Great. Now what?" I still didn't know a thing about the gardens Eli had mentioned or how on earth to get to Capri. Desperation pushed me to stop a woman hurrying by, tugging a little boy by the hand behind her. The kid, maybe seven years old, seemed to be trying his level best to slow their progress, literally dragging his feet.

"Excuse me," I said, reaching out to touch her before she blew past. She jumped to a stop as though she'd only then noticed me standing inches away.

"Good heavens, you scared me half to death," she said, hand to her chest. "What is it?" She glanced at the kid, yanked his arm so he'd stop fidgeting. "Marco, stop it." Then to me she said, "I'm sorry. I'm in a hurry. I don't mean to be rude."

The woman was probably ten years older than I was, with jet

black hair pulled into a high ponytail. She was thin, probably from chasing after her son, who was pulling her arm again, tugging her in the direction he'd been fighting against not two seconds before.

Wait. Was that Italian? "Are you speaking Italian?"

"*Si. Sicuramente. Che vuoi?*" she said, but my brain heard, "Yes. Of course. What do you want?"

Cool.

"*Sto cercando di andare a Capri ed ai giardini di Augusto,*" I said. But what I'd thought in my head was, "I'm trying to get to Capri and Augusto's gardens."

The woman huffed, her gaze darting to the shops and signs around us. Her dark brows rose, and she pointed across the wide street to a tourist office.

"*Li, domanda a loro,*" she said and my brain translated to, "There, ask them."

"*Grazie.*" I hardly got the thank you out before she turned on her heel and marched away, her son dragging his feet behind her once again. *Ahh, kids.*

The traffic between me and the other side of the street was like floodwater, swift and unending—too easy to get swept away. Or run over. Eli was waiting in the gardens, wherever they were, and despite my being able to move faster than light, time was ticking away.

The desire to be across the street swelled an instant before my will moved me. The next moment, I landed directly in front of the office. The picture window was filled with advertisements for touring destinations all over Italy. I spotted a poster-size ad up in the left-hand corner with the word "Capri" three inches tall across it.

Capri's an island. Who knew?

Centering my attention on the poster, I scanned the smaller, inlaid pictures, the marina, the cable car, the piazza, and there in the lower corner was a shot of the Gardens of Augustus. "Perfect."

With my next heartbeat I stood at the edge of the same wide terrace I'd seen in the picture. The ground was paved in terracotta tiles and I leaned against the railing like so many tourists around me, gazing down hundreds of feet to the ocean below. The water was so blue, so clear, that I could see the rocks beneath the surface.

"Well done, Emma Jane."

I spun around. "Eli."

His smile plumped his cheeks and creased the corners of his eyes. He held his hands clasped in front of him, just as he had less than five minutes ago, standing on the head of the Great Sphinx in Egypt.

A warm Mediterranean breeze swirled up the side of the cliff, fluttering the edges of his jacket, shifting through the luminous black strands of his hair. He looked so damned pleased with himself.

"Y'think? You know, I've never been here before. I didn't even know Capri was an island. I almost didn't make it."

He dipped his chin. "That was the point. To force you to think on your feet, to use your instincts, your innate abilities to track and hunt."

"Yeah? Well, here's some news. Apparently I speak Italian now," I said.

"You are able to understand all languages," he said. "Some are more difficult to speak. It's a simple matter of training the tongue."

"Nifty," I said. "So, where to next?"

He held out his hand, and this time I didn't hesitate. The moment my palm settled into the soft heat of his, the scene around us changed. My feet wobbled on the new surface, the lava stone path not as even and smooth as the terracotta terrace had been.

There was a small fountain in front of us now, and the path we stood on traced in a circle around it. We'd moved deeper into the garden. Trees and flowerbeds filled the rolling landscape, the grass meticulously cut and lusciously green, the air fragrant and sweet on my tongue.

Without warning, the skin on my wrist flared hot. I flinched, jerking my hand from Eli's. My wrist was on fire. Or at least it felt like it.

I turned my hand, staring down at the mark Tommy's sword had tattooed onto my inner wrist. It looked the same. The skin wasn't even red. I rubbed at it, but the mark still flamed, sending jolts of heat up my arm.

Concern darkened Eli's face. He turned, scanning the gardens and the winding paths. "Stay here." He took a step, and before the next one, he was gone.

I scanned the garden pathways, focusing on a line of people ten feet away just as Eli reappeared at the end.

The group leisurely walked the flower-lined path toward a small curve where the gardens edged the cliffside. At the front of the crowd the female tour guide led the way, holding a canvas sign at the end of a tall pole that read, "Bedford Corp."

The moment Eli materialized next to the group, a tall man in the center stopped and turned. He looked to be in his early- to mid-thirties, athletic, with corn-silk blond hair, cut short and feathered to the side. A professional, responsible-looking man, he wore a short-sleeved blue shirt untucked from his beige cargo shorts.

The handsome man's bright blue eyes turned cold, narrowing on Eli. The tourists parted around him, continuing on their way with only one or two looking back at Eli. After a flick of the other man's hand, they kept moving.

I was close enough, but I couldn't hear a word they were saying.

Eli crossed his arms across his chest; the other man folded his hands behind his back. The conversation was boring for its lack of gestures or outward enthusiasm. They could be discussing tax laws for all the energy they were putting into it.

Then suddenly, the other man's eyes shifted. He looked past Eli's shoulder, directly at me. Despite the warm Mediterranean weather, a shiver trembled over my skin, turning to solid ice in my gut.

Eli vanished, then reappeared next to me a moment later. "We have to go," he said.

"Why? Who is that?" My gaze flicked back to the handsome businessman on vacation just as he vanished.

"Oh shit."

"Exactly," Eli said. He took my hand.

"No. Wait. That was a Fallen," I said.

"Yes."

"You know him," I said, sure of it. "Who is he?"

"The Duke of Bedford."

"The Fallen who killed Jeannette?"

"Yes."

My eyes went to the Bedford Corp. group. The happy, leisurely tourists were suddenly headed my way. All of them—except the lady with the sign—and they didn't look happy or leisurely anymore.

"You must let me take you from this place."

"Those are demons, aren't they?" I asked.

"Yes."

"You're interfering?"

"No. I'm simply ending our training session and returning you to your home," he said.

The horde of people was twenty feet back, but picking up the pace. They came toward us, shoulder to shoulder, eight bodies wide, men and women, snarling, backs hunching. Their hands melted and reshaped as they moved, forming into long, sharp talons.

A stink cloud of brimstone rolled like an invisible wave before them, washing over me so I couldn't breathe without taking it into my lungs. Bile rocketed up my throat, and I swallowed on reflex.

"You're asking me to run from a fight?" I asked.

Eli glanced behind him, then back to me. He sighed. "Yes."

"Well...just this once...I'm okay with that."

The next instant, the snarling, seething horde of demons vanished.

CHAPTER TEN

It was noon when I opened my eyes and heard someone in my room...eating. Fear snaked through me. The last thing I remembered was being charged by a bunch of stinky, drooling, pissed-off demons.

The green digital display on my alarm clock flashed 12:01. Five and a half hours of sleep does not make for a happy Emma. From behind me, jaws snapped and crunched and mashed: *crackle—snap—crunch—chomp-chomp-chomp*. It sounded like the Rice Krispies guys with a case of 'roid rage.

"Ahh, Mary Kate, Ashley, you were such cute kids. What happened?"

Hey. I know that voice.

"I think Michelle could really use a hug from her uncle Jesse."

Bob Saget? I rolled over.

"How the hell did you get in here?" I asked Tommy. He sat next to the bed at my vanity, which was really just a cheapo desk with a lighted, trifold mirror on top and all the makeup brushes, foundations, eye shadows, and blush I hardly ever used scattered around it.

Tommy lounged with his dirty Converse sneakers propped on the edge of my bed. The jeans looked the same as the last time I'd seen him on Mount Washington: faded, raggedy, with a hole in one knee. His blue, snug-fitting I'M WITH STUPID T-shirt was speckled with red Doritos dust.

"Hey. Are those my chips?"

He twisted the bag, then glanced at me. "Yeah. They're a little stale, though. You should get one of those bag clips."

Afternoon sun streamed through my bedroom window, adding a gleam to Tommy's pale blue eyes, making the dark circle around the iris all the more intense. Soft, sandy-blond curls brushed over his forehead and neck, his cheeks flushed with health and youthful vitality. He winked at me.

Crap. The man was too cute for his own good, and he knew it. That's just irritating. I tugged the covers up to my neck. "I'll try again. How. The *hell*. Did you get in here?"

He laughed. "How do you think? We can go anywhere, Em."

I shoved my foot into his and knocked his grimy sneaker-feet off my bed. They hit the floor with a loud clomp and knocked him off balance on his chair. "Hey."

"Hey, yourself. This is my bed…and I'm *in* it."

His gaze moved to the comforter I clutched as though it were the key to my chastity. "What's the big deal? You've got clothes on under there." His brows bobbed and his smile turned lecherous. "I checked."

I peeked under the covers. Pink tank top over white, and tan shorts—I was still wearing the clothes from my trip around the world with Eli. I didn't even remember getting home this morning, let alone crawling fully dressed into bed.

"By the way, you've got some"—Tommy motioned to the

corner of his mouth with his pinky—"I think it's dried spit."

I scrubbed the back of my hand across my mouth. *Crap.* "Get out, Tommy."

"Nope. Can't." Tommy straightened, crumpling the empty chips bag, then reached to trade it for the remote sitting on my vanity and turned off the TV. "We need to talk."

He brushed the chip dust from his hands and shirt, then swiveled in the chair toward my bed. He leaned forward, elbows on his knees. "What happened with you and Eli before he brought you home this morning?"

"I don't know." I was still battling a serious case of sleep-fog. "Last thing I remember, we were standing in the gardens on Capri. Eli says, the lesson endeth here, and we split. Next thing I know, I'm waking up to the sound of you munchin' down on my food while you're reliving your childhood with the poster twins for eating disorders. I have no idea how I got here or when."

I left out the part about Eli's chat with the Fallen angel and the fact he'd just let him go. Tattletale isn't my color. Besides, I owed Eli for snatching me out of the path of an oncoming horde of snarling demons in tacky leisure shirts.

Tommy shook his head and leaned back in his chair. "Eli probably pushed you to sleep. He's done that for me sometimes when I've had a particularly scary-ass day and I can't put it out of my head long enough to fall asleep."

"Oh. Well, that's disturbing." I didn't like having blank spots in my memory. It's one of the main reasons I don't binge drink. That and the wicked hangovers…and the whole killing brain cells thing. That's bad, too.

"Forget it," he said. "You'll be grateful for it the first time he doesn't do it and you wake up in a cold sweat from a dream of some red-face bastard about to slice off your head."

"I bet. Yet another perk of being the consequence of my mother's one-night stand with a fallen angel."

"That's not what I meant, but…never mind," he said. "What did you do to Eli after I left?"

"What do you mean, to him?" I shoved the covers back and swung my feet to the floor. "I didn't do anything to him except chase him around the world. Why?"

I went to my chest of drawers and rummaged for clean underwear.

"So you didn't…" Tommy hedged. "I mean, you guys didn't…?"

Hand to my hip, I turned to glower at him. "Finish the sentence. We didn't what?"

Tommy rubbed his palms against his thighs, pressing back in the chair. He sighed. "C'mon, Emma. You're not a virgin. You know what I mean. Did you two…do it?"

"*Do it*? What are you, thirteen?" Honestly, did he think I was stupid or just a slut…or both? Never mind that jumping Eli's sexy angel bod was the first thing I thought of every time he popped in beside me.

"Just answer the question," Tommy said.

I turned back to my open panty drawer. "None of your business," I said, just as I found my midnight blue, boy-cut undies and the soft-wire blue bra to match.

"It's totally my business," Tommy said as I crossed the room to my closet. "If you seduce him and he falls, it'll be up to me to kill him. I don't want to have to kill my magister, Emma."

I snagged my striped Dodger-blue buttoned blouse with the half sleeves and French cuffs. I liked the style, with the darts and running seams down the front from under the breasts. It made me look hour-glassy. A few hangers down, I grabbed my dark chocolate, wide-leg crop pants. They hit me a half inch below my knee, and the wide leg gave the illusion of being a skirt without the inconvenience of forced, ladylike modesty.

I turned to catch Tommy eyeing the panties in my hand. *Guys. Sheesh.* "Eli and I are just getting to know each other. He's teaching me how to use our advantages just like he did for you. We're no different than the two of you."

"Like hell." He snorted. "I'm not the cause of an angelic war."

"Neither am I."

"Your gender is." He knotted his arms across his chest and slouched in the chair. "Women are like angel crack, and all angels are addicts. You keep waving yourself under his nose, he's bound to take a snort."

I made a disgusted *tsk*. "Graphic much? I'm not waving myself under his nose. If you remember correctly, none of this was my idea. Anyway, Eli said you're just as much of a temptation as I am. Not everything has to do with sex, Thomas. Sheesh."

He stiffened. "Don't call me Thomas."

"Get over yourself." I shook my head. "I have a client in less than an hour. I need a shower, coffee, and food. You don't qualify as any of those things so…shoo."

I started for the door, deciding not to wait for him to leave. He'd found his way in, he could find his way back out.

"Do you seriously believe that garbage?"

I shuffled to a stop. "What garbage?"

"That men affect them the same as women," he said. "I mean, are you seriously that naive?"

"You're saying he lied?" I almost laughed. "Angels lie?"

Tommy didn't even crack a smile. "Yeah, that's exactly what

I'm saying. They're angels, Emma, not God. He didn't make them perfect. They just look that way."

"Angels lie," I said, still trying to wrap my brain around it.

"Listen, I'm sure Eli wants to believe what he told you is true," Tommy said. "Hell, maybe he does believe it. But that doesn't change the facts. It doesn't change history."

Two more steps, and I was able to lean a shoulder against the doorframe. Tommy had swiveled all the way around in the chair to face me, his back to my bed.

"Eli told me that my being an illorum is just as seductive to him as being female," I said. "And that he's learned to control his passions."

Tommy shrugged. "Let's hope so. Maybe it's true in a way. Heck, I'll admit to a little man-crush on Joe Doerksen—"

I shook my head. "Who?"

"*El Dirte*," he said, with a big smile and heavy Spanish accent. It didn't help.

I shrugged, and Tommy waved my confusion away. "He's a fighter. Anyway, as much as I admire the guy, I don't want him to have my babies, you know? No matter how much Eli admires us, me, for what we are and what we have to do, when he looks at you he sees something different, something…more."

Just thinking about the handsome angel sent a warm rush through my body, but I shut it down, guilty, hoping Tommy wouldn't read my thoughts at that moment.

"Eli's been at this a long time," Tommy said. "There's only so much a guy can take. You think it's a coincidence you're the first female illorum he's had to train in five hundred years?"

"What, you think he planned it?"

Tommy shrugged. "Maybe. He's an angel, Emma. Nothing's

impossible."

"I'm sorry, but you're the one who stumbled his way onto my doorstep with a demon hot on his heels. Not Eli. It was your neck I saved when I picked up your stupid sword and got this friggin' scar on my wrist. Thanks for that, by the way. The way I see it, this is all *your* doing. Not Eli's."

"You've been around Eli enough now," he said. "You really think I was alone when I ran down your street that day?"

I blinked at that. Had Eli told him to come to my house because he wanted me to be marked? I couldn't believe that. I didn't want to think about it. "Why didn't you just teleport away from the demon? Why lead him anywhere?"

"I'd already been hit," Tommy said. "The brimstone was in my bloodstream. That stuff screws with our abilities. It's kind of what holds angels in the abyss. When the Fallen call the captured angels out as demons, their systems are saturated with it. I think that's part of what makes them nuts. I know it's what makes them slower than us."

"But if Eli was with you, why didn't he get you out of there? Why didn't he help you with your wound?" The image of Tommy bleeding on my foyer floor flashed through my brain and made my stomach pitch. "You could've died."

"He couldn't take me out of a fight. He's not allowed," Tommy said. "Besides, I always got the feeling seeing us sliced up by demons is kind of a turn-on for angels. And after what he told you, I bet I'm right."

"That's sick," I said, swallowing the surge of fear that choked at the back of my throat. Eli had claimed he was just ending our lesson early on Capri, conveniently taking me out of the path of a charging horde of demons. I'd wanted to believe him. But even though it hadn't technically been a lie, the line he'd walked was pretty thin—thin enough some would say he crossed it. I pushed the thought from my mind, worried it would show on my face and Tommy would start asking more questions.

"You're damn skippy, it's sick. They aren't built like us, Emma," he said. "Their brains fire differently. That's why mixing between us is nothing but trouble."

"What do you mean, he wasn't allowed to help you? Says who?"

"Everyone says." Tommy sighed. "We're in the middle of a cease-fire in Heaven. The angels pretend all the Fallen are locked in the abyss and the Fallen pretend they don't care that their brothers cut the metaphysical bonds between them. The Fallen are completely off the angels' radar, shunned. Unless they knew each other before their fall, an angel and a Fallen could stand side by side and not know it."

"But the angels know their brothers are still falling," I said. "I mean, hello, we're the proof."

"Knowing it and admitting it are two different things," Tommy said. "If they admit the Fallen are still wandering around knocking up human women, then they'll have to fight. The war would start all over again, and this time they'd have to do it without being able to use their bonds to find them. Their own shortsightedness and pride screwed them."

"But we can sense the Fallen," I said.

"Exactly. When the angels realized nephilim had the ability and the willingness to go after the Fallen, they figured we were the answer to their problem." Tommy uncrossed his leg and leaned forward. "If they could clue us in to our natural abilities, arm us with a sword and call it a gift, we would go after the Fallen on our own, and they could claim innocence."

"But if the angels actually help us by interfering in a way they can't explain as harmless interaction," I said, thinking ahead, "then the cease-fire is broken, and the Fallen will fight back with everything they have. Pretty thin line."

"Anorexic." He straightened. "Which is why we have to be careful. One slip and everything could change. Angels can be just as emotional and stupid as humans. Eli's been working behind the scenes since the beginning. That's a long time to sit by and watch your enemy enjoying the one thing you want just as much."

"Right," I said, but my thoughts were drifting to memories of Eli talking to the Fallen in the garden, then blinking me out before the demons could reach me. He'd recognized the blond guy as the Fallen who'd killed Jeannette. He must have known him before his fall. Had they been friends?

It didn't matter—Eli had interfered. There was no way to argue around it. *Crap.* What if Tommy was right, and I really was the cause of a coming war?

"What?" Tommy asked.

My eyes turned to his, snapping me out of my private thoughts. "What, what?" I don't know what expression I'd had on my face, but he must've read something there.

"You look like you just tripped a nun."

I pushed my shoulder off the doorframe. "Nothing. I was just… thinking."

"Emma, if something happened with Eli, you need to tell me," he said. "If we're caught off guard, we're dead."

I scoffed. "Eli would never hurt either of us."

"Not now, but if he fell…" Tommy shrugged. "I don't know, Em, something happens to them. Maybe it's being shunned by their brothers or being ignored by God. Maybe it's just plain greed and gluttony. Whatever it is, they change. Nothing matters more to them than what they want, and they'll go through anyone to get it."

"Not Eli," I said.

"You don't know, Emma Jane," he countered. "It might not take much. Maybe even a kiss, and the Eli we know could be gone."

"A kiss? And the award for melodrama goes to…"

Tommy stood, rolled a shoulder. "All I'm saying is we might not realize he's about to fall until it's too late. You can't always depend on him to resist. You can't count on him being strong enough to turn away from the brink."

"What am I supposed to do?"

"Don't give him a reason to fall," Tommy said.

"You think I am?"

"I think he's already doing things I've never seen him do before," Tommy said. "He's already taking risks because of you, and for all we know, it might not take more than that for him to slip."

There was nothing I could do about it. My gender wasn't going to change. And the way Eli made me feel, well, that I could work harder to ignore. But for now, after the damage I may have already done, I couldn't think about it anymore.

"If you were so worried, maybe you shouldn't have taken off after that demon when Eli told you to," I said, shifting the blame. I was half-human, after all. *Sue me.* "Did you at least catch him?"

Tommy shook his head. "No. He's an old one, faster. Made it back to the conference hotel before I could catch up."

"So whoever sent him now knows about me." Perfect. I always wanted to be a target when I grew up.

"Don't worry about it. My televangelist Fallen angel dad is gonna be in Pittsburgh in about two weeks for the same kind of religious conference they had in New York. I met a guy. He's got a way to get me close. If everything works out, the Fallen who sent that demon will be too worried about his own head to be coming after yours."

"A guy, huh? I hope you're right."

The bathroom was the door next to my bedroom, and I headed for it, wanting this entire conversation over with two minutes ago. "I have to take a shower before my client gets here."

Tommy stepped into my path, stopping me. "If Eli falls, it won't mean he loves you."

I angled back. We were standing too close now. "What's that supposed to mean?"

He shifted, giving us both a little more of a comfort zone. "When they fall, it's not like the movies. They don't fall to be with their true love or anything. It's physical. It's *sex*—pure and simple. It's what they've been denied, and once they taste it, that's what they crave. That's *all* they crave. They'll take it anywhere they can get it, and angels, even fallen ones, can get it…anywhere."

Goose bumps chilled up the back of my neck. I pulled a breath through my nose and fought to keep my nauseous reaction to myself. "Fascinating, Tommy. Now if you don't mind, I've got to make a living so I can keep us both in Doritos."

I pushed past him and into the bathroom. Just as the door closed, Tommy said, "He doesn't care about you that way, Emma. I love him too, but he's not one of us. He's not nephilim. Don't forget that."

CHAPTER ELEVEN

"Where you goin'?" Tommy asked, and I jumped, jerking the steering wheel of my Jeep so hard, I nearly drove into a tree.

"Holy—crap." I swerved the car back onto the road and slugged Tommy, who'd suddenly appeared in the passenger seat.

"Ouch. Hey."

"Don't ever friggin' do that again. Got me?"

"No doubt. Sheesh," he said, rubbing the sore spot on his bicep.

Then it dawned on me. He'd traveled fast enough to land in a moving car. *Cool.* It'd been nearly two weeks since my trip around the world with Eli. Two weeks of squeezing in combat practice between clients, two weeks of testing out my strength, my speed, my enhanced psychic gifts. I'd only been attacked once since the last demon got away, but I'd managed to slice off her head in the handicap bathroom stall in Walmart.

I still felt like I didn't know what was going on half the time and could never really shake the fear of being ambushed by some berserk demon. Luckily, I faked normal better than most people. I'd had years of practice.

"What, are you stalking me or something?"

"I like to think of it as keeping an eye out for you," he said.

"Right. They've got laws against it."

He shifted to a comfortable position in his seat, slouching. "So, where are you going?"

"To the library," I said. "I thought they might have copies of the yearbooks during the years my mom taught high school English in McKeesport. She's always been all about her job and her family. If a horny angel wanted to get close to her, he'd have to come at her through one or the other. I'm betting job."

I glanced back and forth between Tommy and the road. He nodded. "Makes sense. So, you figure you'll look over the yearbooks and see if you notice any wings or halos?"

I scoffed. "No." *Smartass.* "But I thought there might be some candid shots of my mom. If she was having an affair at school, someone might have caught a photo of them together. Plus, I can check male teachers who were only at the school the year I was conceived, then gone the next year."

"Actually, that's not a totally idiotic idea," he said.

"Gee…thanks. Careful, that kind of gushing praise will just go to my head."

"I know." He stretched his arm out to drape it over the back of my seat and tried to lounge his legs a little more. A Jeep Wrangler isn't made for lounging. "Where's your sword?"

I tipped my head and caught his following glance to the hilt laying on the backseat.

"You're taking it in with you, right?"

"Nah. Doesn't really go with the outfit. Yes, I'm taking it in, nag."

"That's Mr. Nag to you," he said, and shifted his gaze out the window.

The conversation quieted. Several seconds ticked by without a word, but when we were almost to the library, I said, "Don't you, um, have someplace to be?"

He shook his head. "Not until tonight. Besides, I've been doing this gig for a while now. Maybe I'll recognize someone or notice something you don't."

That wasn't it. My gaze flicked to him again as he shifted once more in his seat. His leg bounced on his toe, his hand tapping a counter-rhythm on his knee. "Why are you so wired?"

He looked at me, and all his nervous motion suddenly stopped. "Nothing. Why?"

"For one thing, you're tagging along with me to a library," I said. "So?"

"You're a jock, Tommy. I mean, you might be a nephilim warrior now, but you'll always have the mindset of a jock. Jocks are allergic to libraries."

"That's so prejudiced." His face pinched in offense, mouth agape. He was faking it. "Don't label me. I'm a whole person, not just the beautifully toned athlete you see on the outside."

I rolled my eyes. "Right. Okay, Mr. Toned Athlete, what's got you so keyed up you can't sit still?"

He followed my quick look at his knee—bouncing again. It stopped, and he swung his gaze back to me. His smile bloomed across his handsome face, dimpling his cheeks and twinkling in his eyes. I almost sighed. *So cute.*

"I'm done," he said. "I mean, I will be by this time tomorrow."

"What? What do you mean?"

"That guy I told you about," he said. "My connection—he came through. Got me tickets to the televangelist's seminar. Second row, left side. Close enough I'll be swimming in demons."

"Won't the Fallen and his demon minions sense you?"

"They won't do anything in a crowd like that," he said. "The crowd's actually a bonus, like a no-fire zone for both sides. I can get close enough to sense him, to know for sure he's a Fallen. While I'm at it, I can scout out how many demons he's called up as bodyguards. It's perfect."

"Does Eli know the plan?"

"Yep," he said, his knee resuming its anxious bounce. "I can't wait. You know the first thing I'm going to do when I get my life back?" he said. "I'm taking my whole family out to dinner. Mom, Dad, my pain-in-the-butt sisters, and my nephew. Hell, maybe I'll even include that guy Jill married. I don't care, as long as we're all together, out in public, and I don't have to worry about demon attacks or Fallen angels anymore."

"Not going to be cheap. Can you afford it?" He'd mentioned coming to and from work, but never elaborated on the details. Like what he did and where.

"Yeah," he said, indignant.

"Cool. Where did you say you work?" I asked, oh-so-slyly.

"I didn't," he said. "But I work at a movie theater."

"Yeah? Which one?"

His gaze drifted out his window. "Uh, the one over on Route Fifty-One."

"There's a movie theater on Route Fifty-One?" My brain mapped the busy road. "Where?"

He swung his gaze back to me with a huff. "It's an adult theater, okay? It's open late, we don't get a lot of heavy customer flow, and they're flexible with my hours."

"You work at an adult movie theater? You mean, like porn?"

"Not porn," he said, his shoulders stiffening. "They're artistic films. Mature, relationship movies. Graphic romances."

"Riiigght." Laughter bubbled through my chest. "So what's your job, selling tickets? Working the concession stand? Handing out moist towelettes?"

"I run the projector. Sometimes I have to clean the theater between showings." He grumbled his answer, knotting his arms across his chest as he stared out the window.

"Clean up? Ewww," I said, fighting hard not to let my amusement show too much. "Opens a world of possibilities behind the reasons for the sticky floors, huh?"

"You don't want to know. Trust me," he said, then shrugged. "It's an easy job. I'm away from people, so nobody's at risk. And it's only temporary. After tonight, I'm going back to my old life."

He shifted to face me again, his pent-up excitement returning. "I've been practicing my pitch all these years. Keeping my arm strong. There's nobody in the majors that can touch my fastball now. A hundred and eighty miles per hour. I clocked it."

"The speed's because of your nephilim strength, isn't it?" I asked.

"Well, yeah." He tsked, like the question was stupid. "No human can throw that fast."

"What if your abilities go away once you kill the televangelist? I mean, provided he's the Fallen who fathered you."

Tommy shrugged.

Not so stupid now, huh?

"So, I'll pitch normal speed. I was all-state my junior year, Emma. I would've gone pro if"—he glanced at the illorum mark on his inner wrist—"this hadn't happened. And like I said, I've been practicing. I'm as good as I ever was. Better."

There was a note of desperate worry in his voice, like I was stomping doubt all over his happy hope garden. Truth or not, after eight years battling demons and fallen angels, he deserved whatever hope he could manage.

"You're right," I said. "After all, you've got that awesome athletic bod going for you."

He snorted. "That's right."

Our eyes met, and the mood shifted. My smile tempered, and my tone turned somber. "I mean it, Tommy. With everything you gave up to do this, you deserve a good life, the life you dreamed of."

He reached over and tucked my hair behind my ear. "Thanks, Em. I think we both do."

I nodded, keeping my gaze steady on the road. I wasn't sure I agreed with him on the second part. I'd had a pretty good life up to this point. Still did, as far as I could tell. He'd lost everything at eighteen. I couldn't imagine.

"I want it all, " he said. "A fantastic career, a ton of fans screaming my name. I want to collect friends like a magnet in a pile of paper clips and never let them go. I want the other stuff too, stuff I never thought I'd want eight years ago. To start a family. Kids. I want a wife, someone I can trust, who understands me."

His hand slipped from my shoulder to the back of my neck, his thumb caressing over the fine hairs. A warm shiver quivered through me, stirring sensations low in my body. It wasn't that I wanted to be his "someone," but the way he touched me, the soft sexy tone of his voice, awakened all my body's girl parts.

I looked sideways at him, my smile suddenly out of control as I turned in at the library parking lot and straight into an open spot. "So you'll get me season tickets, right? Wherever you land a pro contract?"

He laughed and caressed his thumb against the back of my neck. "You bet. Box seats. You'd look good up there with all the players' wives. "

I laughed with him, even as a flutter tickled through my belly. Tommy and I had grown close fast and talking like this, like we could have a future together one day, made me feel normal for the first time in a long time. "I'd like that," I said.

He shifted in his seat, moving closer, his gaze focusing on my lips for an instant before flicking to my eyes. "I'm glad you're with me, Emma. I wish I'd known back in high school how amazing you are, but I'm glad I got a second chance to find out."

My breath caught and I sat stone still as he leaned closer and pressed his lips to mine. Heat swirled inside me, pulsing through my veins with the racing beat of my heart. His tongue traced along my lips and I opened them to him, my brain melting as he deepened the kiss.

The taste of his last cinnamon Fireball tingled on my tongue, and the masculine smell of his cologne scented my every shaky breath. Muscles flexed and slicked between my thighs and for a few wonderful seconds, I forgot about the world.

And then he broke the kiss, leaning back just enough to see my eyes. "You're perfect for me."

My face warmed and my smile stretched wide. "You say that now; wait until you taste my cooking."

Tommy laughed and sat back in his seat. "I'll cook if you do the dishes."

"Deal."

He gave me a nod, his smile big and happy. "Okay. But first we have some research to do." He hiked a thumb toward the backseat where my sword handle and sheath rested. "Grab that."

I did, but I had to get out to strap the belt through the loops on my jeans. The hard handle poked the small of my back, but my

GENIUS BY BIRTH, SLACKER BY CHOICE T-shirt covered it. Tommy shut my door for me when I stepped out of the way.

Carrying my purse over my left shoulder kept my right hand free to draw the sword. The purse felt weird on my other side. Not that the sword felt any better.

The lady at the checkout desk looked our way as we walked by, her green eyes smiling. She was probably only a few years older than me, her strawberry blonde hair in a cute pixie cut. "How are you?" she asked.

"Great. Thanks," I said, following Tommy to the woman at the reference desk at the center of the library.

I brightened my smile. "Hi. Do you have a copy of the McKeesport High School yearbook for nineteen eighty-five?"

"No. Eighty-four," Tommy said.

I blinked at him, confused.

"You were born in eighty-five, right?"

"Right." I turned back to the pudgy, caramel-haired woman behind the desk. "Nineteen eighty-four."

Her long hair was pulled into a tight ponytail at the crown of her head, grayish white strands streaking through the darker color. Despite the fact that we were standing, towering over her by several feet, she still managed to look down her nose at me. Her puckered brows grew tighter by the second.

She tsked and pointed off behind her to the left, her shirt shifting over her double-G-sized boobs with a swooshing sound.

"Bottom shelf, last aisle in front of the computer room," she said. "You can't borrow them, though."

"Why?"

Her mousy brown gaze narrowed, looking me up and down. "Because *some* people don't return them and they can't be replaced.

We're missing several years because of a few thoughtless borrowers, and now decent folks have to suffer."

She said it like I'd been one of the people who'd ripped them off. I wasn't. Honest.

"We can photocopy pages though, right?" Tommy asked.

The woman rolled her big shoulders. "I suppose. But don't break the spines. And don't bend the corners of the pages."

Tommy shook his head. "No. We won't."

We walked around the large oval reference counter, feeling her eyes tracking us until the rows of bookshelves hid her view. Zigzagging through the shelves to the back aisle, we came to the windowed computer room and made a left toward the far wall.

At this time of day the computer room was empty. Except for the two librarians, Tommy and I practically had the entire place to ourselves. The sound of a soda can clunking through a vending machine in the snack room echoed off the quiet walls. The library wasn't empty, but close.

"It's not here," Tommy said, pushing up from his squat.

"No way." I knelt, checking for myself. Running a finger along the spines, I counted through the years—seventy-nine, eighty, eighty-one, eighty-two, eighty-seven… *Crap*.

"It's not here." I sat back on my heels and swung my gaze up to Tommy. "Coincidence?"

He shrugged. "Probably. It's not the only year missing."

I wasn't so sure, but then again, I'm convinced Oswald didn't act alone and I've always been suspicious of that moon landing footage. I *heart* conspiracy theories.

"You could try the school," Tommy said.

I got to my feet. "Yeah, but the school librarian won't be nearly as nice as our friend at the reference desk."

Tommy laughed, turning to lead our way back along the computer room wall. We were five steps from the wide center aisle when a nauseating odor filled my nose.

"Uck, did you fart?" As soon as I asked, I knew that wasn't it. "Oh no."

Tommy drew his sword, knees bent. His steps turned cautious, silent. He motioned for me to stay back. I nodded and slid my hilt from its sheath, willing the blade to form. I dropped my purse, adjusting my grip on the sword.

The stench of rotten eggs grew thick enough to taste. I gagged, my stomach churning. Bile threatened at the back of my throat and I swallowed it down, shadowing two steps behind Tommy, turning right into the main aisle. Rows of bookshelves lined the aisle on either side of us.

Adrenaline coursed through my veins. My reflexes were on hyper alert, keeping me on my toes. We paused, listening, moving as one fluid battling force, first and second wave, instinct choreographing us more than conscious thought. But there was no one there. With each passing second my muscles tightened, ready to thrust, block, jab.

Nothing happened.

I couldn't hold the intensity. I straightened, let my sword drop to my side. *What the—*

"Oh," someone said to my right.

I jumped, twisting to face back down the aisle we'd just come up. A woman holding children's books stood at the far end of the aisle next to where we'd just come from. She dropped the books and held up her hands in surrender. She looked like a mousy schoolteacher—short, butterscotch hair; bland conservative blouse, slacks; and sensible shoes. She was maybe three inches taller than me, with an athletic build a lot like mine.

"Uh, sorry?" she said, her dark eyes flicking from my face to my sword. She looked at me like I'd just licked a light socket for the zesty charge. I tucked the sword behind me.

"No. It's okay, we were just…Um…" I had nothing.

"Is that a sword? Did you bring a weapon into the library?" she asked, stepping toward me, craning her neck trying to see what I hid behind my back. *Busted.*

I shrugged and stepped out of the main aisle between the bookshelf and the computer room wall again, bringing the sword out where she could see it. "Um, yeah. It is. We were at a Renaissance demonstration and…" *Crap.* I went blank. My bullshit skills were on the fritz.

"Emma," Tommy said from the center aisle. I looked for him over my shoulder, but I'd gone far enough down the side aisle I couldn't see him around the corner.

"Don't worry about it," the woman said, and I looked back in time to see her draw a dagger from a sheath at the small of her back. "I brought one, too."

"Oh, shit."

She lunged at me, thrusting the twelve-inch dagger straight at my gut. I arched, jumping backward and swinging my sword down in front of me to block. Metal clanked against metal, knocking her dagger arm to the side. Her momentum drove her forward anyway, her free hand reaching up, lightning quick, to snag my neck.

Her grip was superhuman, and my hand went to her wrist on reflex. She squeezed, cutting off air, and my brain raced for options. Girl instincts rocketed to the forefront, my nails scratching and digging at her hand. But she wasn't fazed, her fingers tightening, her nails cutting into my skin.

I kicked at her, panic keeping me from thinking to use my sword. My foot landed hard against her shin. I kicked again and caught her in the gut. She huffed, but didn't let go.

Her sweet, schoolteacher face twisted in rage. I could see now her dark eyes were really a deep purple. I'd think they were pretty… if she weren't trying to kill me.

"Filthy-blooded nephilim," she said, before she slammed me hard against the bookshelf. "I'll snap your head off your neck."

Books rained down on us, knocking my shoulder, bouncing like boulders off my head. The big shelf rocked from the force of the impact, and she used my neck like a handle to slam me the other way against the glass computer wall.

Air exploded from my lungs on impact and a sharp crack sounded. I winced, eyes shut against the pain jolting across my shoulder, radiating through my body. Something had broken. I hoped it was the glass and not me.

The demon lifted me in front of her, shaking my body like a German shepherd would a cat. She wasn't much taller than I was, and she had to lift me high to keep me hanging. She managed. My feet dangled, scraping the floor, almost touching, but not enough to let me get a foothold and leverage to pull away. My vision tunneled, blackness closing in as my lungs burned for air.

Something inside me shut down. Instincts, born from the melding of my blood with angelic grace, took hold. A tingling swell of power coursed up from the depths of my being. I couldn't give up. Not to this…thing. *Never.*

I swung my sword, bringing it around in an arch, hard and sure into her side. The distinct wet *thunk* as the sharp blade cut through meat and bone reverberated up my arm. It was like hitting a tree trunk. But her scream was human, shrill, and she bent with the blow.

Her grip only grew tighter.

My sword was stuck in her side for a second. I had to wiggle and jerk it to get it free of her body. She should've gone down—I'd nearly cut her in half—but she didn't. For a split second, the exact moment my blade popped out of her, relief made her lower me. I found my feet quickly.

My knees wobbled, but they held long enough for me to lift my sword between us. My elbow swung back, gaining momentum to drive the point deep into her gut. My nephilim strength shoved her backward, her nails gouging my neck as her grasp slipped away.

She didn't scream this time, but the air gushed out of her, and she doubled over the sword. Her hand opened on her dagger, and it clanked against the linoleum floor. She grabbed the blade of my sword and raised her head to meet my eyes.

Her pretty purple irises had turned demon yellow, glowing, the pupils now ink-black vertical slits. She snarled at me, showing inhumanly sharp white teeth. Then she took a step, the move driving my sword deeper into her body.

"Die already," I said.

"You first." Her voice was raw, growling. Then the bitch punched me, popped me right in the nose.

The force sent me sailing backward and brought stars flashing in a circle around my head as I slid on my butt across the center aisle. One of those rotating magazine towers crashed against my back, stopping my slide and showering metal and paper over my head. I crumpled on the floor, the metal tower across my legs, magazines scattered over my back and shoulders.

I couldn't catch my breath. I needed a second, just a moment to fill my lungs. The deep inhale raced down my throat, and with it went blood and spit. I took another fast deep breath. Bloody air was better than nothing.

A loud clank and rattle—like the sound of metal hitting and sliding across the floor near my feet—drew me up an instant before someone lifted the magazine rack off my legs. I heard the rack crash down the aisle, slamming into a far-off bookcase.

My sword. I'd lost my grip when she sent me flying. I'd left it stuck in her belly, but I could see it wasn't in her anymore. She must have pulled it out and thrown it. Shifting my gaze in the direction I'd heard the clamor of metal, I saw the hilt now sticking out from under a scatter of magazines.

Just as I reached for the sword, her iron-hard grip latched around my ankle and yanked me hard. The demon dragged me free of the debris. I rolled to my back, bringing my other foot up to drive into her elbow.

Like the crack of a wooden bat, her bones snapped. She screeched, her wails piercing my ears like ice. She let my ankle go, protecting the broken arm against her body. I rolled to my belly, scrambling back for my sword.

My fingers purchased metal, tugged the grip into my palm a half-breath before the demon's steely fingers fisted in my hair. She yanked, snapping my head back, bringing the rest of my body flying backward over my legs so my feet were under me again.

Big mistake. I found my footing and twisted, ignoring the sharp bite of pain as my hair ripped out by the roots. I backhanded her, the solid pommel of my sword driving into the side of her head.

Black goo splattered from her temple. She staggered back, and I glanced down to see way too many of my straight, blonde strands stringing between her fingers. The demon stumbled, teetering on her feet as she turned to face me. She held her head where the oozing blood still flowed, streaking down her face and neck. Her other arm hung at a strange angle, useless at her side.

More thick goo blackened her side and stained the front of her shirt at her belly. She panted, glaring at me, spittle mixed with demon blood bubbling at the corners of her mouth with her breaths.

I gave a quick wipe to the dampness under my nose with the back of my hand. My wrist and forearm came away smeared with blood. The coppery taste trickled into my mouth, down the back of my throat. Warm, wet streams traced my chin and neck. Pain throbbed in my shoulder. My neck burned like acid.

I pushed all thoughts of my injuries from my mind and double fisted my sword. *Ready*.

Somewhere in the back of my mind, I knew Tommy was fighting farther up the aisle. I'd caught glimpses of metal flashing, bodies launching toward him, falling back. Blood, red and black alike, splattered the floors, the shelves, the books. Sounds of battle echoed loudly through the small library, but for me the world went suddenly silent.

The demon woman roared at me, like an elephant trumpeting the charge. She reached for the long magazine rack, cumbersome with the wire holders swinging around the center pole. She hefted it on her hip, holding it like a jousting pole, and charged.

I blinked, and time shifted, slowed, or maybe I just moved that much faster. I watched her come, every step, every subtle shift of muscle, and I waited. Waited. The tip of the rack only two feet from my gut, I spun to the side and brought my sword home to its target.

The cut was clean, quick, and over before her scream left her lips. Butterscotch hair, button nose, and glowing yellow demon eyes came and went—came and went—as the demon's head rolled and bounced into the bottom of the nearest bookshelf. Then the whole of her turned to a steaming pile of goo.

"Emma," Tommy said, breathless. I turned to see him panting in the middle of the aisle, sword loose at his side. Black ooze dripped from his blade, taken from the pile of goo on the floor to his left. Farther back another heap smoldered. He'd fought two and come away without a scratch. I'd barely survived one…and mine was a chick.

"You okay?" he asked.

I nodded without really thinking about the question or the answer. Adrenaline seeped away, and pain swelled up to match its retreat. I winced and doubled over, bracing my hands on my knees. *Crap.* I couldn't get a good breath, and my whole face felt like I'd run headlong into a Mack truck. I let my sword fall to my feet. I couldn't stop shaking; my heart raced like a gerbil on a wheel. Not a good sign.

"Just take deep slow breaths," he said, but I could hear the laughter in his voice. *Jerk.* "You'll get used to it. After fifty or so fights like this, that is."

I swung my gaze to the side to see him walking toward me, his hand swiftly twirling the grip of his sword in his palm like a tennis player does his racket. His smile brightened, dimples going deep, sky blue eyes sparkling with relief.

Then he stopped. His brows drew tight and the brilliant handsome smile flattened. He looked down, and my gaze followed, both of us seeing the long sharp metal point jutting from his chest at the same time.

"What is that?" I said.

Tommy's gaze swung back to mine, his eye questioning as though he'd had the same thought. The blade twisted, boring a hole, and his knees buckled, dropping him to the floor. He knelt there for several seconds, staring at me. Someone yelled his name.

A second later I realized it was me.

He fell forward, face first, no life left to even lift his hands against the impact. He bounced when he hit, jamming his face in insult against the hard floor. Blood pooled around his head almost instantly. I stared at him, hands still on my knees, sword flat on the floor beside my feet.

Slowly, my gaze lifted to the figure standing where he'd been. He was big, dark hair and even darker eyes, dressed like he'd just stepped out of the gym. His mesh shirt and bicycle shorts strained over muscles bigger than my head. Where had he come from? How had we missed him? It didn't matter. He snarled at me, just as the female demon had, his teeth too white, too damn sharp.

His body shifted, his long legs stretching over Tommy's body, bringing him toward me. The long dagger in his hand dripped brilliant red with Tommy's blood.

I should've screamed. I should've gone mad with rage and heartache. I should've let loose my revenge and sliced him to ribbons before his slow demon brain even knew I'd moved.

I didn't. I let him come.

I reached for my sword on the floor at my feet, felt it heavy and solid in my grip. A sudden sense of meaning snaked down through my heart and into my gut as the demon came within reach. A feeling of destiny that I'd never felt before welled inside me.

I exploded in a rush of speed, swinging the long blade in a wide slanting circle as I went. My body spun, the extra momentum traveling up my arm, driving the sword easily through the bottom of his chin and out the top of his head. Half his face slipped off.

I finished the spin, three-hundred-and-sixty degrees, and stopped with a quick plant of my toe back where I'd started—just in time to see the bastard drop.

CHAPTER TWELVE

"I don't know who called the police and paramedics." My eyes did a slow blink at the black zippered body bag on the gurney in front of me, trying to wrap my brain around the fact Tommy was inside. They wouldn't let me ride with him to the hospital, or wherever they were going to take him. But Eli asked the attendants to give me a few minutes with him before they left. The "no" on the guy's lips had faded into a "yes" at the angel's request and the two men walked to the side of the ambulance to wait without questioning.

Eli's arm warmed around me. He scooted closer on the bench seat. "It doesn't matter."

I swung my gaze to him, my body numb. "I couldn't find his sword. I don't know what happened to it."

"His soul took it back from whence it came," Eli said. His smooth voice rippled through me, soothing the edges of my tattered emotions. But it was just a voice, normal, human, not the intense blissful stroke of an angel's voice.

I could've used the sweet numbing escape, the sense of carefree comfort he could offer. But it wouldn't be real. Eli could distract me, turn my thoughts and feelings to other, more carnal things, but nothing would change. Tommy would still be dead.

As tempting as those blissful sensations were, I couldn't, wouldn't ask Eli to share his angelic touch with me. I wouldn't run from this. I owed it to Tommy. *Eli* owed it to Tommy. We'd needed Eli today, really needed him, and he hadn't come.

"Where were you?" I asked, turning my gaze back to the long black bag.

"I came the moment I realized," he said. "I've always felt his need before. I should've felt yours. I didn't. I can only guess you were relying on each other and didn't reach out to me until there was no one else."

"He was worried for me," I said. "If he'd been fighting on his own, he wouldn't have dropped his guard."

"Alone, the battle would have been different, but not necessarily the outcome."

"That's not true. He would've reached out to you instead of thinking about me," I said, desperate to find where we'd made our mistake. "You would've known he needed you and come to help. You could've done something."

"No," Eli said. "There's nothing I could've done. I have witnessed the last breath of countless illorum. My presence has been little comfort. Given the choice, I believe Thomas preferred seeing you in his final earthly moments."

"Given the choice, he'd prefer to still be breathing," I said. "I know you can't pick up a sword and fight, but you could've, I don't know, used your powers somehow. Maybe if you'd been there, the demons wouldn't have attacked. Maybe you could've snatched him out of there before it was too late."

"No, Emma Jane." He caught my chin between his thumb and

the crook of his finger, turning my face to his. "Understand this. I cannot interfere. What I did for you in the gardens of Augusto I should not have done. I've told you, it's forbidden."

"Yeah, but you did it anyway," I said. "You used your powers to get me out of there before the demons could attack. You could've done the same for Tommy."

"The distinctions I made that allowed me to act were thin, at best. Many of my brothers didn't agree. Pointing to our active training that day and claiming ignorance to a coming attack was my only excuse. And it wasn't a good one."

"You told your brothers you didn't know the demons were about to attack?" I asked. I knew he'd lied, but I couldn't get used to the notion. I shifted back enough to pull my chin from his hold.

"Yes. And not very well," he said. "The reasoning was flimsy, yet it was far more than I would've had today. There was nothing I could do...for either of you."

"You got in trouble for helping me in the gardens?" The only punishment I knew for angels was the abyss, and that seemed kind of severe for a little white lie that ultimately saved my butt.

"I was...warned." He glanced out the open back doors of the ambulance then back to me. His jaw tightened, and his brows drew together. "I'll be monitored for a time. Until they're satisfied my prejudices are well in hand. Today should go far in proving my resolve."

My gut twisted. "You let Tommy die to prove a point?"

Eli flinched as though I'd slapped him. "No. Emma Jane, I..." Anger and resolve warred across his face. "No. Do not, for one instant, believe that I didn't love Thomas—that I would not trade my life for his. Trust me when I say, there was nothing I could have done to save him. Nothing."

My rational brain knew he meant every word, but inside, I was aching. Logic and reason were hard to accept when my broken heart was doing the thinking. "Then what're you doing here? I mean, what good are you? You can't help, and I seriously don't need an audience."

I caught his flinch from the corner of my eye, and regret made me look the other way. I stared at the body bag, at where Tommy's smiling pale blue eyes should be underneath. I wanted to see his eyes again, that smile. *This can't be real.*

"I'm here because I care about you, Emma Jane, just as I cared for Thomas," he said. "I'm here to do what I can, however small and unimportant my efforts may seem to you."

I felt his hand move my hair at my neck, felt his warm fingers feather my skin before a sharp jolt of pain sliced through me. I jerked away.

"Those scratches are full of brimstone," he said. "You need holy water."

"I don't have any," I said, reaching up to pull my too-short hair around to cover the wounds. "It's fine. I'll take care of it later."

The punch to my nose and the scratches on my neck were my only injuries. I was sore in spots, probably bruised pretty well, but Tommy had been killed. I was lucky, and I knew it. I certainly wasn't going to sit there complaining.

Eli stood, leaning over the gurney, reaching past me to the zipper at the top of the body bag.

"Hey. What're you doing?" I wanted to see Tommy again... alive. I knew I couldn't have that, and so I wasn't sure I was ready to see him any other way. I'd held his head in my lap until the police arrived. He'd already been cold, lifeless even then. He'd died almost instantly. It all seemed like a foggy dream in my mind.

"You need holy water, now. You can't allow brimstone to fester in your bloodstream. Thomas always carried a vial." He pulled the zipper to Tommy's chest.

"If you're talking about his necklace pouch, that's his," I said, using my fear of seeing Tommy's lifeless eyes again to fuel my indignation. "You can't just take stuff off his body."

"On the contrary, this is one of the few things I can do." He pulled the edges of the bag apart, and I couldn't stop myself from looking.

I don't know what I was hoping, that it wasn't really Tommy inside there, that there'd been some mistake and he was just unconscious? I don't know. It didn't matter. It was Tommy inside. No doubt.

The edges of the dark bag cupped around his face, framing all his light blond hair. He lay with his eyes closed, his long lashes shadowing his cheeks, his lips in a soft relaxed line, almost a smile. There was no blood. Why was there no blood?

His handsome face was untouched. There was something about it that bothered me. I figured it was seeing him so…normal. He could've been sleeping and looked exactly the same. He wasn't sleeping, and the knowledge clogged my throat. My breath shook. I was suddenly cold, despite the warmth of the sunny day.

"I repaired the damage his body suffered to avoid unwanted questions." Eli pulled the leather strap from around Tommy's neck and worked the tiny pouch free of his T-shirt. He cupped the pouch in his hand for a second, then pulled the necklace free. He zipped the bag again, and this time, I made myself look away before the zipper hid Tommy's serene face.

"I don't want it," I said, guessing he planned to offer me the necklace. "It's not yours to give."

Eli settled beside me again. "It is. I gave it to Thomas years ago. It didn't look like this then—I'd made it for Jeannette. Thomas didn't appreciate the feminine quality so I altered its appearance to his tastes."

I looked at the necklace he dangled. The leather strap was a silver chain now, the pouch a long, purplish crystal with a decorative metal top. Sunlight streamed in through the back of the ambulance and sparked off the liquid inside the crystal.

"This is the way the vial looked when I gave it to Jeannette." He twisted off the top, overturned it onto his fingertip. He held it straight again so the water wouldn't spill, then dabbed his wet finger to the bridge of my nose.

The skin warmed and tingled, broken cartilage crackled and straightened. He tipped the crystal onto his finger again and dabbed the scratches on my neck. The warm tingles started there, too, the flesh knitting itself back together, dissolving some of the bubbling brimstone that hadn't already been sealed beneath my quickly healing skin.

"Drink what's left," he said, offering the vial to me. I swallowed the small shot in one gulp and handed the crystal back. The holy water heated down my throat like brandy, sizzled through my veins, the sensation tracking its path down my neck, along my arms, down my chest and belly, and warming through my legs. I stopped hurting…physically.

"I can change the vial into any form that suits you. But I want you to take it. Keep it with you always," he said. "Tommy would want you to have it."

The mention of his name tightened my chest. I swallowed as heartache slowly hardened my resolve, boiling my sorrow to anger. This wasn't right. Wasn't fair. Tommy was the better fighter. He'd given up so much of his life already. He shouldn't be the one in that bag. *I should be.*

"Change it back to the way he liked it," I said. If it was from Tommy, I wanted it to be the way he'd worn it. I wanted it around my neck when my sword sliced through the neck of the Fallen who had ordered his death. I'd get him for this, for taking Tommy's chance at a normal life, for the dinner he never got to have with his family, the nephew he never got to know. I'd get the bastard who did this…for Tommy.

When I looked back to Eli, Tommy's tiny little pouch on its leather strap sat in the palm of his open hand. I took it and tied it around my neck.

"Do you know anything about the Fallen who sent these demons?" Eli asked.

"Not much. But I will," I said. The guy was definitely on my shit list. One last look at the black zippered bag, and I pushed the thought of Tommy lying inside from my mind. I just couldn't keep thinking about it. I had to let him go.

Eli shifted his knees to the side so I could squeeze between him and the gurney and out the back doors of the ambulance. The angel followed behind me. "I'm so proud of you, Emma Jane."

I glanced back at Eli as I tucked the necklace inside my shirt. "For what?"

His smile beamed. "For heeding your call. For putting your duty above your sorrow." He reached out and stroked my cheek. His touch sent a distracting shudder straight to my center. I ignored it.

"You're an amazing woman, Emma Jane. Truly the flesh-and-blood finger of God. You humble me."

"Dude, you've got it all wrong. This isn't duty. This is revenge."

His smile dimmed, his hands slipping into the pockets of his slacks. "I understand your need to find some kind of balance to handle your loss. But I assure you, the soul-deep need you're feeling is the divine ordinance within."

"Um…no. It's really not." I mean, if anyone would know it'd be me, right? This was straight-up coldhearted need for revenge.

"Your emotions are still too charged to understand how deeply your nephilim blood leads your—"

"Eli, stop." I didn't want to hear it. What I was about to do, what I wanted to do, was for Tommy. No one else. "I'm not the grand, noble woman you think I am. I'm not some saint. I'm not your Joan of Arc. I'm just…me. I'm pissed. I'm human. And I want to do some very bad things."

"What you believe of yourself has little bearing on what God sees in you," he said.

Damn, the guy was determined. Whatever. "Fine. You know what? It doesn't matter. If you want to think there's more to me wanting to take this guy down than there is, do it. Just…stay out of my way. I'll call if I need you. Otherwise, I'll do this on my own."

"Miss?" I turned at the sound of the male voice behind me. A uniformed cop stood waiting, pen and pad in hand. My stomach dropped and rolled, like I'd gone down a giant roller-coaster hill. I knew that feeling. It wasn't just sorrow and frazzled nerves. It was something else—a sixth sense, a nephilim sense.

I realized in that instant he was a nephilim, and that he didn't know. I wasn't going to tell him…or anyone. Maybe he'd be one of the lucky ones and never be called. I shifted my belt, making sure the hilt was safely at the small of my back and away from his accidental touch.

"Yes?" I said.

"I need…I need to ask you a few questions," he said, his breath hitching for a second as though something inside him had made it catch. His eyes did a quick scan of me, head to toe, and he took off his cop hat and tucked it under one thick, muscled arm.

His nametag read D. Wysocki, and he had the bluest eyes, like actual sapphires, emphasis on the blue fire. His hair was short, light brown like coffee and cream, and his body was thick. He wasn't fat, more like he'd wrestled in high school a few years back.

"What's your name?"

"Emma Hellsbane."

Officer Wysocki wrote it down. "The EMTs check you out, Emma?"

I tilted my head, wondering why he'd asked. He waved his pen at my face and T-shirt. "That's a lot of blood. Is it yours?"

My hand went to my nose and I glanced down at my blood-splattered shirt. I'd forgotten. The pain was completely gone. "Yeah. I'm fine, though. Bloody nose."

"Good," he said. "The librarian says you came in with the stroke victim. You knew him?"

"What stroke victim?"

Wysocki flipped his pen to point at the ambulance behind me. I turned and looked over my shoulder just to make sure. They thought Tommy had died of a stroke? I guess having your heart drilled through could cause a stroke. Kind of like saying a guy hit by a bus died of kidney failure. Well, yeah…after bus tires crushed his kidneys.

I realized Eli had cleaned up more than just Tommy's appearance—the same way Tommy had said the angels had cleaned up Coach Clark's murder all those years ago. I looked to Eli to confirm, but he was gone.

"Yes," I said, turning back to Officer Wysocki. "We were

together. Tommy was…a really good friend."

"I see. Sorry for your loss," he said, and just like that my throat closed and tears suddenly stung my eyes. I tried to smile, but I couldn't hold it.

"You going to be okay? You need me to call someone?" he asked, obviously seeing the tears welling up.

I shook my head. "I'm fine."

He nodded and went back to writing in his little policeman's pad. "So his name's Tommy? Tommy what?"

"Thomas, actually." I swallowed, trying to get the stupid waver out of my voice. "Thomas Saint James."

"Saint James," he repeated, still nodding and writing. "Good. And what can you tell me about the vandals?"

He thought the demons were just a couple of vandals? What, did he think some stupid kids had scared Tommy into a stroke? No friggin' way. I wanted to set the record straight, make it known that nothing scared Tommy—ever. But what was the alternative? To those who didn't know him, the stroke was a believable story, and that was more important than an illorum's reputation.

"Uh, I don't know. Not much, I guess," I said, not sure what he thought I knew, or what I could say that wouldn't get me an overnight stay in a padded room.

He sighed, and his gaze swung up to me. Frustration showed in the way he jerked his hat from under his arm and dropped both hands to his sides. "Can you tell me how many vandals there were? What they looked like? What they said? Anything to help us catch them?"

My thumbs hooked on the front pockets of my jeans. "So, you think they got away?"

"Do you see them around?" he asked, scanning the small

parking lot. A flicker of movement on the roof of the library over the front entrance drew my eye. There was a man standing on top of the building. Did anyone else think that was strange? I glanced at Wysocki and back to the guy, who stood with the toes of his black dress shoes jutting over the edge of the gutter.

My heart jumped to my throat. The man's pale, almost white hair fluttered down to his elbows, his black, ankle-length jacket moving around his legs with the slight breeze. He was six-four, maybe six-six, with broad shoulders, big feet, and thick hands that he clasped behind him as I watched.

And he was staring at me. At least it seemed that way. He wore dark sunglasses, but he was definitely looking in my direction. And he was defying gravity by perching all his weight on the flimsy metal gutter. He couldn't be a Fallen. I made a mental check of the mark on my wrist, the one meant to warn me when a Fallen was near. It didn't even tingle. So this was an angel—a seraphim. *An angelic rubbernecker. Nice.*

I looked back to Officer Wysocki, who was now looking at me like I might get that padded room after all. He didn't see the man on the roof. People miss so much of what goes on around them. I had, too, until a few weeks ago.

"Uh…what was the question?"

"Listen, I don't know what's going on here, but something smells," he said.

It's probably the brimstone.

"There's a lot of property damage in there, shelves toppled over, books everywhere, blood and some kind of black slime all over the place. There's a glass wall, at least two inches thick, shattered. Now, I want some answers or we'll see if a ride to the station in the back of my squad car helps jog your memory."

"No. Okay, wait." I seriously did not want to be trapped at the police station for the rest of the day. I had things to do, fallen angels to kill. "I didn't get a good look at them. They were hiding between the shelves. When they started making trouble Tommy and I ducked behind some tables and I cracked my nose against one of them. There was a lot of blood and I guess the scare was…" I swallowed hard, hating the lie. "I guess the scare was too much for Tommy. I don't know why they were there or what they wanted."

"How many were there?"

Crap. Whatever cover story Eli had worked up with his powers, he hadn't clued me in. "Listen. I just lost someone very close to me. Everything's still kind of a blur. Tommy and I weren't the only ones in there. There was a lady at the reference desk. Have you talked to her?"

The officer tucked his hat under his arm again and flipped through his pad until he found the page he wanted. "The librarian says she thinks there were four of them. But she can't remember anything else. Can't even tell me if they were male or female. And no one can figure out what that black stuff is that's on the books and floor. What do you know about that?"

Dead demon guts, I thought. But I said, "Nothing. I don't know what it could be."

"Of course not." He stared at me for a second or two, one eye narrowing, his head tilting to the side as though he were weighing his thoughts about me. Finally, he closed his notepad and jammed it into his back pocket.

He used both hands to settle his hat on his head and then propped them on his hips. "Okay. Off the record. Tell me what happened."

It was all I could do not to laugh out loud. *Yeah, 'cause that's how it works.* "I don't know what you mean, officer. If that's all you need, I'd like to go home and grab a shower. I want to call Tommy's parents. Let them know."

He reached for me when I started to turn away. "Wait, I'm serious. Totally off the record. I know something's not right about this scene. I can...I can feel it." He glanced around as though he was worried someone might have overheard him.

"Officer—"

"Dan," he said. "My name's Dan Wysocki. I mean it. Just between us."

And the angel on the roof. I glanced at the ominous-looking man above us. Obviously, Eli wasn't the only one being watched now. But why me?

"There's nothing I can tell you," I said. "Really." At least, I couldn't if he wanted to keep his normal, happy life.

He pointed at me, like he'd pinned a bug. "You said nothing you *can* tell me, not nothing *to* tell me. I'm a cop, Emma; I notice the way people word things. It matters. Please. This isn't the first...strange disturbance call I've gone on. I've seen that black slime at another scene. And when we met I had this sensation in my gut...I've felt it before. It means something."

Dan looked to be in his early- to mid-thirties. There was a tan line on his left ring finger and his wallet was fat enough to bulge his back pocket. A family man.

"You married, Dan?" I asked.

"Divorced."

"Kids?"

"Five," he said. "Four boys and a girl."

I rolled my eyes. "Go home, Dan. Forget about the black slime and witnesses who can't remember anything. Go home to your kids.

Be a dad. Be a cop. Live your life. And don't pick up any swords."

"Did you say swords?"

"Yeah." No way he knew what I meant by it.

"There were marks at the last scene. Gouges left in a telephone poll and a bus stop bench. Like something long and sharp had cut into it," he said. "Our weapons guy said they looked like sword strikes. Neither of the librarians remembers seeing any weapons, but I saw the same kind of marks on a couple of the bookshelves in there."

Crap. I fought the reflex to touch my sword. "Oh, yeah? Fascinating. I have to go."

"Hey." His sharp tone stopped me again. "I could haul your butt downtown and *make* you tell me, you know?"

"How? You going to torture me? Put me on the rack? Use thumbscrews?" I said.

There was something about Officer Dan Wysocki I liked. Maybe it was a kindred species thing. Maybe it was his pretty eyes, or his solid stature. He looked like the kind of guy who didn't back down easily, didn't scare easily. I liked that. Which was why I wasn't going to tell him a damn thing.

"Listen, I know whatever happened here isn't…normal," he said. "I can't explain it, but I could feel it when I walked in and smelled that black goo. Like that stench should mean something to me. I don't know how you're involved, but if you need help, just let me know. I think you're supposed to let me know."

Okay, this was starting to creep me out. "Thanks, Dan. I've, um, really got to go now."

He straightened. I could almost see him go from Dan Wysocki, confused nephilim, to Officer Wysocki, dedicated cop.

"Yeah. I've, uh, I've almost got everything." He pulled his

notepad out again, snagged the pen from his breast pocket, and triple-clicked the end. "Let me see some ID and give me your phone number in case we have any more questions or need you to identify suspects."

"You won't find any suspects, Dan," I said, and his gaze flicked up to mine. His two personas battled in his eyes for a moment before the cop took hold again.

"We'll do our best, Miss Hellsbane. I'll need that ID and number."

I gave him my number and driver's license, and he finally let me walk away just as the ambulance pulled out with Tommy's body in the back. I stood at the driver's door of my Jeep, watching the big square vehicle make a left out of the lot and then a right onto the main street and away. No lights, no sirens, just a quiet retreat. So *not* Tommy.

Tears wet my cheeks and stung in my chest when I turned back to unlock my door. But seeing a ginger-haired angel squatting on a thin branch of a nearby tree nearly stopped my aching heart dead.

"Holy sh— What do you want?" I swiped my cheeks dry with the back of my hand.

His eyes were ghostly white, the irises so pale they looked like chips of eggshell in cotton. He wore the same long jacket as the angel on the roof, except it was white, as were his slacks, his shirt, and his shoes. The choice did wonders for him. His rich, reddish hair lay in stunning waves against the stark white of his back and shoulders.

I glanced across the parking lot and noticed another angel had joined my audience. Dressed in the same dark black as the angel on the library, he stood on the roof of a blue Golf convertible, not even bending the cloth top with his weight.

Yet another angel, blond hair past his shoulders, dressed in a pinstriped gray suit, his arms folded across his chest, stood on the sidewalk, looking odd for the normalcy of it. If not for his white eyes, I might not have pegged him as an angel at all.

I looked back to the nearest angel, who was still squatting in the tree, knees to his chest, arms wrapped around them. "You're wasting your time. Eli's not going to screw up. I won't make him fall."

The angel gave me a slow blink, reminding me of an owl. His eerie white gaze stayed fixed on me, no sign he'd heard or understood. I glanced to the others, their pale faces all watching me, their solemn expressions unchanging.

Stimulating conversationalists. "Fine," I said, opening my door and climbing behind the wheel. "You want to watch? Watch me send one of your bastard brothers to the abyss."

CHAPTER THIRTEEN

I didn't need to know what was on the other side of Tommy's apartment door, just that there was another side. The speed at which I could move actually gave me more time to make decisions.

Eli had said it was some weird space-time thing. I didn't really understand. Somehow, moving that fast, I put myself out of sync with everything else. So, once I was on the other side of the door, I'd have time to take in my surroundings and decide where I wanted to stop, thereby avoiding the chance of stopping inside something unpleasant...like a wall.

Not that I thought there'd be a wall directly on the other side of the door, but you never know. As long as I kept moving, I was golden. It had taken a while to get used to, but I had it down now.

After a deep breath, I pictured myself standing on the other side of Tommy's apartment door. Then I took a step. With my next I slammed hard into the door. I hadn't passed through it—I'd run faster than the speed of light right into it.

That hurt.

A lot.

But the door didn't give an inch. I ran so hard into it every molecule of breath exploded from my lungs and stars spun in circles behind my eyes. If not for a reflexive head flinch, I would've broken my nose again.

Staring at the door, my mouth agape, I looked to Eli, who had appeared beside it. "What was that?"

"*That* is what I was trying to tell you," he said. "There's still a lot you don't know, and I can't possibly tell you everything at once. Some things must be learned as you go—with me at your side. That's why I'm here…on earth."

"Whatever." I'd taken a quick shower to wash off the blood and demon gunk, gotten a fresh set of jeans and T-shirt, and headed over to Tommy's place the second Eli had given me the address.

"So spill it," I said, knotting my arms across my chest. "What just happened?"

"You have to remember you're not pure human," he said. "Your angelic half encompasses equal amounts in your system and makes you, or at least that half of you, susceptible to the same rules as your father."

"Which has to do with this…how?"

"Free will," he said, then gave a nod toward Tommy's door. "This is the physical threshold to a human's private realm. Access to it cannot be gained by use of angelic power unless the angel has already been welcomed in."

"I thought that was just demons and vampires." I shook my head at the sentence. Weird to think I'd used demons and vampires in a serious conversation. *Moving on.*

"It's true for anyone possessing angelic blood."

"So that's why Tommy didn't just pop into my house that first day?" I said. "I'd never invited him?"

"Exactly."

"But after he'd been invited he could pop in any time he wanted."

"Yes," Eli said.

"So, can I walk in the normal way?"

Eli leaned a shoulder against the doorjamb. "Of course. Humans ignore others' free will every day. You're still half human."

I was pretty sure there was an insult in there, but I let it slide and reached for the doorknob. It wouldn't turn. "It's locked."

"Of course," Eli said. "Thomas was very diligent about security."

"Do you have a key?"

He looked away. "No."

"Where's a lock-picking kit when you need one?" I stooped to look at the deadbolt keyhole.

"Will this do?" Eli said, and I looked to see him holding a lock-picking kit in a convenient black-zippered carrying pouch. He gave it to me.

"Cool trick," I said, more than a little impressed. "Can you make anything out of thin air?"

"I didn't make the lock kit," he said, brows furrowed. "I went and retrieved one for you."

"You stole it?" *Holy klepto, Batman.*

His shoulders stiffened, head high. "I didn't steal it. I borrowed the kit from the manufacturer. It won't be missed. I can return it when you're finished."

"Oh. Well, that makes all the difference." *Not.* Angels lie and steal. Who knew? My gaze dropped to the open kit in my hand. Eight different tiny little tools fit snugly into pockets on either side. They looked like itty-bitty screwdrivers, except they each had weird squiggly ends that wouldn't fit any screw I'd ever seen.

I had no idea how to use them. "Too bad it didn't come with an instruction manual."

"It did," he said, pushing from the wall. "I assumed since you asked for the kit you knew how to use it."

I opened my mouth for my clever retort about "assuming," when someone behind me yelled.

"Hey!"

I turned.

"What're you doing there? What's that you got?" The man climbed the last two steps to the landing on Tommy's floor at the end of the hallway just as I slapped the little leather case closed and shifted my hands behind my back. I shook it, hoping Eli would get the hint and take the incriminating evidence. He didn't.

"Uh, nothing," I said. "I just stopped by to get something out of my friend's apartment."

The beer-bellied man waddled on skinny, bowed legs toward me. His dirt-brown shorts came to the wrinkled knees of his legs. His black socks covered his calves, and he wore a dingy gray tank top that looked like it'd been on him for decades.

"Oh, yeah? Whose apartment? What's friend's name?" he asked in accented, broken English. Maybe Russian? He raised the little ball of his chin, and the large, beaklike nose above it. His bushy black eyebrows creased to a point over his small brown eyes and his thick comb-over shifted back.

I hiked a thumb at the door. "Tommy Saint James."

"He in there?"

"Uh, no." *He's dead.* My chest gave a quick pinch to remind me. I shook the pick kit at the small of my back, my mind screaming for Eli to take it. *Take it!*

When he didn't, I glanced behind me. *Crap.* Eli was gone. My gaze went heavenward. *Thanks for the heads-up, magister.*

"I'm owner of building. What your name? Lemme see what you got there." The greasy landlord tried to reach around me, and his bulging belly bumped my arm. *Eeww.*

"Emma." Rather than let him touch me again, I showed him the lock kit. It just wasn't worth wanting to scrape my skin off later.

He took the kit and opened it. "Why you have this? You trying to break into apartment?"

"No." *Yes.* "No, I wasn't. I was just…"

"I'm calling police," he said, turning back down the hall, taking my stolen lock-picking kit with him. "You wait here. Police coming now."

I sighed. "Screw this."

What's the use of having superhuman-angel powers if you can't use them to get yourself out of a jam? A half second later, I was outside on the street at my Jeep.

Tommy's apartment was on Mount Washington. The area had a close community feel—a lot of big houses built close together, with brick porches and small, fenced yards. The neighborhood boasted some great architecture, too, beautiful Queen Anne–style homes, a few Victorians, but most were good old American Foursquare.

The huge old houses had been sectioned into apartments long ago. One last, longing look at the window to Tommy's place, and I pushed the key into the door lock of my Jeep.

Eli popped in beside me. "You're leaving?"

I jumped, and the key popped back out. "Where were you?"

He lifted a card-size pamphlet between us. "Getting the instruction manual. It took me a few minutes to find. They print it in a separate building from where the kit is made. Why do you ask?"

"Because I got busted by the landlord, that's why."

"You shouldn't have been trying to break in," he said.

"Ya think? Or maybe I shouldn't have been trying to break in without someone watching my back."

"Ignoring free will never ends well," he said. "Besides, as I've told you, I cannot interfere."

"I'm not asking you to interfere. I'm just saying a heads-up would've been nice. Maybe a, 'Hey, Em, you're about to get busted by a disgusting hairy egg with legs.' Y'know, or words to that effect."

He closed the small distance between our bodies, and despite the heated city around us, the scent of fresh spring air, wildflowers, and sun-warmed fields enveloped me. I closed my eyes and inhaled a quick, guilty breath. Did all angels smell this good, or was it just Eli? I didn't want to know.

"Emma Jane, now more than ever I must temper my actions," he said, his voice a soft conspirator's whisper. "Even now I am watched, judged. I cannot give the council cause to question my control."

I opened my eyes and met the ice blue of his gaze. "The council? Tommy said they were just other angels, seraphim. What's the council?"

His eyes shifted to his right, and I looked. The angel from the tree at the library squatted on the cross arm of a tall telephone pole on the other side of the road, his arms wrapped around his knees. The long tails of his white coat hung below him, fluttering like a flag in the wind. His ginger-red hair shifted past his shoulders.

"The council of seven," Eli said. "Seven archangels privileged with having our Father's ear. Interpreters of His word. *That* seraphim is one of the council's watchers. A seraphim, but tasked with a mission by the council."

"A spy. How can you be sure?"

"I can sense it."

"You don't talk to God yourself?"

He looked at me. "Yes. But, like you, I do not always understand His answer. The council serves as our advisers, our arbiters, and our judiciary. Their word is not to be questioned."

"Don't sweat it," I said. "I'm pretty sure that one up there's watching me. I guess we both can't be trusted."

"No." Eli's back stiffened. "He's not watching you."

"Yeah, he is. At least it looks like the same one I saw at the library. One of them, anyway. Same creepy white eyes."

Eli glanced between me and the angel on the pole, the skin at the top of his nose wrinkling, his mouth a flat serious line. "You must be mistaken."

He seemed so sure. Too bad he was dead wrong. "Uh…no. I'm not. I'm telling you, Eli, the guy wasn't more than eight feet away." I jabbed a finger in the angel's direction. "That's the guy who was sitting in a tree at the library. I asked him what he wanted but I got nothing. He didn't answer."

"Of course not. Fraciel would never deign to speak to someone like you."

I gasped. "Rude."

Eli blinked as though his mind tripped over itself trying to puzzle out the reason for my offense. "You're the result of sin, Emma Jane. He won't notice you. He refuses. How would you say it? You're not even on his radar?"

"Okay. I get it," I said. "Kudos on the colloquialism, by the way."

"Thank you."

"You're still wrong," I said, and watched Eli go all stiff again. Too bad. "Your buddy Fraciel might be too good to speak to me, but he and his three friends were still thumbing their noses at gravity, and generally weirding me out, watching every move I made with those white eyes."

"Who were the others?" he asked.

"How should I know? They weren't wearing name tags."

He shook his head, his gaze drifting back to Fraciel on the streetlight. "That can't be. Something's changed."

A chill raced through me, like cold iron pumping in my veins. My mind flashed to Eli snatching me from the sharp-toothed, long-clawed grasp of death on Capri. "Because of what happened in the gardens?"

Eli looked at me, and I knew without reading his mind, he'd been thinking the same thing. They suspected it was my fault Eli was acting strangely. And maybe it was—Tommy had predicted as much. Maybe they were just waiting for proof.

"My passions are well in hand, Emma Jane," he said, reading the thoughts swirling loud and clear on the surface of my mind. "Don't waste another moment on worry."

He was right. They could watch all they wanted. We weren't going to break the rules, no matter how good Eli smelled.

I turned and stared up at Tommy's building, pushing the spying angels from my mind. I needed to get those tickets for the televangelist's seminar or at least the name of the guy who was getting them for him. The answer was there, inside his apartment a few feet away. If only I could figure out another way in. And then I saw it.

"There's a fire escape." I may not be able to pick a lock, but I could break a window.

"Someone will undoubtedly call the police," Eli said.

"Then we'll have to move fast. Lucky for us, we're good at that." I thought of the metal landing outside Tommy's window. I took a step, everything blurred, and with my next I stopped right outside. An instant later the world caught up to me. Eli was already waiting, casually sitting on the thin railing.

"It's not unlocked by any chance, is it?" I asked.

His eyes closed as he shook his head.

"'Course not." I tried the window anyway. It was locked, but after pressing my nose to the glass, I realized it was one I could pick. "I need a credit card. There's one in my purse under the backseat of the Jeep."

Two heartbeats later, Eli held out the card to me. I pushed against the window and slipped the card between the old rubber seal. It took a little bit of wiggling and shaking the window, but within a few minutes, I'd managed to push the casted metal lock the other way. *Look out, Thomas Crown.*

With the window open, I climbed inside and turned, waiting for Eli to follow. He didn't. "You coming?"

"I can't."

"You're kidding me," I said. "All the years you two were together, Tommy never invited you into his place?"

"He did. But after you were marked, Thomas...revoked his invitation."

I couldn't be certain what would've made Tommy upset enough with Eli to do such a thing, but I had a pretty good idea. In the end, no matter what he'd said, Tommy didn't trust Eli. He didn't trust any of the angels, and after spending the day with my angelic tail, I was beginning to have the same opinion. I just couldn't lump Eli into that category, no matter how much Tommy had warned me.

"But he doesn't really live here anymore," I said.

"His essence still protects his home," Eli said. "A human's essence, the power of their will, can linger for years in a home, even longer around favorite objects. All of Tommy's earthly possessions are inside there. His will still holds me out."

I thought about that as I stood on Tommy's kitchen chair next to the window. I closed my eyes, listened, felt, smelled. I could sense him, a subtle current in the air, a familiar pressure against my body, like the sixth sense that tells you someone is near…only fainter.

I inhaled deeply, taking in the scent of Tommy's home and with it, the scent of the man himself. Cheap, powdery male cologne, a faint scent of stale water, and the warm smell of his skin hinted on the air that filled my lungs. Eli was right. There was still so much of him here.

"I'm sorry, Eli. I'll hurry." My stomach soured for the pained look on Eli's face. He'd loved Tommy, and they'd had a falling out because of me. It was my fault he wasn't welcome in Tommy's home, my fault Tommy had died with his long friendship with Eli strained.

"The heartache of loss is suffered only by the living, Emma Jane," Eli said. "Thomas has moved beyond such things."

I nodded, turned, and stepped down off the chair, trying to believe him.

Afternoon sun lit the small room with soft, filtered light. There were clean dishes in the dish rack and a dirty spoon and bowl in the sink, cloudy dried milk marking both. Tommy's last meal at the apartment, as though he'd only stepped out a moment ago.

My throat clenched, and my chest hurt. I closed my eyes against the sudden sting of tears and pushed past my emotions.

Tommy wouldn't have wanted this. He'd want me to figure out which Fallen had ordered his death and take the bastard's head. Yeah. I could do that.

Damn, I missed him.

I banished the thought before it pulled me down again and

stepped into the living room, touched the back of the couch. He'd used bedsheets for curtains on the two living room windows, and they were tied back, allowing the sun to light the room. He hardly had any furniture, just the basics any growing boy needs—couch to rest his butt, coffee table to rest his feet, twenty-inch TV on a stack of plastic milk crates, and an upholstered wing chair for guests.

The coffee table in front of the couch was about the messiest thing in the apartment—half-opened newspapers, magazines with sections cut out, notepads, and crumpled notepaper piled on either side of a hefty-sized laptop.

"Nice." I sat on the couch, perching on the edge in front of the computer. Now I knew where all his money went.

This is what I'd come for. Whatever Tommy had on his Fallen and on Mr. Ticket Guy should be on the hard drive. But thanks to his greasy landlord, the police were probably on their way. I closed the monitor, snagged the power cord, wrapped it all up, and headed back to the kitchen.

The moment I stepped into the hall, I knew I wasn't ready to leave. Not yet. I'd known of Tommy for years, but I'd only gotten to really know the guy behind the handsome jock-star smile over the past few weeks. I wanted more, and standing in his apartment, I knew this was my last, best chance.

I turned down the hall, past the bathroom, and into the one and only bedroom. Carrying the theme "less is more," there wasn't much in the way of furniture: a bed, a chest of drawers, a nightstand, a lamp, and an alarm clock. Hugging the laptop to my chest, I plopped down onto his bed, letting the springs bounce me. I leaned over and took a deep whiff of his pillow.

"Tommy," I said, recognizing the scent of his shampoo.

Sirens wailed softly in the distance. They might have been going anywhere, but chances were they were coming for me. I had to leave, but it felt so final. I knew I'd never come back here. Tommy's apartment would be cleaned out once the police notified his parents.

I pushed myself to my feet, but before I could take a step something fluttering on the wall near the door caught my eye. "Holy crap, Tommy. What were you doing?"

The world map he'd thumbtacked to the wall was at least four feet tall and six feet long. He'd taped photos along both sides and a few on the top. Each photo had a piece of red yarn trailing from it to some point on the map. I followed the strings out to the pictures. They were all candid shots of people I didn't know. Except for one. Me.

The string connected to my picture led to Pittsburgh on the map. It was a hideous photo of me, but then they always are. Not that it mattered. He'd written "Marked" across my body. It wasn't a recent photo, either. I looked maybe fifteen.

"Wait. I *am* fifteen in this picture," I said, standing on tiptoes to get a closer look. I wasn't wearing my glasses. I'd gotten contacts when I turned fifteen.

There was a second string leading from Pittsburgh that connected to the picture below mine. After a few seconds staring at the blurry photo I recognized the young man. "Officer Wysocki."

He was younger in his photo, and nothing was written on it. Why had Tommy taken the photos so long ago?

I stepped back, reviewing the entire display. Several of the pictures had the same word, "Marked," written across them, but most had nothing.

"He was tracking nephilim and illorum," I said to myself. There were hundreds of them all over the world, United States, Europe, Africa, China.

My skin warmed, a sense of connection coiled in my belly. I'd lost Tommy, the only person in the world who knew what I was going through, who understood like no one else. But I wasn't alone. And I knew, just like that, why he'd done it. He didn't want to be alone either.

Take it, Emma Jane, Eli said, his rich voice rippling through my mind. *He'd want you to have it. Leaving the map and photos will only create unwanted questions.*

"Right." He didn't need to tell me twice. Setting the laptop on the floor, I popped out the thumbtacks and carefully rolled the enormous map. I'd just gotten the laptop back under my arm when someone pounded on the front door.

"Hello? Anyone home?" *Crap*. I knew that voice. Dan Wysocki. *Sheesh!* Weren't there any other cops on duty today? "This is the police. Open the door."

"Wait. I have key," I heard the greasy landlord guy say. "Master key. I let you in."

The lock rattled as I climbed onto the chair at the window. Eli had already vanished from the fire escape. I heard the door slam against the wall when Dan pushed it open, heard their feet shuffling against the wood floor as they rushed in.

My heart raced, pulse going a zillion miles a minute. With the map under one arm, the laptop under the other, I got a foot through the window, my mind screaming—*get out, get out, get out*.

And suddenly I was.

The moment my torso and head were past the window's threshold my anxiousness triggered my angelic speed. I flew across the metal fire escape, the hard railing catching me straight across the gut. Sheer willpower and wicked-awesome balance kept me from tumbling head over heels to the alley two stories down. The laptop wasn't so lucky.

"Hey. You!" Officer Dan said.

I glanced back into the apartment before I could stop myself and saw Wysocki pointing at me from the kitchen doorway. "You."

"Crap." I willed myself to the alley below. The world blurred and a blink later I was there, standing over the spilled guts of Tommy's monster laptop. "Oops. Think that can be fixed?"

"Emma Jane," Eli said suddenly beside me. "Run!"

"Right." I scooped up the laptop and ran.

CHAPTER FOURTEEN

"Is there any hope for it?" Eli nodded at the smashed remains of Tommy's laptop lying on the folded map in my lap. We'd teleported to Olympia Park a few blocks over from Tommy's place on Mount Washington to wait for Officer Wysocki and his buddies to leave so I could get to my Jeep.

I glanced at him sitting on the playground swing next to mine and then down at the ruined laptop. "I don't know. Maybe. My cousin Gretchen knows a guy. I'll call him when we get back to the Jeep. My cell's in my purse under the front seat."

Eli nodded but he wasn't looking at me. I followed his stare to the jungle gym playset about eight yards in front of us where the red-headed angel from the library, and outside Tommy's apartment, perched. The small play roof the angel stood on was hard plastic and colored bright yellow to go with the brilliant primary colors of the rest of the playground equipment.

He looked enormous standing atop the pint-size set, his long, blood-red hair stirring over his shoulders, his white coat fluttering around his calves. His expression remained a constant mask, his unblinking white-blue eyes staring at us, his lips a flat line and his hands clasped loosely in front of him. In an instant the other three library seraphim joined him. One squatting on the green guardrail of a twisting tube slide, another balanced on the head of a spring-mounted hobbyhorse, and the third standing effortlessly on the two-inch-round metal rod of the monkey bars.

The Council's spies had followed me.

I pushed my swing sideways toward Eli, my gaze glued on the angels. "I gotta tell ya, between you and your brothers, you definitely got the good looks in the family."

"They wouldn't agree," he said. "They are exactly as our Father created them, exactly as they were when the finger of God last touched their flesh. They are…perfect."

I tried not to let his idea of perfection give me a complex. "So, why all the alterations for you?"

"I shortened my hair and lightened the color to appear more human," he said. "To walk among you and better aid my illorum."

I looked at his coal-black hair. "You lightened it?"

He smiled, but it didn't stick. "Even the blackest human hair color never truly reaches the midnight blue my hair once was. The… *alterations* weren't fun. I had to shorten the length of many of my bones as well, mostly in my hands and feet."

I took a better look at the redhead's hands, big palms, long, slender fingers, then I looked back at Eli. "Well, I think you upgraded. Especially the eyes. Ginger over there is way too creepy."

Eli stiffened, his hand lifting, touching his cheek. "My eyes?"

He didn't know? Of course not. The man had zero ego. Why would he bother looking in a mirror? Or maybe he just didn't want to notice. "Your eyes are darker. I mean, they're still unbelievably light, but theirs…theirs are unearthly. They barely have any color at all. Trust me, eyes need color."

"I didn't do it on purpose." He glanced at me then back to the angels watching us. "They must've darkened over time. The more we interact with humans the more…tainted our spirit becomes. We grow weaker, slower. The difference is miniscule but gradually it begins to show in the color of our eyes. I didn't realize it'd become noticeable to anyone else."

I reached over and took his hand, squeezed. He looked at me. "You have beautiful eyes, Eli, and a beautiful spirit. I know it comes at a cost, but I wouldn't be able to do this without you."

He smiled and this time it lit his face. He pushed his swing toward me, our shoulders bumping, our heads close. "Thank you, Emma Jane—"

"Elizal," the redhead said, and we jumped apart. It sounded as though he stood right next to us. We looked and the angel hadn't moved from the top of the little playground roof, hands still clasped in front of him.

"Fraciel?" Eli said, as though he wasn't sure the angel had actually spoken either.

Before my brain could make sense of it Eli was standing at the base of the playset in front of Fraciel. He cupped his hands behind his back, gazing up at his seraphim brother.

"One of your pets was put down today," Fraciel said.

Eli bowed his head and looked up again. "Yes."

"The one that remains to you is female?"

"Yes."

The angel farther back, the one standing on the tube slide, stood. "We believe it is best you put her down as well, and return home."

I was suddenly on my feet clutching the computer and map to my chest. "Excuse me?"

No one even looked my way.

"I will not," Eli said.

The long-haired blond on the hobbyhorse said, "It is not for you to decide."

Eli's gaze shifted over his shoulder. "I will not take human life. Father forbids it."

"It is not human," the blond said, his white eyes narrowing.

"She is half human." Eli turned his back to him and faced Fraciel. "Her soul is human. Father alone decides her time on this earth."

"And the Council," the angel on the tube slide said, his snow-white hair drifting off his shoulders, caught in a soft breeze. "The Council's word is the word of Father. You accept this as truth, do you not?"

Eli blinked, his gaze shifting to the distant seraphim. He didn't answer right away. Instead, he seemed to think for a moment and then finally said, "Yes. Has the Council dispatched you with a new commission since last we spoke?"

The burgundy-haired angel balancing on the monkey bars finally spoke up. "Magisters do not question the envoy of the Council. Magisters obey."

"No," Fraciel said before Eli could respond to the other angel. "We have not been charged with a new commission. But the state of affairs has changed since we last imparted the Council's concerns."

"It has not," Eli said. "Thomas was killed. But Emma Jane's duty remains unchanged. Father blessed her with courage and a divine calling to fight the corruption of His creation. She has not failed that pursuit. She endeavors toward it now…to this very day."

The tall angel lowered himself to a squat, his pale face nearly level with Eli's. "Its efforts toward redemption and the protection of your spirit are not interchangeable. It is a danger to you, Elizal. As was the last female. Perhaps more so after suffering the loss of the male for which you had grown too enamored. We do not want to lose you—*I* do not want to lose you. Come home, Elizal. Allow your brothers to heal your spirit. There will be others to aid when you are strong again."

"My spirit is secure. My place is here," Eli said.

Fraciel stood, his face tense, brows creased together. He exhaled. "It is in pursuit of a Fallen?"

"She is," Eli said. "She has tracked him to this city and will soon devise a way to draw close enough to dispatch him to the abyss."

The blood-haired angel stiffened. "Then we will wait to report our findings to the Council. See that it finds this Fallen soon, magister. And see that you do not one day meet his same fate."

I blinked and all four seraphim were gone. Eli's shoulders visibly dropped and he lowered his head as though he'd been holding his breath.

I stepped up beside him. "Thanks for going to bat for me. I know that couldn't have been easy."

He didn't say anything, just nodded, and a smile flickered across his lips.

"What would you have done if the Council *had* told you to kill me?" I asked. My stomach fluttered, worrying for a half second over his answer.

Eli raised his head, meeting my eyes. "I pray we never find out."

"Right." My exhale blew out a little shaky and I stepped away.

"The police have left Thomas's apartment. It's safe to return to your Jeep," he said.

It took a second to figure out how he knew. Then I remembered his gift for reading human thoughts. "You coming?"

He shook his head. "I...need a moment."

"Right." I nodded, tried to smile, but emotion clogged at the back of my throat and tightened through my chest. I took another step away. "Well, I'm going to head home, so...that's where I'll be. Gonna call my aunt, see if my cousin still knows that computer guy. Maybe do some Internet searches, see what I can find on the Fallen Tommy was going after."

"Try hard, Emma Jane. Please," he said, and then he was gone, just like his brothers.

"Right. No pressure."

• • •

"Hi, Aunt Sara. Is Gretchen still seeing that Will guy?" I pinched the cell phone between my cheek and shoulder and shifted gears, keeping up with the busy midday traffic. Something beeped and I glanced down at the dashboard gauges. I needed gas. *Crap.*

"Oh, no dear, I'm sorry," she said. "They broke up a few months ago. Why do you ask?"

I glanced at the pile of computer and techno guts spilling over the passenger seat next to me. "Just having some computer problems. Thought I might be able to swing some free geek assistance."

"Well, Justin knows a lot about computers too. He's always showing me how to take care of those bothersome virus alerts."

My cousin Justin took a website design course in college and had been the reigning family computer guru until his sister Gretchen started dating Will, an *actual* computer guru. With Will out of the picture, it seemed Justin had reclaimed his title. *Long live King Justin.*

"I think my problems are a little out of Justin's capabilities." I came to a stop at a red light.

"You could come by if you want and let him have a look. Everyone's here to watch the game and we'd love to see you. It seems like months since you made it for game day," she said. "You know, you and Lacey are always welcome. Since your dad passed, you girls never make it in time for the game."

It was true. The Sunday ball game parties were typically a guy-motivated get-together. Mom wasn't really a sports freak like the rest of the family. After my dad passed away she didn't see a reason to endure the game portion of the day, and Lacey and I took after her in that respect. We saw the family at major holidays and family reunions, but on game days we'd take full advantage of our reputation for late arrivals and show up just in time for the post-game celebration — or commiseration, whichever the day called for. Post-game was when we really got to be together as one huge family anyway. I'd missed the last few game days, figuring I'd go the next time. Now I didn't know if it would ever be safe for me to go again.

The attack in the library had been aimed at both Tommy and me. I wasn't just an innocent caught in the crossfire anymore — I was a target. It didn't matter if the Fallen Tommy had discovered months ago was really his father. He was after me now too, and until I could figure out how to get close to him and take his head, anyone near me, everyone I loved, would be in danger. If I couldn't get the name of Tommy's ticket guy off his computer, I'd figure out another way. I wouldn't risk my family.

The light turned green and I was moving again. "Thanks, Aunt Sara, but I've, uh, I've got a couple clients today. Maybe next time." My chest pinched; I knew it was a lie but wished with all my heart that it wasn't.

I heard a click and then my uncle Greg said from another phone in the house, "Is that my little Emma Jane? Are you finally gonna come root for the black and yellow with us and make this a real party?"

"Hi, Uncle Greg. I'm sorr—"

"Aw, c'mon, Emma. You're just like your mom," he said, not bothering to let me answer. "You both have that special something, able to liven up a room just by walking through the door. Especially if the room is full of men." He laughed, totally clueless how creepy he sounded.

Uncle Greg had always been the king of inappropriate comments. He meant well, but sometimes it seemed like the circuit between his mouth and brain wasn't always making a good connection. Then again, as a kid, I'd always wondered if he had a thing for my mom.

"Greg, hang up the phone, dear. You've drank too many beers and the game hasn't even started," Aunt Sara said. She knew her husband, and she loved him anyway, faulty brain-mouth circuit and all.

And then I had a thought.

"Uncle Greg, wait a minute. Do you remember my mom ever having that effect on anyone specifically? I mean, besides my dad," I said. "Like say, I dunno, twenty-three years ago?"

"Emma, what are you asking?" Aunt Sara said, loyalty making her tone suspicious. "After your mother and father married she never looked at another man."

"Except for that guy she met working on that political campaign," Uncle Greg said, and then the pop of a beer can tab crackled through the connection. "'Course, that was more him looking at Carol than the other way around. Can't say I blamed him. Carol, all fired up the way she was over teachers' issues and politics back then, she was getting a lot of people's attention."

Aunt Sara clicked her tongue. "What on earth are you talking about? I don't remember anyone paying any extra attention to her, or vice versa."

"Sure, you do," Uncle Greg said. "Don't you remember when the governor was running for reelection? Carol and a bunch of her teacher friends spent all their free time helping out and going to all those campaign shindigs. That guy, uh, Isaac...something, started hanging around. We all thought he was a spy for the other guy's camp."

"I have no idea what you're talking about," Aunt Sara said.

Eli had said the Fallen wipe the memories of the women they've been with. Could my angelic father have wiped Aunt Sara's memory of him too? My mom and her sister were close—best friends close. It didn't make sense Aunt Sara wouldn't know if a strange man was making a play for my mom.

But then, maybe their closeness is why Aunt Sara didn't remember. What good would it do him to wipe Mom's memory if her sister would remind her anyway? I guess my father didn't count on my uncle Greg's creepy inappropriate interest in my mother.

"I'm not crazy, woman," Uncle Greg said. "I bet we even have a picture of the guy. Where's the scrapbook?"

"It's out in the cabinet in the living room," Aunt Sara said. "I don't know what you hope to find. I'm the one who put all those pictures in there."

Uncle Greg didn't stop to argue. I heard the clunk when he set down his beer can and the huffing and shuffling as he searched for the book.

My heart skipped. A picture? Could it really be that easy? If not for Tommy's smashed laptop, I wouldn't have even called.

Tommy had searched for years and come so close, but not close enough. I'd been marked a little more than two weeks ago, and I might have already discovered the name and photographic proof of the Fallen who'd fathered me. Of course, if it was really him I'd still need to find him somewhere in the great wide world. But with a first name, a picture, and people who actually remembered details about him, I'd have a good place to start.

"Ha!" Uncle Greg said, his voice fading and shaking as though he was walking with the phone. "I told you we had a picture of him."

My heart leapt to my throat. I held my breath as I drifted to a slow stop at another light.

"Let me see that," Aunt Sara said and I realized Uncle Greg must've brought his extension and the scrapbook into the same room as her. "I'm the one who took that picture. Nobody there was interested in Carol romantically."

"What about this guy?" Uncle Greg asked.

I waited for the couple to come to some verbal conclusion but my curiosity got the better of me. "Uncle Greg, could you send me a copy of that photo?"

"Sure, honey," he said. "Give me a second and I'll snap a picture of it with my phone and text it to you."

I was coming up to a gas station on the right so I flicked on my blinker and pulled in. After turning off the Jeep I sat for a moment, waiting for the picture to come through.

"I have no idea who that is," Aunt Sara said. "He wasn't working with Carol's group, I can tell you that."

"Okay, Emma," Uncle Greg said, ignoring his wife for the moment. "Did it go through?"

My phone beeped. "Got it. Thanks."

I thumbed the touch screen to open the text and photo. It took a minute to recognize my mom, twenty-three years younger, standing among a clutch of people posing for the photograph. It was taken indoors, the group standing in three short rows. Behind them in the near distance, leafy green ferns grew from long planters on top of a stone wall and gave the feel of a public location.

"I'm telling you, Sara, that guy had something to do with the fund-raisers or politics." Uncle Greg's voice rumbled with leashed temper. "I mean, I figured he was working on the campaign. He was around enough. You even asked him to be in the photo, but he was camera shy or something. Hell, I talked to him every time we went down there. Isaac was his name, or maybe it was Ivan. No, it was…it was one of those *I* names…Damn, why can't I remember?"

"Which guy, Uncle Greg?" I asked.

"The guy walking behind the group there," he said. "His face is kind of blurry, but you can see him right over your mom's shoulder."

Until that moment I hadn't noticed the man in the background. He hadn't been posing with the group, but he'd looked at the camera when the photo was taken.

Nearly a foot taller than my mother, he was blurred by motion, the details of his face hidden except for the cornflower blond of his hair and beard. But his blue eyes had caught the light and flared in the picture like two small gas-lit fires. He wore a white shirt with a black tie and slacks.

He could've been anyone.

A minivan pulled in behind me, and I watched through my rearview mirror as the driver and passenger hopped out. The passenger, a woman, dashed inside the convenience store while the man who'd been driving began pumping gas.

My attention flicked back to my phone. "You said his first name was Isaac, Uncle Greg?"

"Well, I don't remember him," Aunt Sara said with a final denial.

"Yeah. Isaac. Isaac…" Uncle Greg's voice trailed off as though searching his memory. "Aw, hell. I can't remember. It was Isaac something."

Aunt Sara sighed. "Never heard of him."

Isaac. My gaze fell to the blurred photo of my angelic father. Did he still go by the same name? How many women had he seduced since this photo? How many half siblings did I have? The questions whirled through my head, each one spawning a new thought. But like an island amidst a raging sea, one crystallized above them all.

Could I kill this man?

CHAPTER FIFTEEN

"Hey."

I refused to turn, just kept my eyes on the numbers rolling over the gas pump, like I hadn't heard a thing.

"Hey, aren't you Madame Hellsbane, the psychic?"

Most times I get a kick out of being recognized. This wasn't most times. I tensed my cheek muscles, forcing a smile as I looked over my shoulder at the guy standing next to the minivan. "Hi."

"It is you. I knew it. Hey, honey…" Mr. Minivan, in his tie-dyed T-shirt and faded jeans, turned, yelling to his honey, who was still in the convenience store. He spun back to me. "She's gonna be thrilled. We're big fans."

"It's great to meet you," I said, practiced professional smile in place.

I seriously didn't have time for this. I'd just gotten a huge clue to the identity of my angelic father and I still needed to figure out a way to get close enough to take out Tommy's. I needed to get home and do some serious Googling. Plus…I needed gas.

The problem was, in my business, reputation was everything.

And this guy seemed nice. Nice enough to have a lot of friends. Plus, he kind of reminded me of Tommy. Maybe I was just seeing what I wanted to see.

But he was tall like Tommy, over six feet, with the same thin, gangly, long-limbed build, though Tommy had been more muscled and about ten years younger. My tie-dyed fan kind of reminded me of a high school science teacher, with his hawklike features and his silver wire-framed glasses.

"My name's Kyle." He offered his hand, and I shook it over the top of my other, still on the gas pump. "You probably remember my wife, Sherry. You did a three-card reading for her at the big Beltane gathering last year. Waited two hours in line to see you." His smile brightened. "It was great, by the way. Dead on."

I nodded with a polite "good to know" smile. Even if I didn't do thousands of readings a year, I'm horrible with putting names to faces.

The gas hose clicked off, and I yanked the nozzle out of the Jeep, turning to hook it back in the pump. "It was great seeing you again, Kyle, and I'd love to say hi to Sherry, but I'm kind of in a hurry…"

"Kyle?" a woman's voice called, two beats before she joined us between my Jeep and the gas pumps. Seeing her tie-dyed shirt and jeans, I made the giant leap that she was Kyle's wife.

"Ohmygod…You're…you're…"

"Madame Hellsbane," Kyle said, translucent brows high on his forehead, smile wide and bright. "I tried to tell you."

Sherry rushed toward me, shouldering Kyle out of the way. She grabbed my hand and shook it hard enough I thought she'd loosen my arm from my body.

"It is you—do you remember me—I can't believe you're pumping gas like a normal person—I'm such a fan—you're shorter than I remember." Words gushed out of her like she'd taken a verbal laxative.

I didn't mind much. She was a sweetheart with twinkly milk chocolate eyes and a cheery smile. And she clearly liked me. Always a big plus.

"Of course," I said, amping up the professional smile a few watts. "Sherry, right? We met at the Beltane gathering last year."

Her jaw dropped, eyes wide. "That's right. That's right. You remember."

I would've admitted to gleaning the info from Kyle if he called me on it, but he didn't. Typical. People only pay attention to about half of what they say.

"Ohmygoodness, would you use your powers to tell us if we're going to get pregnant soon?"

Crap. I exhaled, smiling as I said, "Sure."

The moment I agreed, a strange unease settled in my stomach, like the first hint of nausea. I scanned the small gas station lot on reflex. Cars passed by on the streets, stopping and starting with the stoplight. People pumped gas and strolled in and out of the convenience store, going about their business without so much as a glance in our direction.

Forcing myself to ignore the sensation, I took Sherry's hand in mine. She reached for her husband. This would be the first time I tried foreseeing the future using the full angelic powers I'd been born with but only recently had begun to explore. I wanted to see what I could do on my own.

Eyes closed, I opened my mind to Kyle, then Sherry, their thoughts swirling fast and chaotic on the top of their minds. With questions about pregnancy and the wish for babies fresh in their thoughts, the couple's hopes, worries, and fears rushed through my mind, filling my body with the sensations of their emotions. My stomach tightened, lungs squeezed, and a dull ache started at my back. Together, they were carrying a ton of baggage.

Please let it take this time, Sherry thought, and her doubt twisted my gut.

What if I'm not a good dad? I heard from Kyle, and his anxious emotion turned my veins to ice.

I pushed harder, pressed through the hazy layer of unfocused musings to the deeper echo of more concentrated thoughts. Within seconds, I learned they'd been trying for five years to get pregnant. There was a problem with Kyle's sperm count, but pregnancy wasn't impossible and their determination was undeniable.

And then, *Was Richard Hubert right? This is all our doing. We can fix this. We have the power within us to achieve perfection of the mind and body,* Kyle's voice whispered through my mind. My heart stuttered at the mention in his thoughts of Richard Hubert. I opened my eyes before I could stop myself. The couple stood with their eyes closed, Kyle clutching Sherry's hand with both of his.

The power is in me. I believe. The power is in me. The mantra-like chant echoed through Sherry's mind. I shifted my gaze to her. She and Kyle were desperate, clinging to any spark of hope. Richard Hubert, Spiritualist of the Faith Harvest Church, had given it to them. It seemed wrong.

"How do you know Richard Hubert?" I asked.

They opened their eyes together, blinking slowly, like they were trying to reason out why I'd asked.

"We…we just came from his afternoon sermon," Kyle said. He dug into his back pocket, and handed me a twice-folded brochure. The edges of the folds were white and ragged from riding in his pocket, but I opened it to the front page and was met by a smiling photo of Richard Hubert.

He had the same jock-star good looks as Tommy. His thick build reminded me of a farmer, a man whose muscle and mass came from hard work rather than hours in the gym.

The photo caught him with his mouth open as though he'd been talking when they snapped the picture. His gaze skyward, his eyes bright blue, joy shining through clear as the sun. He had the same creamy butter-blond hair as Tommy, and the same rich curls, too. The biggest difference between father and son besides the age was that Richard Hubert wore his hair in a long ponytail at the base of his neck.

"He's amazing," Sherry said. "We've been watching him on TV for pretty near a year and when we heard he was gonna be right here in Pittsburgh, well, we just had to come and see him in person."

"You met him? Like face to face?" I asked, wondering for one horrifying second if Sherry could have been the fallen angel's latest victim.

"Sure, well, I mean, close enough," she said, blushing. "We didn't have great seats but we could still see him. Would've loved to actually shake his hand, but they rushed him off right after the sermon. Never got that close to him. Doesn't matter—it was still amazing. There's something about him. I just…believe. He makes sense, y'know? Some say he's…well, they say he's an angel."

"Seriously?" How had anyone found out? Was Hubert telling humans what he was? That couldn't be good.

Sherry nodded, quick and eager. "Yeah. And, well, normally I'd assume they meant it metaphorically, but after meeting him, listening to him…I don't know."

"Right." My gaze flicked to the pentagram on the silver chain around her neck. "I thought it was a Christian revival thing?"

"No," Sherry said, her hand fluttering to her necklace, fingering the pentagram charm. "Faith Harvest is an open-faith church. Believers in God in all His forms are welcome. It really is amazing."

Yeah. So she kept saying. *Amazing.*

"There's an admission coupon in there. Everyone who attends one of his sermons gets a brochure to spread the word," Kyle said. He wagged a finger at the paper. "You can have it."

"Thanks," I said, folding the brochure along the same worn seams and shoving it into the back pocket of my jeans. It might come in handy if I couldn't find the guy who'd promised to get Tommy into the sermon.

I sighed and took Sherry's hand again, refocusing on the task. I was sure with their strong-willed determination and the powerful medical regimen they'd committed to, Sherry would eventually get pregnant. That was as close to predicting the future as I'd ever been able to do. I smiled and opened my mouth, ready to give my reading, when another voice tickled through my mind.

The power is in me. I believe. The power is in me. The voice was softer, barely there, like a shadow following so close behind Sherry's thoughts it was nearly indistinguishable. Every notion flittering through Sherry's mind echoed in the thoughts of this other voice. As though this other mind shared every contemplation and emotion Sherry had, knew and thought only what passed through Sherry's mind first.

My gaze dropped to her flat belly. A tiny little voice, an unfinished mind, cocooned in silence except for the thoughts and feelings of the one that surrounded it. *Holy Cow.* "You're already pregnant."

Sherry's thoughts stopped cold and with it the echo of her baby's thoughts. Her smile trembled at the corners of her mouth before taking hold.

"I am?" she said.

I am? her baby's thoughts echoed.

"I hear…" I stopped myself before I spoke crazy out loud. "I mean, I get the strong sense of another life joining yours and Kyle's. And I believe that life is already with you."

Sherry turned to Kyle, his eyes wide, his chest stiff with his held breath. "I'm pregnant," she said. "We're pregnant."

I'm pregnant. We're pregnant, the wee voice mimicked. The sweet sound of it puttered through my mind, and I closed the door between us.

Sherry laughed, tentatively at first, before the emotion rolled through her body like a runaway snowball, shaking her slight frame and infecting Kyle. His breath exploded, his laugh bursting out of him like a champagne cork. They threw themselves together, hugging and kissing, utterly confident I was right.

I was.

How powerful was this ability? I'd tapped into the mind of a person who was barely a person at all. What more could I do? How far was my reach? The possibility sent a cold rush across the back of my neck. I shivered. A blanket of goose bumps tingled over my skin.

My powers were only a shadow of what the angels could do. These powers were new to me, mostly uncharted, untested. But there were illorum out there who'd been at this for decades, maybe longer. Who knew how much more there was to discover, how much more those seasoned illorum had learned?

The Fallen had sinned and continued to do so, but we, their children, were their most devastating offense. What kind of monsters had the Fallen unleashed on the world? Our fathers had to be stopped.

"I have to go," I said, turning my back to the couple and heading around the front of my Jeep. "It was nice meeting you. Good luck with the baby."

A warm breeze swept across the lot as I opened the Jeep's metal-framed door. The heady scent of gasoline, mixed with the teasing aroma of French Fries and burgers from the neighboring fast food joint, flavored the summer air. But underneath, like decaying wood beneath the pretty plastic siding on a house, was the rancid odor of rotting eggs, ruining the sun-warmed scene.

"Brimstone." I scanned the lot again, my vision touching for a moment on the two cars parked near a pay phone next to the exit. Two people sat in the front seat of one, though I couldn't make out details. The other car looked empty. There were a few others parked in front of the store and at the far pump. Nothing out of the ordinary. I shifted my gaze to the street, to the people walking by, to the traffic stopping at the light, then driving on.

The hairs at the nape of my neck tickled with the feel of being watched. My heart thumped faster and faster by the second. The demons were close, whether I could see them or not. The risk of witnesses was all that stopped them. I was relatively safe in the busy convenience store lot, but cowering by the gas pumps wouldn't get me any closer to Tommy's Fallen. I had to get home, where I could safely surf the Internet for answers.

I climbed in behind the wheel and slammed the lightweight door closed. Kyle and Sherry waved as I pulled onto the main road.

No one was following; I was almost positive. Glancing back between the long strips of electrician's tape that patched the slices in my back window, I kept an eye on the cars leaving the lot behind me. None pulled out after I passed. None of the cars nearing behind me looked like any I'd noticed in the gas station. I was away, clean.

More than halfway home, I made the left into Sycamore Park out of habit. It was a little after three, and the sun was bright, but the twisting road through the park was lined with thick trees, branches arching over the pavement like the roof of a tunnel. Sunlight dappled through like a strobe light. I knew the road by heart, and during the flashing instances when my vision was obscured, I drove by memory.

Almost at the end of the park, the road made a long, blind bend to the right around a steep hill. I turned the wheel just as the street began to straighten out, and a blur of movement caught my eye to the right. Before I could think, something shot down the hillside beside me and onto the road. I stomped the brakes and the clutch together, screeching to a stop, but not before I plowed into the large, solid obstacle.

God, what was that? What had I hit, a dog, a deer? I could taste my heart at the back of my throat. My hands clenched so tightly on the steering wheel, my knuckles whitened. I peered over the hood and saw the mangled bicycle in the middle of the road. *Oh God, oh God.* I'd hit a kid.

Despite my foot on the clutch, the Jeep had stalled, but I turned the ignition off to make it official. I didn't want to look. I knew I'd hit him hard. My windshield was shattered, my hood dented in the shape of his shoulder and torso. I unhooked my seat belt and opened the door, slipping out.

My feet hit the pavement, though I couldn't feel it. My chest squeezed, making my racing heart work harder, as I walked around to the front of my Jeep.

The right headlight was broken, and so was the blinker on that side. Glass and yellow-orange plastic littered the blacktop, glinting in the sunlight that speckled through the trees. The bike was at least ten feet ahead, and when I reached it I could see the red paint from my Jeep on the handlebars and the flattened pedal. The front wheel was bent in half. The frame looked like a giant hand had tried to wring it dry.

Like a dream, a warm breeze swirled through the leaves overhead, ruffling my hair, skittering twigs and forest debris along the road to make scuffling sounds that echoed through my ears. The noisy silence was deafening.

Where was the kid?

The thought hit me as hard as I'd hit him. I spun on my heel. He had to be somewhere behind the car. I ran, my gaze scanning ahead, searching the sides of the road. How far had he flown? Dear God, how could he have survived it? What if he hadn't?

I couldn't breathe. I wasn't sure how I was moving or even thinking. Cold sweat wet the back of my T-shirt, tracing down my spine and under my arms. Stumbling over nothing, over my own sneakers, I ran down one side of the road scanning the hillside, behind trees in tall clumps of grass, and then back up the other until I reached the Jeep.

Where was he?

"Stupid nephilim."

I spun, glancing up, following the direction of the voice. There he was, sitting on a low branch of the overhanging tree, his right leg bent wrong, his right shoulder sloping, dislocated. He held the branch in front of him with his left hand, though black ooze seeped from between his fingers and gashes on his forearm.

He looked twelve years old. His head was dented, as though the bone was shattered under his hair, and demon blood darkened his forehead and trickled in a slow stream down his cheek. His smile was everything wicked, his boyish face scratched and dirty. His eyes glowed yellow in the shadows of the thick leaves, the pupils black vertical slits.

"You're not human," I said, relieved for a half second before I realized the alternative meant I had a battle on my hands.

"Neither are you," someone said from behind me. The stench of brimstone swamped over me, churning my stomach.

I turned, using the momentum to draw my sword and call the blade, swinging blind and hitting nothing. When I'd stopped my spin, my gaze landed on another boy, maybe sixteen, with ash blond hair and the same creepy yellow eyes. They weren't bothering to hide their demon features. There was no one besides me who'd see. Not good.

The demon in front of me chuckled, having jumped clear of my swing. He pulled a red bandana from the back pocket of the jeans sagging halfway off his ass and tied it around his forehead. He adjusted the shoulders of his long-sleeved shirt, a picture of an ugly scarecrow's head stretching across his chest. As casually as if he were picking up a dried leaf, he bent to pull a switchblade from his sock. A flick of his wrist opened it.

"You ready to throw down, illorum?" he said, though his smooth voice and articulate speech made the vernacular seem out of place.

"Throw down? What's that…gang-slang?"

"You could say that," a third boy replied, stepping from behind the thick walnut a few yards in front of my Jeep. He wore the same kind of red bandana tied around his wrist, his upper body bare except for a maroon, down-filled vest.

Three. Yeah, that could constitute a gang.

This third boy looked older than the other two, maybe eighteen or nineteen. His head was shaved, leaving only a dark shadow of new growth. His darker, tanned skin made me think Hispanic.

Though in truth, nothing about him was real. This was just the body he'd chosen when his Fallen had called him forth from the abyss.

He reached behind and pulled a foot-long dagger from the sheath strapped to his back. A beam of sunlight hit the blade, and the demon twisted his wrist to make the light flash off the gleaming metal.

"You may think of us as…the cleanup gang," he said, his refined, eloquent tone belying the young streetwise persona he'd chosen. His thin lips curled to a smug grin. "Our deliverer detests messy ends. You see, our brothers erred in only dispatching your ignorant boyfriend. It now falls to us to repair their mistake and send you to join him."

My boyfriend? They meant Tommy. "Your deliverer is the same one who sent the demons to the library after us?"

The boy gave me a courtly bow. "It matters not. Your male companion is no more, correct? The command now stands that your life be forfeit as well." He shrugged as though my death couldn't be helped. "Our deliverer wishes you removed from the planet."

And there it was, the target that had been on Tommy's head had officially shifted to me. I was out of time, and I still hadn't seen the Fallen Tommy was after with my own eyes. I opened my gift to touch the twisted mind of the oldest boy. *Uzza and I will distract her so Neria can jump down and take her head from behind.*

The thought swirled along the top of his mind and his yellow eyes flicked to his blond compatriot across from him. Their gazes met, and I knew without listening in, the blond understood the plan.

The young men closed in on me, dagger and switchblade brandished for the attack. Their smiles were mirror images, the glints in their yellow eyes reflecting the excitement swelling inside them. Vivid thoughts of slicing my skin from my bones swirled faster and faster through their rotting minds, taking more and more of their conscious thoughts. I'd bet their gang brother wasn't any different.

They were losing it. Their lust to hurt me, to cause me excruciating pain, warmed their bodies and fogged their judgment. I held my ground, my stomach roiling, knowing the pleasure they'd take in hurting me. My hands trembled, legs wobbly, but I kept my sword in front of me, double fisting the hilt, point up and ready, trying hard not to breathe in the thickening stench of brimstone.

These weren't the demons that'd killed Tommy, but they worked for the bastard who'd ordered his death. The thought rolled around in my mind, gaining speed, kicking up friction, stirring anger. They were an extension of the Fallen, his eyes and ears, his weapon. As surely as if the Fallen wielded the switchblade and dagger himself, these demons were under his control. His will was theirs. Killing them wouldn't be like cutting off his arms, but it would feel almost as satisfying.

Determination as cold as iron hardened my spine. I wanted them dead, gone, and the cool, steadfast desire flicked some sort of switch deep inside me. Like freeing a wild animal, some long-suppressed part of me stirred through my veins, triggering instincts I hadn't known I possessed.

A soft thump sounded behind me, and my breath caught in my chest, my heart pounding like a drumbeat in my ears. It took all my willpower not to flinch. I knew the boy, the demon I'd hit with my Jeep, had jumped down from the tree. He was behind me, ready to strike just as the other demon planned.

I didn't look, but I'd bet money he'd already healed his broken leg and dislocated shoulder. Their plan would work if I didn't do something fast. I had to move or be moved upon. All that was human inside me suddenly gave way to those strange instincts.

I spun, judging height from memory, distance from the sound of his feet shuffling toward me. My blade met cloth and flesh, slicing deep across the child-size gut. He stumbled back, his arm clutching across his belly, his other hand holding what looked like a three-pronged meat hook. *Holy crap, what had he planned to do with that?*

Before I could finish him, the two I'd put at my back moved in. The sweaty arm of the blond demon latched around my neck, choking my air supply. The stench of brimstone triggered my gag reflexes. My stomach churned, bile threatening at the back of my throat. A sharp, burning pain stabbed at the top of my thigh. I tried to scream, but I couldn't get enough air to give it voice.

"Such sweet, sweet flesh," the boy demon hissed in my ear. "Female flesh. If not for its wicked temptation, the abyss would be an empty hollow."

I dug my nails into his arm, clawing at his skin, but it didn't do any good. I swung my sword, wild, panicked, but the demon stood at an angle I couldn't reach. He inhaled long and loud through his nose as though he was breathing me in. He moaned, then nuzzled his face against my cheek.

I cringed at the smell and feel of his sweaty, rancid skin. Then he opened his mouth and licked me from jaw to temple. I squirmed harder, frantic to get away, my skin crawling. The fat line of his saliva warming against my skin began to burn.

"Mmm...tasty," he said. "Think I'll take a pound of your sweet female flesh for later." His body jerked beside me, the knife in my thigh slicing up then down. My brain screamed. Pain beyond imagination ripped through my body—stealing my breath, my reason.

I thrashed against him, against the chokehold he had on me. I couldn't get free. My mouth gaped, tears stinging down my face.

My body went rigid, the agony unlike anything I'd ever known. My lungs closed, my nerve endings screaming. I couldn't get away, and I couldn't make it stop.

A final slice and the demon yanked the chunk of meat from my leg. My mind spun, dizzy, pain throbbing with every hard thump of my heart. Hot blood drenched my leg, survival reflexes already numbing the limb, blocking the worst of the pain to keep my body from shutting down, allowing my brain to continue functioning.

The edges of my vision darkened, and I struggled to stay conscious. The demon bent, tilting me with him to stab the chunk of flesh that had fallen to the ground. His distraction loosened the grip he had on my neck as we straightened again, and that strange new side of me rushed to the forefront, capitalizing on his mistake.

I had just enough slack to shift my weight, and before I knew how I'd done it, I'd raised my hands straight out, double-fisting the hilt of my sword so the long blade tucked back along my side. One hard thrust, and the sharp tip plunged behind me into my captor's gut. I gave the hilt a hard twist, and the blade bored a hole through him. His arm dropped away from my neck, his hand going to grope at his belly.

A forward step, then I spun, adjusted my grip, and jerked the sword skyward. The unearthly sharp blade sliced through meat, muscle, and bone like wind through trees, breaking free of the demon's body at the shoulder. My weight shifted, and I swung the sword straight across, my nephilim strength slicing head from neck with ease. The demon collapsed to the blacktop—dead.

Little of my human half held sway inside me then. I felt the older boy charge. Chin down, calling on the same sense of time and space I used when I teleported, I swung the long blade. I knew where he was, knew where to aim without ever meeting his eyes. I just knew.

The sword caught him under his arm as he ran at me. The blade sliced up at an angle, breaking through the flesh at the top of his opposite shoulder. The wound wasn't at his neck, but the effect of removing his head from his body was just the same. He tumbled forward, his momentum carrying him down to his knees, and death crumpling him to the pavement. His top half slid a few feet farther, his dagger skittered past me, the clanking metal sounding loud against the blacktop.

Nephilim senses hummed, adrenaline thrummed though my veins. I still smelled live demon. The boy I'd struck first wasn't dead. I turned to where I'd left him holding his nasty three-pronged weapon. He wasn't there. The warrior angel inside me faltered—I was in demon-killing mode. Finding none, my human half wanted to take control again.

My arm relaxed, lowering my sword to my side. I scanned the hillside and trees, making my way to where he'd stood when I'd sliced open his belly. Ooze steamed on the ground. He'd bled a lot, but not enough, and the thought stirred the warrior within, pumping my heart, coiling my muscles. Yeah. I wanted to fight.

The realization jolted through my head and stopped me in my tracks. I'm not a fighter. I'm a run-and-hider. How could I have such diametrically opposing instincts? It was too weird, and the more I thought about it, the more my human half bubbled to the surface. Heady adrenaline seeped away at the same time, leaving me trembling from head to toe in the middle of Sycamore Park.

The demon's escape irritated all the way down to the pit of my stomach. But standing there waiting to be attacked again was just stupid.

"Fine. Run and tattle on me to your deliverer, you little prick," I said, the last of my illorum anger simmering through my veins. "Tell him I'm coming. Tell him he's next."

I willed my blade to disperse, sliding the hilt smoothly into the sheath at the small of my back as I went to my Jeep. I was behind the wheel, seatbelt fastened and turning the key before most people would've realized I'd moved. I shifted gears, turned the wheel, and drove around the twisted pile of bike still lying in the middle of the road.

My leg throbbed as adrenaline washed from my bloodstream, the pain coming back full force. The bleeding had stopped, and I suspected I was already beginning to heal. I figured the fact the demon used a knife instead of his claws meant no brimstone had gotten into the wound. But holy crap, it hurt.

Pain tightened across my shoulders, starting a cold sweat up my spine. But it wasn't just pain that had my jaw tense and my hands strangling the steering wheel. It was something else.

My sixth sense niggled at the nape of my neck; something wasn't right. The stink of brimstone filled the inside of my Jeep, souring my stomach. Too strong. When the cloth roof of my Jeep suddenly peeled back, I knew why.

My heart leapt into my throat, and my chest squeezed. The missing demon boy was a little different now, four inches taller, red skinned, fanged, and muscle-bound. He'd shifted into his full demon form, desperate and *really* pissed.

He ripped the cloth top past the middle roll bar and wrapped his arm around it to hold on. I swerved, trying to knock him loose, but his grip was firm.

"You die today, illorum," he said, his voice raw and gravelly.

His muscled arm swiped at me, and I managed to dodge and swerve at the same time. He missed. Struggling for balance, his long, talon-like claws snagged the passenger seatbelt.

The Jeep veered to the right, and I looked back to the road in time to swerve back. The polyurethane nylon belt unraveled fast until it reached the end, then snapped, sliced through by the demon's wicked-sharp claw.

The sudden release sent the demon reeling backward, arm flailing, fighting for balance. He threw himself at the Jeep and held on as I swerved again, running off the road, aiming for trees with low branches to knock him off. He hunched forward, his body crawling over the open top of my car toward me.

Exactly where I wanted him to be. "See ya, sucka."

Clearly, the demon didn't know this park the way I did. He didn't notice the old river stone tunnel until a half second before I jerked the wheel. I took out my side mirror against the wall and the demon's head and shoulders against the low arch.

Black demon ooze exploded over the passenger seat, covering the windshield, the dash, the floor, and Tommy's computer.

Crap. That probably wouldn't do the laptop any good.

CHAPTER SIXTEEN

"What were you thinking?" Eli said, having the nerve to sound indignant as he gingerly sprinkled holy water over the raw muscle and meat on my thigh.

"I was thinking that I'd hit a kid. What'd you want me to do, keep driving?"

"Yes," he said, dabbing my leg too near to the wound, trying to catch runaway water.

I hissed, swallowing my sissy-girl whimper. My leg was healing fast, new skin growing pink and tender as I watched. There'd be no sign of the injury tomorrow, but today, it still stung. I tugged the towel I'd draped over me, hiding my pink cotton underwear as I laid on my couch. My jeans were toast. There's no patching a fist-sized hole like that. *Dammit.* I liked those jeans. *Friggin' demons.*

"What if it'd been a real kid?" I said.

Eli sat back on the coffee table, his ice-blue eyes sliding up to mine. "This is war, Emma Jane. Casualties are inevitable. The greater good must always come first. Without our illorum warriors, the whole of the human race is lost, never mind one small boy."

His somber, unflinching tone chilled through me. "You don't really mean that."

"Life is precious," he said. "But it is the soul that's priceless. A soul is never sacrificed. The gift of life it clings to, however, is a gift to all humans, not just itself."

The couch cushion propped behind my shoulders slipped, and I shifted my head on my hand to compensate. Eli went back to drizzling holy water. Stretched out the way I was, laying on my side, I could see the gentle care he took each time he touched my thigh. Time and again he'd rest the bottom of his hand against my skin and the warmth of it fluttered through my belly, then lower, flexing the feminine muscles of my body on reflex.

I closed my eyes, looked away, forced myself not to think about it. "You'd sacrifice your life for the greater good?" I asked him.

"My life and soul are one and the same," he said without looking up. "I am now as I am in Heaven, as I am before God. I have no mortal life to sacrifice. My spirit manifests the physical form you see. I can just as easily release the matter called forth and become purely spirit. But your eyes won't register a difference."

"Well," I said, having had enough of his tempting touch and heartless philosophy. I pushed up straight on my hip. "Isn't that nifty. Maybe if you had a mortal life, you wouldn't be so quick to consider it expendable."

Our knees brushed when I swung my feet to the floor, sliding my legs between the couch and the coffee table where he sat. Eli's confusion showed in his wrinkled brow and in the narrowing at the corners of his eyes.

"Emma Jane, what I do, what I ask of you, I ask because I so love and treasure human life," he said. "I ask that you value your survival above a single human, so that you may live to fight that which threatens all human existence, that which threatens all immortal souls."

"Whatever. I just can't accept that anyone else should sacrifice his or her life in my place. So don't count on me throwing someone under the bus for the greater good." I stood, clutching the edges of the towel together at my hip. "Besides, I thought you said we were doing this to *prevent* a war."

"A war between the angels and the Fallen, yes," he said, standing with me. He gathered the used gauze and the clear glass decanter of holy water he'd brought. "But make no mistake, an angelic war will endanger humans as well. They are, after all, at the very core of the turmoil."

"Right," I said, tucking one corner of the towel behind the other so it stayed snug around me. I made my way across the hall to my home office, Eli heading for the kitchen to drop off supplies before joining me.

Tommy's computer was on my desk where'd I'd left it before Eli had shown up and declared I wasn't healing fast enough on my own. Demon blood had left big, blotchy black stains on the shiny metal top. Some of the stains were edged in brown rust, with holes eaten straight through to the keyboard where the thickest globs had sat. Who knew demon blood was so corrosive?

I dropped into my desk chair and opened the hole-ridden lid of the laptop. "Aw, hell."

The power button had been right under one of the burn holes, not that it would've mattered. If Gretchen's computer guru boyfriend was still around I doubted even his mad computer skills could bring the charred and gutted computer back from the junk pile.

"There's something you need to see," Eli said, suddenly beside me, his arms gripped around an enormous book. He set it on the desk in front of me.

Three feet tall, two feet wide, and at least a foot thick, the book was bigger than any I'd ever seen. And I could swear it was getting thicker as I watched. It was bound in some sort of soft hide, pale, almost flesh tone. In the center was a large circle of blood-red wax, dish-sized and mostly flattened, as if by a huge stamp.

The design in the wax was an intricate mix of geometric patterns, one inside the other, points used again and again for each shrinking shape inside the next. The outside hexagon encased the rest, a pie-cut circle at the center, inside a rectangle, inside a hexagon, inside a larger rectangle, inside a six-point star. Its tips touched the corners of the outside hexagon, each vital end ringed in a perfect circle all the way down to the center. I stared, my eyes noticing new shapes within the old ones, intersecting lines seeming to shift, highlight, then fade.

I blinked, shook my head to break my stare. "That's cool."

"Yes."

"What is it?"

"The Book of the Lost," he said, cracking open the cover. The first page was blank, except for two short lines of decorative symbols.

"What's it say?" I asked.

"'Herein is scribed the sacred sigils of the Fallen. May their spirits be damned.'" His voice was soft, reverent. He lowered his gaze. After a moment he turned the first age-yellowed page, and then the next and the next.

Each page held four columns of names written in English, or so my eyes saw, and more than fifty rows. Beside each name was an intricate angelic symbol, some so similar it was almost impossible to tell them apart.

"These are all the Fallen?" I asked, turning page after page of names.

"These are the Fallen who have yet to be dispatched to the abyss," he said. "After their spirit is chained, their name is erased."

My hands smoothed over the open book, fingers splayed. The hairs on my arms tingled. Power, energy of some kind hummed between the ancient sheets, tickling over my skin, vibrating through my blood like sound through water. "It feels…alive," I said.

"It is forever in flux," he said. "Forever changing. Names added, others erased. It is…without end."

"So it is getting bigger."

"Yes. For centuries the book was half as thick, but in recent years…" His voice trailed off, and when I looked at him I saw the soul-deep sorrow in his eyes. The weight of loved ones forever lost, deepening the frown lines on his face.

"I'm sorry, Eli. It must be rough."

He reached out and ran his fingers over one of the names. "Many were friends, all were my brothers, and now they're lost to me."

"Can't you talk to them?" I said. "Convince them to stop, you know, sinning? Get them to ask for forgiveness? They can be forgiven, right? I mean, if they really repent their sins?" It didn't seem fair only humans could play that particular get-out-of-Hell card.

His steely blue gaze slid to mine. "Since the beginning, I hadn't spoken a word to any Fallen before that day with you in the gardens on Capri."

Seraphim, even those working as magisters, weren't supposed to speak to the Fallen or even acknowledge their existence. But he'd done it that day; he'd broken the rules…for me. I swallowed hard, trying not to think about it. "What'd you say to him?"

"I asked that he spare you. Nothing more," Eli said. "It was more than I should have."

A drop of ice plunked into my gut like a heavy stone in a deep lake. I was a danger to Eli whether either of us would admit it or not. Tommy and the Council spies had been right.

I licked my lips, my gaze shifting back to the book, wanting to look anywhere but into Eli's beautiful, pain-filled eyes. "Maybe if you guys tried talking to those who slipped—"

"Not slipped. Fell." His voice was suddenly fierce. I glanced at him and saw how his pain had burned into anger. "They made a choice. They turned their backs on God, on their brothers. Lust of the flesh meant more to them. Their redemption is no longer my concern."

"And you can't put yourself in their shoes? You can't imagine how it could happen?" I said. "How you could want...*someone* more than anything—more than air? Want someone so much you'd break every rule, risk every connection? You can't imagine how easy it would be to cross the line?"

Our gazes held for a long moment. His brows tightened and then he glanced away. "It doesn't matter. Repentance is for the individual to appeal. There's nothing anyone else can do for them. None have ever turned back once they unleashed their desires. The Fallen are forever corrupted. So it has always been." Eli reached over and closed the book.

"I know who the Fallen was that Tommy was after." I turned to my computer, left on since this morning. "I can show you a picture..."

After a few clicks and keyword searches, I brought up the web page for Faith Harvest Church. The same photo from the brochure of the blue-eyed Richard Hubert was also featured prominently on the front page. The words "Faith Harvest Church" gleamed in golden letters across the screen, the *T* in faith made to stand out with starbursts shooting from the cross.

They'd used a line of photos as a navigation banner, a picture of a sprawling building bathed in heavenly sunlight signifying home. Underneath the banner was a greeting message in large letters that read, "Welcome to the coming new faith."

"That's him," I said, pointing at the screen. "That's the Fallen Tommy was hunting."

Eli leaned forward, peering over my shoulder, then straightened. "Yes. I know. But I can't even be certain he's one of the Fallen. Tommy had yet to determine—"

"No. He was sure. Don't you recognize him?"

"Millions of angels have fallen," Eli said. "Millions more are brought forth into existence every day. I can't know them all any more than you can know the name of every human ever born."

Okay, that made sense, but I couldn't allow us to slip any further away from finding justice for Tommy. "Listen, he has to be a Fallen angel. I met some people today who were totally wrapped up in every word he said. They clung to his sermons like…like it was gospel. And they said he's not Christian or Jewish or even Pagan. He's calling it a *new* faith."

"It would not be unexpected for a Fallen to maneuver himself into a position of influence," Eli said. "It's been rumored for centuries a movement is in play to empower a new Heaven on earth, thereby usurping power from God."

"Right." I snorted. "Like that would work."

Eli shifted his hands behind him, his expression neutral.

"How?" I said.

With an eloquent roll of his shoulders he said, "By turning people from God. By shifting their faith to something…other than the intrinsic divine."

"And God would just let it happen?"

"What would you have Him do? Force the love of His creation? Take back the gift of free will?"

"He could fight back."

"He is. Through you."

Whoa. No pressure. "I told you already, Eli, I'm going after this Fallen for Tommy. Whatever grander plans you people have for me you can keep to yourselves. I'm not your girl. I'm taking the bastard's head because he killed my friend." I pushed back from my desk to stand, readjusting the towel to keep things G-rated. "Plus his demon minion totally jacked up the cloth-top on my Jeep, so he's got it coming. Those things cost a fortune."

"How will you get close enough? You don't have the ticket Tommy was counting on or the name of his contact."

"I've got the general admission coupon," I said. "And I've got mad seat-jumping skills."

"Security will likely be…determined."

"So will I," I said. "I'm going to go grab a shower before it's time to go."

I moved to step around him, but his hand came up, pressing lightly at my shoulder to stop me. "Wait. Your face…"

My hand went to my cheek on reflex, to the spot where the demon had licked me from jaw to temple. The skin was still tender, but Eli had assured me the holy water I splashed on it while he took care of my leg would keep it from scarring. Vanity made me worry all over again.

"What's wrong? It's not healing?" I said.

"It's fine." Eli centered himself in front of me, his broad chest filling my vision. "Just a little red. I can help with that."

With one hand on my shoulder, he cupped the other to my cheek. His touch was tender, his palm warm. He caught my eyes with his, held the gaze, the pure, unbroken blue of his eyes as strangely soothing as his touch. Heat washed through me, warming low in my body.

"Isn't this interfering?" I asked, my voice softer, shakier than I would've liked.

His moist lips lifted at the corners, his eyes crinkling. "I'm forbidden from healing fatal wounds. Healing this small wound will change nothing," he said. "Besides, the Fallen more than anyone would not begrudge me such a perfect excuse to touch you."

My belly fluttered, my heart suddenly loud in my ears. This was wrong. I knew it, but I couldn't make myself pull away. I didn't want to. His touch smoothed the dull ache from my skin, but more than that, the nearness of him made everything female inside me awaken. I liked the feeling.

"The worst problems can start with the smallest mistakes," I said, hoping he had more strength than I did—and hoping he didn't.

Eli closed his eyes, dropped his forehead to mine. "Emma Jane." He whispered my name on his exhale. "Please promise me you'll be careful tonight."

"I will," I said, breathing deep, taking the sweet, summery scent of him into my lungs, willing it to be enough to satisfy the urges he was stirring to life inside me. My hands found his waist before I realized, fisting the soft fabric of his jacket.

"I can't lose you," he said. "Not now. Not so soon after losing Thomas."

"I know." I lifted my gaze to meet his.

"I wasn't honest with you before," he said. "I *can* imagine what my brothers battled before they turned their backs on us. I often do. And I wonder if I am truly stronger or simply luckier. Thomas was right. It was too soon for me to take on a female illorum. But now that it's done…"

He lifted his other hand to frame my face, and brushed his thumb over my lips, his gaze tracking the move. "Don't let them end you, Emma Jane. I won't survive it."

"Eli…" I wanted to promise him—to reassure him. But the only thing I could be sure of tonight was that I wouldn't make killing me easy.

CHAPTER SEVENTEEN

"Ticket for Tommy Saint James?" I said through the little cluster of holes in the bulletproof glass at will-call.

The young woman smiled, looking way too chipper for being locked behind a Plexiglas wall eight hours a day. "May I see your ID, please?"

I dug into my purse and wiggled my driver's license out of its holder in my wallet. Sliding it through the arched hand hole, I said, "I'm not Tommy Saint James. I was hoping I could pick up the ticket for him. He, um, can't make it."

Will-Call Girl looked to be about my age, with spiked, snow-white hair and thin eyebrows drawn on her bare brow. *Her mom must be so proud.*

She eyed my license, her gaze flicking to me then back down. After a few seconds of comparison she wrinkled her nose, sliding the card back through the hand hole.

"This license says Emma Jane Hellsbane," she said.

"I know—"

"Sorry, but we only release the tickets to the person they're left for," she said, apparently offended I'd tried to pull one over on her.

"But he won't be picking it up. He can't," I said. "Trust me. Tommy would want me to have the ticket."

"Sorry." She shrugged, then looked behind me as though I'd vanished the moment she'd dismissed me. "Next."

"You don't understand. Tommy Saint James is dead." I pushed up to my toes to get my mouth as level with the little holes as possible. "No one's going to pick up that ticket."

"Then have him call in and reissue the ticket in your name, and I'll be happy to give it to you…with proper ID," she said, then flicked her gaze behind me again. "Next!"

"But…"

The next person in line shoved forward, a hefty elbow to my ribs sending me shuffling out of the way. I jammed my license back in my wallet and dug for the folded pamphlet the tie-dye couple had given me earlier. Careful not to ruin the admission coupon, I tore along the dotted lines. At least I'd get my foot in the door. After that, it'd be up to me how close I could get.

The David Lawrence Conference Center had opened its doors in 2003. All of Western Pennsylvania's hospitality industry held its collective breath, worrying if it was worth the nearly $400 million price tag.

It was pretty snazzy, seamlessly blending functionality with cutting-edge technology. At least that's what the brochure said. No matter how functionally edgy it was, I figured it'd have to be one helluva party to be worth a $400 million address. The building kind of looked like a big circus tent to me—in a functionally cutting-edge sort of way.

I followed three priests, a rabbi, and a Wiccan high priestess in a form-fitting suit dress into the elevator. Sounded like the start of a joke, but in my business I run into a lot of different religious types at some of the festivals I work. In the same way I'd gained a sudden knowledge of all languages, I kind of just knew people's faith beliefs when I looked at them.

The whole convention was lousy with religious types. Every conceivable religion looked to be represented. I'd never seen so many different symbols on display: crosses, Ankhs, pentagrams, chaos stars, Hamsa hands, Star of David, and Vodoun Veves.

With so many conflicting soul-deep beliefs, tension hummed like a ribbon of electricity through wide corridors, all the way up to the balcony floor beneath the tall sloping ceiling. It tickled the fine hairs on my arms and at the back of my neck, radiating off the multitude of conference goers from every direction.

Yet no one breathed an intolerant word. Who could've imagined so many diametrically different people could come peaceably together under one roof? Faith Harvest spiritualists milled the hallways, handing out pamphlets, talking about "the coming new faith," answering questions, encouraging more. But humans weren't the only ones roaming the halls.

My stomach pitched and rolled, over and over. The place was crawling with nephilim. Most were probably unmarked, but the sheer number helped to keep the army of demons moving around, masquerading as Faith Harvest spiritualists, from getting a clear bead on me. The stench of brimstone was nauseating.

The energy level was high. There were booths set up on the lower level for demonstrations, past-life retrieval, spirit cleansing, ascending classes, whatever. People were eating it up. They'd all been drawn to this new faith Richard Hubert was preaching. The Faith Harvest Church welcomed all souls. Something didn't sit right.

For centuries philosophers and intellectuals have said the root of all evil is religion. Many maintained that the only way for the human race to achieve global peace is to abolish all religion. So, if the eradication of all religion will bring peace, what would the melding of all religion do?

What would happen to the human race if there was only one worldwide religion? And what if God had nothing to do with it?

The thought snaked through me as I got off the elevator on the third floor of the convention center. The doors to the Spirit of Pittsburgh Ballroom were directly in front of me. According to my admission coupon, this was the room where I'd find the Fallen angel who'd ordered Tommy's death—Spiritualist of Faith Harvest Church, Richard Hubert.

I crossed the floor toward the doors, my gaze sliding to the right, down the long hallway, to the far end and the enormous floor-to-ceiling window. It was dark outside, but I imagined the window would be even more impressive in the daylight.

The passageway was littered with people, most seeming perfectly normal, some not so normal, all respectfully keeping to themselves. A group of Mennonites was heading in my direction, two men walking side by side in their blue buttoned shirts, black vests, pants, and shoes, both wearing identical, wide-brimmed hats. Their plainly dressed wives and children trailed behind them. They looked like a family of ducks, with the ducklings all in tow.

The families passed between a congregation of Franciscan monks in dirt-brown robes and a group of Raëlism followers, who believe life on earth was created by extraterrestrials, dressed all in stark white.

My attention slid back to the ballroom in front of me, when something my eyes had caught finally registered in my brain. I glanced back to the right again, behind the group of Franciscans, standing farther back next to the stairs.

He was dressed just as I'd seen him before, long jacket, button shirt, slacks, and shoes all in white. He could've fit perfectly with the Raëlians, if not for those ghost-white eyes. His long Hot Tamale hair hung thick to his elbows behind him, his fine-boned face and sensuous mouth expressionless. *Friggin' angels.*

What was his name? Started with an *F*. Fra—something. I wasn't sure. I waved at him. "Hey, Fred."

He didn't respond, didn't even blink. Maybe he didn't like the nickname. If he followed me into the conference room, I'd ask him. I kept moving with the crowd from the elevator as it pushed forward around me.

There were three wide doors opening into the room. I aimed for the center doors and the teenager standing behind a waist-high ticket box. Two mountainous men in tight black suits and white shirts stood sentry behind the teenage boy on either side. There were two sets of attendants just like them, or close enough, at each of the other two entrances.

I waited my turn, shuffling forward behind an older couple, the man's arm lovingly draped around his wife's shoulders. Their look screamed "old money," gold Rolex, gold chains, pearl necklace and earrings. It just proved no one, not even CEOs, were immune to the allure of religion…if the deity was right.

The young man ripped their tickets, dropping half in the tall box, handing back the other half and motioning them through the doors. "Welcome. May you unlock the barriers to personal health and spiritual healing."

The old guy scoffed, leading his wife through the doors. "For a hundred and fifty bucks, I damned well better."

The moment I was close enough, holding my tired coupon for

the taking, my nose tickled with a hint of rotten eggs. *Demons.*

My gaze shifted to the bouncers, their attention snapping to me, violet eyes narrowing. *Crap.* Both men went stiff, shoulders straightening like guard dogs scenting fresh meat.

"Sorry, you have to use the other doors." The teen ticket taker flicked his head, tossing his bangs from his eyes, only to have the stringy, straight hair slide back over half his face again. "This entrance and the one closer to the stage are for preferred ticket holders only."

I took the coupon back from the boy and edged away, my gaze zeroing on the demon bouncers at the door again. Why didn't they attack? Were they really so worried about making a scene, they'd let an armed illorum into the ballroom? Maybe they were just that confident they could stop me if I tried something.

Maybe they could. I guess we'd see.

My ticket was good at the far door. The double set of demon bouncers let me pass, though not without tracking my every step, glaring so hard I could almost feel their claws scraping against my skin. *If looks were daggers…*

The ballroom was gigantic, easily big enough to fit two football fields side by side. And I was in the cheap seats. No surprise. My ticket was free.

The back third of the room was set with half-circle rows of seats in four sections. The chairs were up a level on tiered platforms stretching to the wall, stadium style. They'd strung a red velvet rope from one end of the ballroom to the other, separating the cheap seats from the preferred ticket holders.

The good seats were on the other side of that rope, and those came with tables…and drinks. They were divided in four sections, arching around a low stage, nearly all the seats filled, as were the more than three hundred seats in the freeloaders' section. The place was packed.

A sapphire-blue curtain hung from floor to ceiling at the back of the stage, lights glowing from behind, giving them a soft, ethereal look. Two enormous speakers hung from either side of the suspended scaffolding above the stage, spotlights strategically positioned, ready for a rock star entrance. The crowd was low-key, conversation humming off the walls like a swarm of honeybees.

Now was as good a time as any to make my move. I crossed the room, past the center, and ducked under the rope. The idea of moving at illorum speed occurred to me right about the time someone said, "Hey, you."

Too late. I kept moving, walking at an angle toward the tables, like I had someplace to go, people expecting me.

"Hey, lady. Stop," the same male voice called from behind. I managed three more strides before I felt his beefy hand clamp down on my shoulder. "Where're you going? This section's for preferred ticket holders only."

I turned, his hand staying on my shoulder until we were face to face. He was as big as I expected from the size and weight of his hand, but he wasn't a demon. *Lucky me.* He smelled like any guy: deodorant, mouthwash, and a little too much cologne.

He was probably military or ex-military, judging by the brutally short hairstyle and the oversized muscle. With my nephilim strength I might be able to wrestle free of him, but I wasn't willing to risk it. Time to put my mad seat-jumping skills to the test.

I glanced in the direction I'd been heading, twisting my expression into one of anxious impatience. *I have someplace to be, people expecting me. I belong.*

"I'm sorry, what did you say?" I looked away and back again.

"Do you have your ticket, ma'am?"

"What? Yes. Of course." I glanced over at my imaginary table and the nonexistent people waiting for me. Seat jumping is all about attitude, and I had gobs of 'tude.

"Can I see it, please?"

"Seriously?" I huffed, patting my pockets, digging into the front two and then the back. "You seriously need to see it again? Why? I just went to the restroom. I don't know what I did with it. It's probably back at the table."

Dressed in the same kind of too-tight gray pinstriped suit as the demon bouncers, the big guy sighed, ready to haul me out of the ballroom. I glanced back toward the tables, feeling my time running out so fast I could almost hear the ticktock of the clock.

And then my luck kicked into gear. Some guy stood up and waved in my direction. Okay, so he was a little to the left of where I'd been aiming, and I knew for a fact he wasn't waving at me… details, details. He'd do.

"There's my brother. See?" I said, pointing. The bouncer followed my gesture and I moved around so he'd give his back to the waver to face me again. It wouldn't do at all for the bouncer to see whomever the guy was waving at arrive before I was free and clear.

"Listen," I said, pouring on the charm. "They checked my ticket not more than five minutes ago. I swear. That stub's so small I don't know where I put it. I just snuck out to powder my nose. Can't you give a girl a break?"

I smiled, sweet, sexy, with a coy tilt of my head, and batted my pretty blues at him. Yes, it was a shamelessly anti-feminist move, but remarkably effective. *Sue me.*

Faced with flimsy proof I had someone to vouch for me and the possibility, however remote, of getting laid, the guy responded to type and let me go with a smile and nod of his own.

I made a beeline for the tables. The lights dimmed, the doors closed, and people filled their seats. My waver's table was full, and so were all the tables in his section. I scanned the other sections, my heart pumping. There aren't a lot of rules to seat jumping, but the biggest sticking point is you have to have a seat to jump to.

Spotlights warmed onstage, casting soft color and muted light as the house lowered to faint honey glows. Just before it grew too dark to see, I spotted my target. In the first row next to the stage, three seats sat empty. Even as I zigzagged my way there, I scanned to make sure no one was moving toward the table.

A bright light spotted onstage as I sat, sending the rest of the ballroom into comparative blackness. I jerked my chair around so I could face the stage. When I looked up, a forty-something man, dressed like a Hindu priest in a yellowish Sherwani jacket with gold trim and white churidar pants, had stepped center stage.

"Welcome, honored seekers of the coming new faith." His voice echoed through the room like an emcee at a wrestling match.

I knew that voice. *Bariel.* The demon Tommy had chased on Mount Washington. He was right—the bastard did work for his angelic father. This close, I could smell the brimstone floating around him like a cloud. His eyes were normal, no sign of the demon slit pupil he'd revealed on the overlook.

The crowd erupted in applause. I clapped along with the rest, but I couldn't keep my focus. Worry jolted through my system, but something else sent my brain off-kilter. My belly quivered. I realized the sensation had been building since I ducked under the rope, and I'd been ignoring it. The weird feeling was stronger now, and rapidly growing more intense.

I clutched my arm around my waist. My stomach pitched and rolled like my insides had hitched a ride on the mother of all roller coasters. I was going to be sick. Where was it coming from? I scanned the people at my table, then the tables around us.

They couldn't *all* be nephilim, could they? But I knew from the strength of the nausea rolling through me that they were. More than four hundred unknowing nephilim in one spot. Why? What would a Fallen angel want with nephilim? A chilling thought iced through me. Could he be preparing a preemptive strike?

"Are you okay?" my tablemate behind me asked. He leaned over my shoulder, his hand light on my back.

I nodded. "Just feeling a little nauseous."

"That happens to some people when they're touched by Arch Hubert for the first time."

"Arch? As in archangel?" That took balls.

I glanced back at my tablemate, and he nodded. He was a thin man with hair plugs all over his male-pattern baldness. He was wearing a burnt rose-colored Sherwani jacket with the same fancy gold trim as our demon emcee, Bariel. They both looked like they'd stepped out of a Bollywood movie. In fact, now that I noticed, most of the men in the nephilim section were wearing the Sherwani jackets. *Must be a fad.*

"No one touched me," I said, the roller-coaster sensation easing as my body grew used to the nearness of so many of my kindred species.

"Not physically," he said. "I meant when he touches our minds. Didn't you feel it?"

I shook my head, a cold wash of fear settling in my gut where the nausea had been. Was it possible for a Fallen to scan the minds of all these people without even being in the room? If he'd read my mind, then he knew I was here to kill him. *Not good.*

"This your first time?" my tablemate whispered.

"Yeah. Why?"

"It's just strange. You paid three hundred bucks and you've never been enriched? I'm surprised they allowed you to skip the induction level."

Three hundred? So there were preferred tickets on top of the preferred tickets? "I've got connections. They told me this was, uh, life altering," I said.

My balding tablemate nodded, his eyes glancing to the stage as Bariel assured the crowd they should feel honored that they were about to be in the presence of the greatness that was Arch Richard Hubert.

"That explains why you didn't feel him touch your mind," the nephilim said. "You're not pure enough yet. The induction cleanses the everyday mortal filth from your psyche. A pure soul like Arch Hubert can't touch a filthy mind. You really should do the induction first."

First? Before what? I wasn't sure I wanted to know. "Is there someone who can help me with the induction?"

He perked. "I can. Or, well, I should be able to after today's session. I'm a Dominion. After today I hope to advance to Throne. Most people at this table are barely Powers. I think a few are only Virtues. I can feel it. Can you?"

I gave him a serious, wrinkled-brow nod. *Sure I can. Whatever.* I had no clue what he was talking about. "So Dominions can't do inductions?"

"Of course not," he said. "Only Thrones, Cherubim, and Seraphim have the purity and advanced enlightenment to perform an induction."

"Wait a second." Dominion, Powers, Cherubim, Seraphim, those were in the Bible. They were all orders of angels. "You're working to become angels?"

"At least. Most of us have ascended beyond that rank…I mean, those of us on this side of the rope." He laughed, glancing at the poor saps in the back of the room. I didn't like him as much anymore. "Of course, not everyone has the intellect to ascend. Most humans will never be even the lowest angel. The induction weeds them out."

"Arch Hubert touches the minds of everyone who's been inducted?" I asked.

His smile turned conspiratorial. "That's what we're paying him for. He touches our minds to get us ready for the enrichment. Sort of opens us up, makes our bodies more receptive. The friend who got you the seat didn't tell you any of this?"

I shook my head. "Wanted it to be a surprise." I smiled. "I'm surprised."

"You haven't seen anything yet. I feel twenty years younger. And the things I can do…"

He was a nephilim, but what he was describing were illorum powers. I caught a glimpse of his wrist. No mark. How was that possible?

His gaze slid to the stage, eyes going wide and glassy. "Here he comes."

I stood with everyone else, a rush of adrenaline charging through the crowd like a wave crashing on the shore. I could feel the power of their excitement thrumming through my veins, tightening my chest.

The room thundered with applause as the man from the website strolled onstage—Fallen angel Arch Richard Hubert. The illorum mark on my wrist burned, flames shooting up my arm, stinging through my brain. I clenched my jaw, kept my scream trapped inside. *Bastard.* My friggin' wrist hurt.

"Thank you. Thank you," he said into the headset microphone. The gizmo hooked over his ear, a stiff wire, barely visible, wrapping around his cheek to the corner of his mouth. His perfect, white-toothed smile beamed, plumping his apple cheeks. Cobalt-blue eyes glistened, brilliant beneath the intense lights.

He wore the same Sherwani-style jacket as the other men, the golden material fluttering around his knees against matching churidar pants. Delicate pale green embroidery wove around turquoise stones and Indian sapphires, sparkling down the center of his jacket, around the stiff collar, and at the ends of both long sleeves.

"I have to tell you," he said. "I have to tell you, my heart is filled to overflowing to see so many striving for a better existence, striving to find the truth beneath the lies your soul has been fed for eons."

Another uproar of applause drowned out his "Amen" and "Thank you." Most people probably only saw him mouth the words. He nodded, raising his hand in acceptance of their accolades.

The man worked the stage like a virtuoso, strolling from one end to the other, making eye contact with the besotted nephilim down front, then coming around center stage to throw a few charming glances to the cheap seats.

His long, curling hair shimmered in the harsh lights, pulled to a ponytail at the base of his neck. The light sugar-cookie color was so much like Tommy's, and the thought pinched my chest. Anger kindled in the pit of my stomach. He was tall like Tommy, too, but then it seemed the larger height was a common trait among angels.

"Now," he said, his gaze scanning the darkness at the back of the hall. "I know why you're here. I know you've heard the rumors.

People whispering about how their life turned around. How after an hour worshipping at Faith Harvest Church, they felt better than they had in years. You're curious. Suspicious. Disbelieving."

The hum of voices softly admonishing those people rose up around me, like a kettle of water brought to a simmer. The nephilim seemed as much a part of the sermon as Hubert.

"We at Faith Harvest Church welcome your doubt. We encourage your questioning intellect. The intelligent mind thrives on reason and logic. At Faith Harvest Church, we don't just want to enrich your soul, but your body and mind as well."

Another burst of applause deafened me, my tablemates whooping and whistling. Hubert's smile brightened. He'd expected the reaction, planned for it, and when the applause had gone on long enough, he took a breath to speak, and all went silent in anticipation.

He was larger than life up on that stage, his voice a smooth satin caress over the audience. They'd have done anything to have his attention. They would've done anything he asked. The angel's voice was like a long drink of wine, relaxing tense muscles, buzzing the human mind, and I had to fight to keep my thoughts focused.

"And how do we do that, you might ask." He paused, wringing every ounce of dramatic effect out of the pregnant air. Soft murmurs hummed over our heads from the seats farther back, the audience's curiosity stirring.

Hubert smiled. "We don't." *Pause. Pause. Pause.* "You do."

The nephilim jumped to their feet, cheering. Upbeat organ music piped a joyous beat through the speakers. But this time, Hubert's microphone overcame the noise.

"You do," he repeated. "The power is in you." The cheers grew louder. An unseen choir joined the organ music, singing praise to a beautiful new day. He strolled the stage, tossing a small wave to this person or that, clasping his hands at his mouth as if praying—he wasn't—as the noise level softened, both real voices as well as piped music.

The excitement calmed, and people found their seats again.

"At Faith Harvest Church," he said, when all was quiet, "we show you how to find that power. It's there inside each of you, waiting to be tapped, waiting to fill you, to move you to a better level of existence. Because you were all meant to be…so much more. So much more." He shook his head, lowering his gaze, feigning sadness. *Oh, he was good.*

"We've all experienced it, right?" he said. "The supreme power of the human mind. Precognition. Déjà vu. What about the power of will? How many times have you prayed and prayed and prayed for something…and then it happened?"

The back of the room rumbled softly, sounding like they weren't sure they wanted to follow where he was leading.

"We're always so eager to give the credit away. Oh, I didn't do that. I'm just human," he said, scoffing. "Exactly. You *are* human, and the power…is in you. The power is in you!"

The people at the front of the room were on their feet again, the cheers louder than any explosion before. Their utter belief in his words was like a force in itself, pushing the rest to believe as well, swirling and rising and filling us. I could feel their angelic power. Could they? Did they know that unearthly sensation was coming from them?

"How about the power to heal?" Hubert said. "A man suffering from terminal cancer meets the girl of his dreams. He decides he won't die of cancer and the tumors go away. How? The power was in him.

"How about the woman in a horrific car accident, losing vital blood by the second, but she doesn't die. She refuses. She won't leave her little girl trapped in the backseat alone. She holds on until help arrives. How?"

"The power was in her," the closer group murmured around me.

"That's right," Hubert said, his voice soft, cajoling. "The power was in her. Just like it is in you. And you. And you. And all of you." He swept his arm across the crowd. "You've seen it. You've tasted it. You know it's there, or you wouldn't be here asking about it, how to tap into it, how to let it elevate you to a higher state of consciousness."

The way he spoke, the sound of his voice, the cadence—it was getting to me. I blinked, realizing my thoughts were slowing, like walking in thigh-deep water. I wasn't bothered by the sensation, and that bothered me. I shook my head, tried to clear the stroke of his warm liquid voice from my head.

"He's hypnotizing everyone," I said.

My tablemate shushed me, and I glanced back to see him staring like an eager puppy at the Fallen angel onstage. This had to stop.

"Humans were meant to be more. The proof has been around you since the beginning of time," Hubert said. "Your ancestors saw it, wrote about it in their holy books…"

"Angels!" a nephilim yelled from across the room.

Hubert snapped in his direction, pointing. "That's right. Angels. The perfection of the human spirit. Pure soul. Perfect health. Eternal life. The goal of human evolution, the highest level of existence. And you have the power within you to rise to it."

"How?" someone yelled from the cheap seats, and the forward crowd rumbled with understanding laughter.

"I'll tell you how," Hubert said. "By letting go of the limitations of mortal life. This is not your first time around. No. Your soul has ridden this mortal coil time and again, striving to rise above it. And every time, the trials and disappointments of living break you down, hold you back, make you believe you can't reach the heights your soul aches to achieve."

Reincarnation? "Seriously?" I murmured.

My tablemate shushed me again. I was really starting to dislike him.

"These people here have done it." He pointed to the preferred section, his finger swinging over my table and back the other way. "I've done it."

Hubert pointed to the back of the room. "You can do it. Right now."

Applause echoed across the large room, more subdued. Those in front mildly happy for those in the back, those in the back unsure what he meant.

Bariel stepped onstage again, crossing to stand in center stage, microphone in hand. Hubert lowered his head as though meditating, his hands clasped in front of him.

"Blessed are you mortal men, for you are in the presence of an archangel," Bariel said. "Feel him stir the power within you."

The Fallen exhaled loudly into his headset, his shoulders heaving with the effort. All at once his head snapped back, his arms flying out to his sides. The spotlight brightened, or maybe it was him, and the crowd gasped.

A moment later, soft moans floated forward from the cheap seats. Someone fainted off his chair and then another.

"Oh my God!" someone cried.

"Not God," Bariel said.

The cries and soft cooing quieted, and Hubert slowly lowered his arms, straightened, opening his eyes. "That was only a taste of what the coming new faith can bring you."

"Teach me," someone yelled from the corner. "I want to be an angel, too."

His gaze shifted to the tables, the ticket holders eager, sitting on the edges of their seats. "My children, those prepared to rise higher, come forth," he said. "Let my spirit enrich yours so that you might enrich others. Together we will alter humanity as a whole and complete the evolutionary struggle."

Everyone seated in the front row of tables stood and a steel cord of nerves knotted in my gut. This was it—my chance to be near enough to the fallen angel to strike. But how close could I get before being discovered? I'd resisted the brainwashing power he was pushing through the audience, but I wasn't sure I'd be able to keep my thoughts straight the closer I got. Still, I had to try. I held my breath and filed along with the others toward the stage, forming two long lines. I followed like I knew the drill.

"Blessed are you. For you are in the presence of angels," Hubert said to the rest of the room. "Behold, these once mortal men and women. They are without illness, without worry, without doubt. They are Dominions and Powers, the second order of angels here on earth. They follow the path I lead, rising higher and higher, and soon will be one with me at my side."

The first two in line stepped up onstage, and Hubert reached out, taking their hands. The threesome closed their eyes, lowered their heads.

To the ignorant skeptic, this was all a huge crock. Hubert was a con artist scamming these people out of their hard-earned money. Looking at the three people standing onstage, a skeptic would claim they'd been swept up in Hubert's elaborate production, compelled to play along. Who could tell?

I could. I could feel his power stretching out to the two unmarked nephilim, seeping into them, searching, tempting, calling to that part of them that was so familiar to him. Like calling like. I stood in line, the truth dawning. He was calling up their angel halves without triggering the illorum mark.

If he succeeded, they'd be nearly as powerful as angels without even knowing it. He'd be in control of them. His own army of human angels.

"I don't think so." I drew my sword, willing the blade to form.

CHAPTER EIGHTEEN

I couldn't let a thing like Richard Hubert build his own superhuman army. The burning flesh sensation on my wrist began to ease. Like the nausea, it was a warning, sounding and then dissipating.

The weight of my sword settled perfectly in my palm, loose at my side. I stepped out of line, heading toward center stage with long, even strides. People glanced, eyes going from my face to my sword, alarm rising through their bodies as I passed. I didn't stop, coming dead center, stepping up in unison with the next two nephilim in line.

The first pair was finished, already walking offstage. I could feel their power, same as mine, snaking out of them, twining through people, through minds, exploring. Power with no direction, no purpose — raw and dangerous. Placing these people in the hands of a Fallen angel seemed the worst possible fate.

The ballroom erupted the moment those farther back caught sight of my sword. Screams echoed through the hall, catching and spreading like fire in a windstorm as more and more people noticed. *Sheesh, it's not like it's a gun. No one is going to get hit by a stray swing. Probably.*

Metal doors banged against the brick walls, frightened people slamming through them, running for safety. Most of the nephilim stood their ground, Hubert having thoroughly screwed with their brains so they valued his Hell-bound life more than their own. They rushed onstage to gather around their personal archangel when most everyone else was running the other way.

The smell of brimstone turned my stomach a second before demon hands latched around both my arms. I glanced behind me. The demons were on either side, both dressed in the same Sherwani jackets as Hubert, peach and purple respectively. The one on my left was a few pounds lighter than his partner, but they were muscle, nothing more. Of course they weren't going to let me get close enough to strike.

Didn't matter. That's not why I'd stepped forward.

"Illorum," Hubert said, parting the protective wall of human nephilim in front of him so there was no one directly between us. "I'm so glad you decided to join the ceremony. I thought you might never move into action. I do hope you're not planning anything… unfortunate."

"Who, me?" I said, feigning innocence. Then I sobered up. "Archangel? Seriously? You're lucky God hasn't struck you down already."

His brows shot up, surprised. He laughed. "God? Oh, you are new, aren't you?"

Crap. And here I'd been going for cocky experience.

"If God were going to raise a finger against me, if He could, don't you think He would have by now?" Hubert said. "There's no God here. The creature you speak of abandoned this world eons ago. He was impotent. These people have no need of a God so

powerless that He'd allow the atrocities of mortal life to keep them
stunted and unable to evolve into the masters of their own destiny,
Gods in their own worlds."

"Yeah, I don't really know about all that garbage, but I do know
you're wrong about one thing. God has raised a finger against you."
I shrugged. "Here I am. Guess which finger."

"Indeed," he said. "Do you believe you'll leave here alive?"

"Uh, yeah. Yeah, I'm pretty sure I will." It'd be easier if I wasn't
surrounded by demons, with one of them squeezing his nails into
my arm.

"Better illorum than you have tried."

"You don't know that," I said.

"You're right. I don't know how good you are." He clasped his
hands behind him. "How good are you, my lovely, young illorum?"

Maybe it was me, but my brain went straight into the gutter.
Good at what? I wanted to be grossed out. I mean, he was only one
step above a demon from Hell. Right? But I was learning demons
don't always look…y'know, hellish. Fallen or not, Richard Hubert
definitely had the alluring angel thing down.

It wasn't just his muscled, manly stature, or his heart-melting,
cool angel-blue eyes, or his smooth as silk voice, or even those
shimmering golden locks a girl could lose her fingers in. It was…
him. Call it charisma, charm, mojo, whatever, the guy had it in
spades. Those cobalt eyes focused on me made my heart pound a
little faster, made muscles low inside me warm and flex.

I liked having his attention. I liked having him talk to me,
ignoring everyone else. I wanted to keep his notice. I wanted to hear
him say my name. I wanted to see his lips turn to a smile for me,
because of me. I wanted to be special to him.

Even knowing it was wrong, knowing his angelic powers were

working me hard and fast, didn't make it any easier to snap out of it. And knowing that pissed me off.

Apparently, anger is an amazing motivator for me. "Tell you what, have your demon dog let go of my arm, and I'll show you how good I am."

The bodyguard still holding my sword arm jerked me hard enough I stumbled back a step. I tried to yank my arm free, but he held firm, his fingers digging deeper.

"My apologies," Hubert said. "Mr. Imad and Mr. Jalil are compelled by a fierce love and loyalty to me. They fear for my safety. To dissuade them would be to insult them."

I scoffed. "Loyalty. Right. Why not? You got their banished asses out of the abyss."

Another hard jerk, and I thought I heard something tear under the skin on my shoulder. Pain stabbed up to my brain, but I clamped my teeth down and kept my yelp bottled up.

"I did for them what I would do for any one of my brothers. Though I cannot say the gesture would be returned in kind."

I huffed. "Oh, I've got a gesture for you."

"We are judged and sentenced by a small group of elitists ruling by ignorance and fear," he said, ignoring my comment. "The Council of Seven has no authority. There is no unseen God for whom they speak. It's all been an elaborate hoax, and those of us who've refused to live by their oppressive, separatist rules have been cast out."

"So, let me get this straight. It's not God who smacked you down for raping human women and screwing with their minds. It's just a bunch of jealous, uptight angels." My hand adjusted for a firmer grip on the hilt of my sword. "And, why? To keep humans from evolving into what? You, right?" Disgust made an ugly noise at the back of my throat.

"They are hypocritical fools, using our progeny to do what they haven't the strength or stomach to do themselves," Hubert said.

"If you weren't raping women, there'd be no progeny to send after you."

"It is only rape if the female is unwilling."

"It's rape if the woman doesn't have a choice," I said, feeling my growing ire tightening my jaw. "Using your angelic charms is like drugging a woman. You take away her ability to think clearly, to make an informed, balanced decision. That's rape."

"That's seduction," he countered smoothly. "It's no different than a handsome man's smile, an eloquent man's poetry, an endowed man's prowess."

"Except a woman can ignore a handsome smile or a snappy come-on line. When it comes to angelic mojo, a girl doesn't stand a chance."

"You seem to be having no difficulty denying the effect."

My mouth snapped shut, and my brain flinched. He was right. I still felt the seductive draw from him, the desire to be the center of his world, to be touched and kissed and…touched by him. But I wasn't about to chuck everything—family, friends, divine mission—and throw myself into his arms.

I could say no.

"I understand your concern." His voice was softer now, as though he'd sensed my brain's falter. "I share that concern. For eons, your species has been kept stilted and unchanging. The moment my brothers realized you would one day evolve to become equal to them, they began doing all they could to alter humanity's course. Spreading false propaganda, twisting truths, and casting out those of us who would stand against them, chaining us in the bowels of the earth where our outcries can't be heard."

"And yet you stand here, surrounded by bastardized human and angel offspring, triggering powers in them they aren't near capable of controlling or understanding," I said. A few of the nephilim looked as though they were following the conversation; most stared like guard dogs waiting to pounce.

"These beautiful souls are the next step in human evolution." He opened his hands, gesturing to the men and women crowding around him. "Their mothers were chosen to take our seed, to advance humanity. With my help, we've compensated for valuable evolutionary time. With my help, our children will become so much more."

I loved my mom. She was the best. But she was just a normal woman, and this guy was full of it. "What if they're not ready? What if by forcing evolution you're skipping a natural, necessary progression? It's like pushing a newborn bird out of the nest. Just because it's got wings doesn't mean it knows how to fly. You can't give these people angelic power without teaching them how to use it."

"Was your education so vast? Would you have your powers stripped because your magister's teachings were lacking?" he said. "Are you any better, any more deserving, any more capable than these people? You would deny them the very thing that gives you confidence to stand here and argue your point with an angel? How very hypocritical of you."

"I didn't ask for these powers," I said. "I didn't ask to be chased by demons, to have my friend slaughtered right in front of me, to have my family put at risk, my life turned upside down."

"That is not what I'm offering these people." He took a step closer, and the crowd around him held their collective breath. Tension spiked, like air pushed into an over-inflated balloon. "I'm offering them the chance to be a part of the greatest thing mankind has seen since the birth of civilization. I am giving them the power to bring Heaven to Earth and live as the gods they were destined to be. I'd offer that same gift to you, if you'd take it."

"Me?" Maybe he forgot why I was there.

"Yes," he said. "There's something about you. Something... different. Your power feels more like my own, more pure."

My thoughts slowed, a dull ache starting behind my eyes, pressure building. It came on fast, pushed against my eyeballs and stuffed my ears. And then it was gone.

"You have a strong will...Emma Jane. No surprise you can resist my charms."

He'd probed my mind. That's what the sensation had been— he'd taken my name from my thoughts. Understanding dawned quickly. He'd forced his will, pushed his way through. That's why it had hurt. I couldn't stop him, hadn't even thought to try. Who knew what other information he'd stolen?

Anger washed over me, thumping through my chest. He had no right. "Stay the hell out of my head, Fallen."

His soft, pink lips curled into a smile, cocky—confident. "I was right. You are different. My, your father was clever."

"My father was an engineer. He was a good man. A *human*. The bastard that raped my mother will be rotting in the abyss before long."

"Such harsh, angry words from someone so curious, so unsure," he said. "I can answer your questions, Emma Jane. I can help you understand, show you the truth. Join me, and I can help you become a force of nature."

Questions? So many rattled through my brain, questions I didn't want to think about. Could he tell me why this was happening to me, what it all meant? Will I ever be forgiven for what I am if I can't find and kill my Fallen father? If I'm too sullied for Heaven and too angelic for hell, where do I belong? Who will want me?

The Fallen had looked inside me, deeper than anyone ever had. He knew the questions I'd been trying not to ask, scared of what the answers might be. If I was damned no matter what, did I want to know?

Yes. I wanted to know. I wanted it so badly, the temptation of his offer tied my stomach in knots. I didn't like *wanting* this much.

I clenched my fist, my gaze sliding to the demon holding my sword arm. Our eyes met, his so human no one would know by looking what he was. The hate I felt for him, for Hubert, for myself, choked at the back of my throat, and I let it fuel my glare. I jerked my shoulder, and he let me go.

"Your power is remarkable," Hubert said. "I'd begun to doubt if such a pure melding of human and angelic spirit was even possible. But with your sword at my side, the mighty will kneel before us, and more like you will rise."

My gaze slid back to him, and the hate inside me flared. The memory of Tommy bleeding to death in my arms stormed through my mind, of my mother seduced by a wicked angel, of these people, consumed by power they shouldn't have. I wanted to stop him, to make him pay.

"I'm not here to join you," I said, my voice deadly calm. "I'm here to take your head."

The Fallen angel stiffened. I could see the war waging inside him, survival instincts urging him to put distance between us and pride refusing to show the weakness. *Good.*

"You're mistaken, illorum," he said. "You will join me or *you* will die this day. Either way, you've done more than you can possibly realize. My brothers will know our mission is within our grasp. We can birth an army formidable enough to put asunder the walls of Heaven."

"Not if I kill the messenger. Ready to see how good I am now?" I raised my sword, both hands tight on the grip, blade high, ready to swing with every ounce of angelic force pumping through my veins.

Hubert didn't budge. The conflict I'd seen in his eyes a moment ago was gone. His gaze was cold, devoid of emotion—ice. "You're a fool."

Maybe.

Movement at the far corners of my eyes made me look. One side, and then the other. I was surrounded.

Demons, I guessed, judging by the pungent cloud of brimstone steaming off them. They stood shoulder to shoulder in a tight circle around us. The brainwashed nephilim huddled close to Hubert's shoulder in front of me, making it difficult to land a blow without slicing my sword through one of them first. I'd manage.

"You will join me, Emma Jane," he said. "I can let no other have you as mother to their legions."

"Mother?" My brain shifted through all the possible implications. "Oh, hell no. Dude, trust me, you are never going to touch this."

My weight shifted, the world slowed, and power suddenly hummed through my veins, giving inhuman strength to human muscle. In that same instant, the circle around me tightened. Demons advanced. I didn't care.

A breath before I swung, someone yelled. "Freeze! Police."

I glanced over my shoulder then turned, my sword dropping to my side, my free hand going up in surrender. Everywhere I looked, all I saw were gun barrels, every one of them pointed at me.

Time caught up, made me blink as my brain struggled, a few beats behind. Police were everywhere, yelling. "Freeze! Drop the weapon! Drop the weapon! Drop the weapon!"

In the snap of a finger, the demons had shifted from seething, threatening beasts to innocuous convention goers. Some melted into the crowd of nephilim onstage; others feigned fear, cowering behind chairs, taking cover next to tables.

The demons set me up. Any visible threat, any justification for my drawn weapon was gone. All that was left was me with my big honkin' sword, threatening to swing at the spiritualist Richard Hubert and his fifty or so *unarmed* loyal followers. I admit, it didn't look good.

I dropped the weapon, put both my hands up in surrender. It didn't seem to make a difference to the adrenaline-pumped cops.

"Don't move! Don't move!" they yelled, edging closer.

"Emma?" someone said.

My gaze snapped to the uniformed policeman among the sea of uniformed policemen washing toward me, guns still drawn.

"Officer Dan?" I groaned.

"Hold your fire," Wysocki yelled. "Hold your fire. I got this. I got it."

No one fired, but they still had a bead on me with their guns. One cop darted forward, grabbed my sword, and stepped back like I might try and snatch it. I released the power I'd sent to call my blade and watched the gleaming metal vanish. The cop holding it nearly dropped the hilt out of shock. I didn't care as long as Dan didn't touch that grip.

Officer Wysocki holstered his weapon, snagging his cuffs from farther back on his belt. "Jeezus, Emma. Threatening a priest? What the hell's going on with you?"

"He's not a priest." *He's a fallen angel.* But I doubted it'd make a difference. Dan spun me around so my back was to him, and I held my hands behind me without being asked.

"You have the right to remain silent…"

The cuffs pinched.

CHAPTER NINETEEN

I think they make the fingerprint ink hard to remove on purpose. Sort of an added humiliation on top of the humiliation of being arrested. The wet wipe Officer Wysocki gave me was practically dry already, and I'd worn holes in it scrubbing at my blackened fingertips.

My stomach dropped when he shoved through the steel door with the itty-bitty window on top, and tossed my official file onto the institutional, gray metal table. It slid a few inches to stop in front of his chair as he sat. "All right, Emma. Want to tell me what was going on today?"

Geez, I wished he'd stay in the room or out of it, so my nephilim senses would stop warning me another of my kind was near. I saw him grimace, so at least he was suffering as much as I was.

"I accidently put twenty bucks in the collection plate, and I was trying to get my change back," I said. "Those Faith Harvest people are real misers."

"C'mon, Emma."

"Okay, okay, Hubert was telling all those people he was an

immortal god and I was just going to test the theory with my sword."
Close to the truth.

"Emma…"

"Speaking of my sword," I said. "I kinda need that back. Um, now."

He made an amused sniff, then looked me in the eye and realized I wasn't joking. "Your butt's going to be on the next transport to the county jail in about thirty minutes, Hellsbane. We don't normally arm our prisoners with swords, or even sword handles. What is that thing anyway, some kind trick weapon? The plastic blade collapses into the handle or something?"

A horrible thought occurred to me. "You didn't touch it, did you? My sword—I mean the handle. You didn't touch it, right?"

I reached for his wrists, my cuffs and the chain they used to attach me to the table clanking against the top as I moved. I managed to snag his right hand, twisting it to see his wrist. No mark. He jerked away before I could grab the other to check.

"Hey. Hey. Enough." He held his hands up and out where I couldn't reach. But I could see his left wrist was clean, too. "What the hell's with you?"

"Nothing." I shook my head, leaned forward so I could reach to scrub my face with both hands. "Bad day. Really bad, long, bad day."

"Yeah. Well, mine hasn't been a bowl of peaches, either," he said. "What was going on in that ballroom? Were they burning something, incense or drugs or something? The second I walked in there I thought I'd puke."

"I don't know." Why should I spell everything out for him? No one warned me before it was too late. Ignorance is bliss, right?

"No," he said. "I just got a weird feeling in my gut. Like…"

"Like you were riding a roller coaster?"

"Yeah, one too many. Almost lost my lunch."

I shrugged. "Maybe you ate some bad sushi."

"I didn't eat any sushi today."

"Bad tuna?"

"Emma." The way he barked my name made me flinch. I hated that.

He waited a few beats, either for me to collect myself or for him to collect himself, I'm not sure which. "Listen. We've had this conversation before," he said.

"You still got kids?"

"Yeah."

"Then let it go," I said. "And while you're at it, how about letting *me* go, too?"

"Tell me something, and I'll see what I can do."

"Seriously?" I said, straightening.

"I might be able to talk to the people at Faith Harvest. I'll vouch for you. See if they'd be willing to drop the charges, since no one got hurt…"

"Sweet."

"First…talk."

Oh. Right. I didn't want to be the one to pop his normal-world balloon. I still wished mine had never been burst. "Fine. No, they weren't burning anything in the ballroom. That's not what made your stomach feel weird. Good enough?"

"Not by half," he said. "You still owe me for letting you get away when I caught you at Saint James's apartment."

My chest tightened at the mention of Tommy's name. I pushed the pain away. "*Let* me get away? Dude, you never *had* me at the apartment. Wait. I mean…I was never there. I don't even know what you're talking about." *Close one.*

He snorted. "Clever."

"And even if I *had* been there, no way would you have caught me." I mean, seriously. I could move faster than the speed of light.

"Yeah. About that." He leaned forward, forearms resting on the table, his big biceps pushing the stretching point of his short cop sleeves. "How'd you move so fast? One second you were standing on the kitchen table and the next you were on the balcony. A second after that you were gone."

"I…uh…" Me and my big mouth. I couldn't think of anything he'd believe. "Dammit, Dan, why can't you just let it go? Trust me, you'll wish you had."

His back stiffened, his brows slamming low over his pretty blue eyes. "Is that a threat?"

"No," I said. "It's a fact. If I tell you the truth, you won't believe it. And if you do, it'll drive you nuts."

"Try me," he said. "I'm a cop, Emma. I doubt there's anything in your little girly life that's going to give me nightmares."

A challenge. Yum. "Girly? Really?"

He shrugged. Yeah, he knew it was a dumb thing to say. I glanced at the big-mirrored wall behind him. "Anybody in there?"

His eyes slid to the side like he'd look but his attention came back to me before he did. "No. Just you and me."

Bullshit. I own a TV. "Whatever. Okay, if I tell you, you have to promise you'll get the charges against me dropped."

"I'll do what I can."

"And I need my sword back," I said, then hurried to add, "But you can't touch it. Someone else has to bring it to me."

"You're not exactly in a position to be making demands," he said. "How about you start talking, and I'll decide what I can do to help you out."

"Fine." I sighed, sinking back in the hard chair. The stupid thing looked like it had cushions on the back and seat, but the blue-green pads were as hard as the gray metal that made up the rest of the chair.

I squirmed, trying to stop my butt from getting any number. "What do you want to know? Where should I start?"

"How were you able to move so fast?" he said.

"I'm not human." I stopped myself. Rethought. "Well, I'm not totally human. I'm half human and half"—I glanced at him, watching his reaction—"angel."

He did one of those slow blinks, the kind you do when your brain hasn't quite figured out how to process the info it just received. I waited.

Officer Wysocki was a decent-looking guy. Great body, solid muscle. Kind of short, but then again, so am I, so I can't really throw stones. He looked like a good solid man, a good cop, a good dad, and I was about to blow his world all to hell. *Yay, me.*

"Okay," he said, snapping out of his stupor. He pushed to his feet, the metal chair screeching against the ugly linoleum floor. "An officer will be in to take you to the transport in about twenty minutes. Good luck in court, Miss Hellsbane. You'll need it."

He grabbed my folder and turned to leave.

"Hey, wait. What about the charges? What about my sword?"

He looked back at me, defeat and frustration stewing on his cute face. "I haven't got time for this. You're not going to be straight with me, fine. I've got better things to do than help you out of your own mess."

"*Shit.* I knew it." Resignation weighed my shoulders, and I slumped. "I knew you wouldn't believe me."

Dan turned and rested on his fisted knuckles against the

tabletop, his elbows locked. "Half human and half angel?"

"Yeah. We're called nephilim. It's in the Bible. Look it up," I said, still slouching.

He straightened. "Yeah. I've heard the term. They were described as giants. You don't look like a giant to me."

"Right," I said, swinging my gaze up to him. "Listen, you said you wanted the truth. You said you knew whatever was going on wasn't normal. Surprise! You're right. So here it is. How about giving me and your gut the benefit of the doubt?"

He sighed, grabbed his chair, and pulled it under him as he sat. "Fine. So which half? Mother or father?"

I shifted forward, the chain on my cuffs catching on the edge of the table, my hands laid in front of me. "Father. Angels are only male."

"So, nephilim are only female?" he asked, and I could swear I heard a tremor of hope in his voice. Did he know?

"No. Nephilim can be either male or female," I said, not wanting to meet his gaze. "Most never realize it. They live perfectly normal lives. No one in the family knows. Not even their mother."

He scoffed. "How's that possible?"

"The Fallen—that's what they're called once they choose to defy God and be with a woman—the fallen angel wipes all memory of his existence from the woman's mind and from anyone close enough to her to remind her."

"Convenient."

"Right." I huffed to myself, *"Bastards."*

"So how did you find out?" he asked.

"My friend Tommy. He was a nephilim, too, but he'd been marked. Uh, called to duty, they say. He was an illorum, fighting to banish the Fallen angels into the abyss, as God had commanded."

"How'd he do that? How was he…marked?"

"The sword," I said. "It's real. The blade appears and disappears with my will. When a nephilim picks up an illorum's sword to do battle, they're marked. Literally." I rolled my arm to show him my wrist and the skeleton key scar. "It's burned into your skin."

"Ouch," he said.

"Yeah, right?" I laughed, though nothing about this conversation was funny. "Anyway, once a nephilim is marked, their angel half and all the powers that come with it are triggered. Y'know, so we're strong enough, and *fast* enough, to fight Fallen angels. We're given our own sword, which is the only thing capable of killing demons and sending the Fallen to the abyss. And it's kind of why I need it back."

"Jeezus," he said on an exhale. He leaned back, staring wide-eyed at me. "That's crazy."

"Yeah. Another thing. God really doesn't like the whole name-in-vain thing."

Dan snorted. "Okay."

I shrugged. "Just a tip."

"Wait. Back up. Did you say demons?" he asked, shifting forward in his chair.

"Yeah. Fallen angels call them up to do their dirty work, like hunting and killing illorum before we can kill the Fallen," I said. "They also use them as bodyguards and to act as emcee at their religious revivals."

"Religious revivals?" I could almost see his mind working. "You mean, Richard Hubert?"

"Well, no. Hubert is a Fallen angel. Bariel…I mean Bob, is the demon. Hubert's second in command. And he ain't the only one," I said. "In fact, if you and the rest of Pittsburgh's finest hadn't stormed in when you did, I'd be sitting here in one of those black body bags. Well, not here…in the morgue, I guess. Right? Whatever. You know what I mean."

"So, those people huddled around him on stage were demons?" Dan asked. "I knew there was something weird about them. I could feel it. Y'know?"

Crap. That's not what he was feeling from them. "Uh, no. They weren't demons. Those people were nephilim. Unmarked. Hubert was working to try and trigger their angelic powers without them becoming illorum. He's got them brainwashed. They'll do anything for him. He wants to make his own nephilim army."

"Why?"

"To bring down the walls of Heaven and rebuild it under his control here on Earth." Wow, felt kind of strange to talk crazy out loud—and believe it.

Dan shook his head and took a deep breath, like he needed to digest the information. "So what was I feeling? It nearly brought me to my knees the second I got close to that stage. I sense it every time I get close to you, too. Only for a second, and then it's gone."

Crap. Crap on toast. Crappity-crap-crap-crap. I did not want to be the one to tell him this. But what choice did I have?

"Dan…you're a nephilim."

"No, I'm not."

"Yes, you are. The sensation you keep feeling is like a warning bell, letting you know another of your kind is near. That's why you feel it around me, and why you felt it today in the ballroom. It's also why you can't touch my sword."

He blinked at me, his face utterly devoid of expression or emotion. "That's not possible." But he knew it was true. I could see it in his eyes.

"I need my sword," I said, but there was no sign he'd heard. "Dan, seriously. I need my sword. It's the only way I can defend myself. Hubert saw the police take it—he'll know I'm vulnerable."

"He won't get in here." Dan sounded distracted, not at all believable, like his mind was somewhere else. I think he was in shock.

"He's a friggin' fallen angel. He fought against God and all the angels in Heaven and survived. You think a few measly metal bars are going to keep him out? He's not above killing to get what he wants. The cops out there, your *human* friends, they're in danger. Dan!" I didn't know if that was true. I knew the Fallen would kill if they were desperate enough, if there'd be no witnesses. Whatever. The possibility was enough.

Life flickered at the back of Officer Wysocki's eyes, and they shifted to me. He blinked, pushed his chair back, and stood. "You're safe here. Relax. I'll see what's holding up your transport."

I exhaled, loud, frustrated. I'd thought he'd believe me. "You're going to get those people killed. You're going to get *me* killed. Dan. Officer Wysocki. I need my sword."

Without looking back he jerked the door open and let it drift behind him, not closing it.

There was only one person left who could help me, but calling him was like asking someone with their hands tied to scratch your nose. I sighed. What choice did I have?

"Eli!"

CHAPTER TWENTY

The Book of the Lost hit the interrogation table with enough weight and force to shake the legs against the linoleum. The chain between my handcuffs rattled.

"Rifion," Eli said, standing behind me.

I leaned forward, scanning the page he'd dropped the book open to. The rows of names were in alphabetical order, and I found Rifion halfway down on the middle row.

"That's Hubert?" I glanced up and behind me. "Wait. How'd you figure it out? You didn't know him when I showed you the website."

"You shared your sight with me," he said, his black brows tightened, ice-blue eyes locked on mine. "How'd you do that?"

I sniffed a laugh. "You're asking me?"

Eli squatted next to me, a hand on the table, the other on the back of my chair. "I've been training illorum for thousands of years and never, never has one had the ability to bring an image to my mind. Whispered words, halted sentences, yes. But that's not what this was. I saw what you saw, as though I were there with you.

The vision was crystal clear in my mind. It's an ability only angels possess."

Okay, he was starting to freak me out. Not a good sign when the crazy in your life is scared for you. "There has to be an explanation. It was probably just a fluke. I mean, I thought if you saw his face, his mannerisms, heard him talking, you might recognize him. That's all that was going through my head: *Does Eli know him?*"

He glanced away, considering the possibility, and stood. "Interesting."

"Right. That's what I was thinking. Interesting." In a totally whacked, abnormal, inhuman kind of way. Exactly the right word. My gaze swung back to the book.

"Well, now you have his angelic name," Eli said.

"Which would be almost as good as not being handcuffed to this table," I said, rattling my own chain for him to notice.

Eli reached out and pinched one of the fat silver links. The chain that looped through the cuffs and held me to the table dropped away, the link he'd touched broken. I pushed to my feet, the back of my legs shoving my chair so it screeched against the floor.

"Cool. Thanks. What about these?" I held up my wrists, tensing the smaller chain of the cuffs between them.

He reached for it, then stopped. "What will you tell the officer when he returns to collect you?"

"I don't have to be here when he comes back," I said. "They'd never even see me leave."

"Don't they have your name and address by now?"

"Oh. Right. There's that." I dropped back into my chair. "This sucks. I don't want to go to jail."

Eli reached for the book, slamming the cover closed before gathering the enormous thing to his chest. "No one was hurt. I can't imagine Rifion will press charges. He wouldn't want the unfavorable attention. You'll be released soon."

"You're leaving?" I said, and couldn't help the little girl quiver in my voice. "But I'm…I'm defenseless here. I don't have my sword and my hands are cuffed. If Rifion comes—"

"He won't. He's got too much at stake to risk exposing what he is to humans. It's not worth it. Now, I must go. I've interfered more than I should. A request has been made for the book. I have to pass it along," he said. "I've kept it longer than I should have already."

"Right." Geez, I was going to be his damnation if I wasn't more careful. "I'm sorry. Thanks for everything. I got it from here."

"I know you do."

"Oh. Wait," I said. "There's something else. Tommy was right. He knew there was something weird about the nephilim he met, the ones working with Rifion. They've had their powers triggered. I don't know how he's doing it, but they aren't illorum. They aren't marked. They're like a blank slate, no direction, no rules. How is that fair?"

Something about Eli altered slightly. He seemed taller suddenly, more powerful. His beautiful face turned hard, calculating. "How many?"

"Oh, uh…I don't know, maybe ten or twelve who actually had some power. But there were a bunch more who were working toward it. Like forty, fifty, maybe more."

"You have to find them, the ones already brought into their power. They'll have to be marked, or…" He seemed to stop and think, but then shook his head. "They must be marked."

"How?"

"Your sword," he said. "Let them touch the hilt. It should do the rest."

"You don't sound sure."

"The illorum sword calls a nephilim to duty, as well as triggers their powers," he said. "These nephilim have already come into their power. It may be too late to imprint their desire to serve."

"Whoa, imprint their desire? That's sounds disturbingly close to brainwashing." I tried to catch Eli's eye, tried to read his reaction. He wouldn't look at me. "Have I been brainwashed?"

His gaze snapped to mine. He looked pissed. "Absolutely not. Free will is paramount. When will you stop questioning—"

"Right. Right," I said to stop his rant. "My bad. Though, I gotta tell you, I don't really feel like I've got a choice here. Either fight or be killed."

"The threats to your life stem from demons and the Fallen who control them. Not us," he said. "The desire to seek and destroy the Fallen is natural to nephilim. The sword simply…enhances the instinct. Humans tend to have selfish priorities. I'm not confident that, faced with the temptation of unearthly power, an unmarked nephilim would choose to use it for the greater good."

Yeah. He was probably right about that. Powers like mine could come in wicked handy in Vegas. I shrugged. "Like you said, the demons will take care of it. Fight or be killed. We just need to warn them."

"Not necessarily." Eli turned away, not meeting my eyes again. I watched him in profile, the Book of the Lost clutched to his chest. "It's the enhanced desire to kill Fallen that the demons sense. Unmarked nephilim are just as easily swayed as normal humans, and therefore, likely little threat."

"So the demons won't bother them?" I said, my mouth gaping. "What a jip." The demons trying to hack off my head every other second were totally the worst part of being an illorum. Not fair these guys got to opt out.

His gaze slid to mine, one brow higher than the other. "It is your enhanced desire that has given you the will to make amends for your father's sins—to make amends for what you are. That desire alone keeps the wrath of God and Heaven from your door."

I swallowed, my throat tight. "Wrath of God?"

Eli dipped his chin. "Indeed. The only thing that stays God's hand against the other nephilim, those who have not been marked, not called to duty, is the fact they live as normal humans, their angelic powers dormant."

"And now we've got a bunch running around, testing out their powers, with no mark," I said. "And a Fallen who's rounding them up and signing them onto his team. Crap. They're bound to piss off the Big Guy. That ain't good."

"Exactly," he said. "You must find and mark them. I know how you feel about bringing others into this...life, but the deed is already done. If you don't act to rectify this, God and His angels will."

"Damage control," I said. "Save the world and stuff."

"Yes."

I sighed, grumbled to myself. "Well, let's hope they left a forwarding address, 'cause I'm a little tied up at the moment." I waved my cuffed hands at him.

"I'll return shortly," he said. "I know a few lawyers. We'll have you out in no time."

Seriously? How mundane. "Right. Thanks," I said, but he'd vanished before I finished.

I'd no sooner adjusted my brain to the fact and settled in for my wait than the metal door to my interrogation room swung open.

A uniformed officer poked his head around the door. "Emma Jane Hellsbane?"

"Yes," I said, figuring my ride to the county lockup had finally arrived. *Oh, joy.*

He leaned back, disappearing for a second behind the door. "Yeah. She's in here."

A moment later the mark on my inner wrist blazed with pain, the sensation searing up my arm like a red-hot branding iron pressed to my flesh. The spiritualist Richard Hubert, a.k.a. the fallen angel Rifion, strode through the door. On his heels followed two uniformed officers. They were both demons—I could smell the rotten eggs like the stench was pumping through the AC, filling the room. My stomach gurgled in protest.

I was on my feet, my back hitting the far wall, before I realized I'd even moved. "How'd you get in here?"

My heart slammed in my chest like a jackhammer. My throat closed, and I had to tell myself to breathe. With my hands cuffed, no sword, and the bad guys walking right past the people who were supposed to protect me, I figured I was pretty well screwed.

"Calm yourself," Rifion said. "I'm not here to kill you. I've come to escort you to your new home." He motioned toward me with both hands, and the two demon police officers advanced on me.

"Hold up. Wait," I said, hands raised, wrists chained together. It worked. They stopped. "My new home?"

"I've decided you are too valuable to remain unprotected." He clasped his hands behind his back. "Panic could easily cause one of my brothers to act foolishly and order your disposal. I'll ensure such a tragedy does not occur."

"You're going to protect me?" I said, gesturing between us. "That's rich."

Rifion tilted his head to the side and rolled his shoulders as though my take on things were immaterial.

"Right," I said. "Well, as much as I appreciate the protective dad routine, I think I'll keep the status quo. You know, where I'm an illorum and you're a fallen angel and I use my neato-bandito sword to send your rapist ass to the abyss, where you belong."

"Your sword. Yes." He made a show of scanning the room. "Where is your sword, Emma Jane? And how will you wield it when you can't even find the strength to free yourself from human bonds?" He tsked. "Really."

I thought about that for a second. I hadn't even tried to break the cuffs. I was still thinking like a human. My hands in front of me, I took a breath and yanked. The metal dug into the backs of my wrist, but the small chain between them snapped.

Cool. "Ouch."

"Mighty warrior," he scoffed, then threw a nod to the two cop demons awaiting his command. "Collect her."

"Wait," I said, the wheels of my brain spinning for escape possibilities. Only one thing came to mind. "Help! Police! Somebody help!"

The demons hesitated and for an instant, Rifion's attention split between me and the door, looking to see if anyone would come. That was all I needed.

Trapped in that little room with two armed demons and a powerful fallen angel, my maneuverability was limited. If I could get away, even make it to the larger room, find witnesses, my life expectancy would improve dramatically.

I focused my will, remembering the route Dan had taken when he led me through the station. On the other side of the door was a large room, a few desks, tables along the walls, a TV mounted in the corner. He'd nodded to a plainclothes cop as we passed, a detective. The room was their office.

My vision narrowed, the world around me blurred, and an instant later, I stood next to the center cluster of desks right outside the small interrogation room. The place was empty. *Shoot.*

And someone did.

Bullets whizzed past my ear. I jumped behind a five-foot-long wall of metal file cabinets just as a screech of bullets drilled the desks beside me. After a courage-sealing deep breath, I peeked around the end to see the two demon cops, guns drawn, shoulders braced against either side of the doorjamb. Lucky for me, these demons couldn't aim well.

Another round of gunshots pounded into the cabinet, sounding surreally crisp and precise, like quick hammer strikes. The bullets exploded out the other side, way too close to my head. I dropped to my knees and scrambled to the other wall. Apparently you don't have to aim well if you've got bullets that go through damn near anything.

I needed my friggin' sword. If TV was any guide, it was probably locked in the evidence room, wherever that was.

With no sword, there was no way I could stop Rifion except to use his fear. After all, the possibility of being hunted down, caught, caged, and torturously experimented on could make a person think twice.

Was it impossible for humans to capture an angel? Maybe. But they'd thought the same thing about harnessing the atom. If he was smart, Rifion wouldn't take the chance.

I was betting Rifion was very smart.

CHAPTER TWENTY-ONE

The plan was the same. I needed witnesses. I poked my nose out just far enough to get a bead on the door from the detective's office into the hall. Across from there was the general squad room and Officer Wysocki's desk. I knew exactly where I was going. I'd sat at his desk for nearly an hour while he'd filled out an endless pile of paperwork. I knew the squad room well, and I focused my will.

I took a step, and the next stopped me exactly where I'd planned—Dan's desk. He wasn't there. *Crap*. But I wasn't alone.

Wysocki's desk was on the windowless end of the squad room. Ducked beside it, I counted ten officers and two Faith Harvest followers in the room. My stomach lurched, then dropped, and I fought the urge to double over with the sensation. The Faith Harvest pair was nephilim.

They stood between the two desk clusters at the center of the room, hands clasped in front of them, heads bowed, eyes closed, wearing the same Sherwani jacket Rifion still wore. They matched each other, both jackets a soft, creamy-rose color, although I was pretty sure one of them was a man. It was hard to tell; they both had long, dirty blond hair that curtained on either side of their faces. Seriously dirty blond, I mean, unwashed. Greasy and stringy. *Ick.*

They looked to be meditating, or sleeping, neither of them flinching a muscle when I'd breezed into the room.

My gaze shifted to the officers, four of them at the far desks, unmoving, staring straight ahead, arms resting flat in front of them. The nearer cluster, including Dan's desk, held only two officers sitting in the same, unmoving pose.

I figured the other empty desk must belong to one of the two officers standing hypnotized at the coffee maker, or the one idling at the opened file cabinet, or the other just standing a few steps from the door to a smaller room. It looked as though he'd been on his way in or out and had simply stopped for no apparent reason.

My illorum mark stung like a fresh blistering burn.

"Imad, watch the door," Rifion said, walking into the squad room at a leisurely, human speed. "Lower your weapon, Jalil. I believe Emma Jane has grasped the gravity of her situation and won't cause us any further difficulties."

The two demons in cop outfits took up position. Imad, I assumed, closed the door from the squad room to the hallway we'd come through, then stood in front of it.

Jalil had crossed to the opposite side of the room, his gun still drawn. He lowered it so the barrel aimed at the floor. He didn't look happy to do it, thick neck muscles twitching, his cheek trembling with a thinly veiled snarl.

I stood, looking back to Rifion. "What's wrong with these men? What'd you do to them?"

Rifion stopped about three feet away from me. He smiled, his face relaxed, happy, as though we were standing on a street corner to catch up. "Whatever do you mean? I've done nothing to these humans."

"Bullshit. Why aren't they moving?" My gaze drifted from one officer to the next. It took a few seconds of close observation, but I finally caught a muscle twitch, knuckles turning white with a hand's tight fist.

I shifted my attention to his face at the exact moment his jaw flexed. Deep furrows creased his brows, his eyes shifting a millimeter, full of rage. I looked closely at another officer and then another. Oh, yeah, these guys were pissed. Something was holding them frozen, but they were fighting it with everything they had.

"Don't you know? The ability is the same within you. Don't you recognize it?" he said. "Can't you sense it?"

I looked to the two greasy-headed nephilim at the center of the room and opened my mind to theirs. My breath caught, their power flashing through my mind as white-hot light. Like the long, ghostly tentacles of a jellyfish, their power stretched out in all directions, boring into the minds of each of the officers.

Stay. Be still. Obey. The commands hummed over and over along the lines of their power, pushing on the will of the humans. And then, as though they'd been waiting until they were sure I was listening, the command changed. *Place your weapon within reach.*

In one single-minded effort, every officer in the room un-holstered his weapon. The ones sitting placed the guns on the desk between their outstretched arms. The officer at the file drawer set his on top of the metal cabinet. The two at the coffee maker and the one standing by the door simply held their guns loosely at their sides. A spark of fear replaced the rage in a few men's eyes. I couldn't blame them.

Dread iced through my veins. "Why'd they tell them to take out their guns?"

"Incentive," Rifion said. "Being half-human, I assume you have a certain...affinity for these mortals. I, of course, do not. Therefore it would be of no consequence to me to see them pass from this world."

"You'd kill them?"

"No." He shook his head, his bottom lip pouting as though the question was ridiculous. "They will kill themselves."

The nephilim's power whispered through the room, tickling along my mind. *Weapons to your temple*, they commanded, and the room of trained police officers helplessly obeyed.

My heart lurched. "Wait. Stop. What do you want? Why are you doing this?"

Rifion tilted his head like a puppy hearing a new sound. "Why? For you, of course. I told you—I will not lose you to another. You will join me or perish."

"But why?" My brain whirled, trying to find sense in his actions. "You're not supposed to do this. I mean, it's not worth exposing yourself. I'm not worth it. I don't even have my sword. I'm no threat to you. Just...leave. I won't follow."

He shook his head, his long golden hair swishing along his back. "Is it possible you truly don't know? Of course. How could you? Your magister would never touch your mind as I did. He'd never dare defy his brother's law and explore your soul. Fool."

"Stop talking in riddles. Just spit it out," I said. "What's got you all hot for me?"

His gaze swung to the nephilim still wielding their power over the room. "You understand what they're doing? They're forcing their will on all these men, as well as anyone who thinks of entering this room. Two controlling ten and more."

"Yeah. So? Color me impressed," I said, throwing as much

biting sarcasm into my tone as I could. "Now tell them to stop."

"You tell them," he said. "Better still—make them."

I snorted. "Sure. Why not? Oh, that's right. I don't have the power to mind-fuck people."

He sniffed, his shoulders shaking with a silent laugh. "I like the term. But you're mistaken. You're capable of wielding ten times the power you feel from my two children."

"So that's it?" I asked, folding my arms over my belly, trying to seem way more relaxed and confident than I felt. "This is all about power? What you think I have, or could have? Dude, if you wanted a nephilim with real power, you shouldn't have killed your son Tommy. You had your own flesh and blood murdered, and you think I'd willingly do anything for you?"

His gaze shifted away. It was the only sign my words had any effect on him. A second later, those cool blue eyes were on me again. He held out his hand. "Join me. It is the only way to save these men. They will kill themselves before you can move to stop even one."

"You're making them do this."

"I'm not. You are."

"Bull." The decision to act and the act itself happened almost simultaneously. I spun, reaching for the gun of the closest man sitting at the desk across from Dan's. In the split second before I could touch him, his big brown eyes shifted to me, terror making the pupils huge. His finger clenched, and the gun exploded with a deafening crack of thunder.

Surprise yelped out of me and I jumped. My eyes snapped shut on reflex as the warm splatter speckled my face, my hair, my shirt. The wet feel on my lips made me want to lick, but I used the back of my hand instead, scrubbing away what I knew must be blood and God knows what else. I didn't want to look, but the solid thump of a body collapsing to the floor made my eyes open.

Blood was everywhere. The officer I'd tried to help lay dead on the floor at my feet. The side of his head was a soft bloody mess. My stomach convulsed, bile shooting up, making me gag. I turned, doubled over, and heaved into the trashcan.

As quickly as I could manage, I straightened, wiping the spittle from my mouth with the back of my hand. I scanned the room, looking everywhere but at the body in front of me. Nothing else had changed. I swung my gaze to Rifion. "Bastard."

He shrugged. "Your love of me is not required. Simply your bloodline, and your womb."

In the back of my mind, I knew my body was trembling. Like a dream, I could feel my hands shaking, my knees wobbling. My chest quivered with every breath. But the rage burning through my head and heart wouldn't acknowledge any of it. "I'm not going anywhere with you."

Rifion's cool blue eyes swung to the nephilim pair at the center of the room. "Children—"

Before he could say anything more, the door to the far hallway flew open, and Officer Wysocki rushed awkwardly into the room like he'd been thrown. He landed on his knees, vanishing from my sight behind the far cluster of desks. Metal clanked against the hard linoleum floor, confirming what I thought I'd seen in his hand.

He had my sword's hilt.

My mind went quiet, focus narrowing, angelic instinct swelling to the surface all on its own. Power hummed through my veins, steeling my nerves. I took a step, and a single thought later I was beside him, scooping my sword from his gloved hand, already willing the blade to form. I breathed a sigh of relief, not just because I had my weapon but because it was out of Dan's hands. He'd touched the sword, yet he hadn't been marked. Not because of the gloves, but because he hadn't tried to use it like I had when I'd saved Tommy. At least it was one less thing I'd have to deal with.

Bullets ricocheted off the wall behind me an instant before one shot hot and fast through my left bicep. The same sensation bit the back of my calf. I didn't slow down to check the wounds. I couldn't.

Instead, I turned to Jalil, the trigger-happy demon cop, who'd held his gun at the ready since he came into the room. His aim sucked, but that wasn't stopping him from working toward an empty clip. Shots rang out in the brick-walled room, twanging off metal desks, slamming with solid thunks and bangs into everything in their path.

My vision tunneled, and I saw him at the end, gun pointed straight down the tube at me. As though the world slowed, I had all the time I needed. His finger squeezed and before it pushed the trigger all the way back, I was on him, my sword swinging.

The heavenly sharp blade met flesh and bone, spattering demon blood as it separated head from neck. My momentum spun me, turning my back to him before his body knew to drop.

The gunshots hadn't stopped. Someone else was shooting, and my gaze snapped to Dan. Still on his knees, fire exploding from the barrel of his gun, he pounded a rapid fire of bullets into Imad, the demon guarding the other door. He didn't know the man disguised as a cop was the least of our worries.

Imad's body jerked and twitched as the bullets pummeled his chest. Dan's aim was dead on, every shot straight to the heart, lethal wounds for a normal man. But Imad had never been a normal man. His body absorbed the bullets like rain on a puddle—a splat of ooze, a hole, and then the flesh healed over. That fast.

Dan emptied his clip, and then dropped behind the desks to

reload. He'd emptied the replacement clip in seconds, unable to accept what his eyes were telling him. Bullets weren't going to kill Imad.

Without the constant hammer of bullets, the silence seemed unreal, like listening through cotton balls, and it took a moment to notice the noise underneath. Someone was pounding on the squad room door. Both doors—the one Dan had forced himself through was closed again. Police from all over the building were outside the room, trying to get in, but were mysteriously kept at bay.

My gaze shifted to the Faith Harvest nephilim at the center of the room, heads down, still focusing their power. Miraculously, they hadn't been shot, but I could feel their power straining in all directions.

They'd kept a kind of protective shield around them all the while, still ruling the minds of the cops in the room. Why hadn't they made the men pull the triggers, blow their brains out, and end them as threats?

I knew the answer almost instantly. They couldn't. Nearly all their power was flooding toward the doors, working hard to convince the determined men on the other side that no matter how hard they wanted to, they could not enter the room. The effort was draining the nephilim. Human will is a powerful thing, and those cops were gaining will with every gunshot they heard.

Movement snapped my gaze back to Imad. With his body completely healed and Dan busy reloading, now was his chance to advance on Wysocki. He pulled his gun, started firing, the hypnotized cop at the corner desk helpless to get out of the way.

The shots drilled through his back, two of them exploding in a red plume from the front of his chest. He slumped out of his chair to the floor, the rest of Imad's bullets hammering the top of the now-empty desk. I had to stop Imad. Nothing else could.

"Dan," I yelled, but the gunshots were too loud, too unrelenting. I had to let him know what I needed him to do. My mind went quiet again, my will focusing.

Power hummed through my brain, stretching out of me, searching for Dan like I'd done when I'd followed Eli around the world. I found him, his thoughts shuffling fast, weighing options, concentrating on getting the new clip into the butt of his gun.

Dan, I said to his mind, and I felt him pause, stunned but listening. *Stop the couple at the center of the room before they force your buddies to pull their triggers.*

I didn't wait to see if he understood—if he'd do as I asked—I just moved, focusing my will on the demon heading for him. I had to get to Imad before he got a clear shot at Dan. The world narrowed into a long tunnel, and I took a step.

My next sent me flying backward, slamming with a lung-crushing thud into the far brick wall. My eyes focused past the ringing stars the impact had sent whirling through my brain, and I caught a glimpse of Rifion, his arm finishing the back swing that had sent me sailing. I slid down the wall, collapsing in a heap on the floor, struggling for a full breath.

"Enough," Rifion said, his voice a rumbling boom even above the sound of bullets shattering walls and ripping through metal. His tall frame towered over me. I glanced up, squinting against the brilliance of his outstretched wings.

They weren't wings in the typical sense, though I could see why they'd been described as such. The enormous translucent spread was more light than physical substance, molecules constantly moving and changing, undulating and coalescing, glimmering and fluttering in a wide halo over his shoulders and down his back to his ankles.

It was…beautiful. The shape of wings was there, faint among the blinding gleam, the shadows playing through the moving ethereal light to form the soft impression of feathers—but not.

"Selfish woman," he said, his handsome face twisted with rage. His hand shifted. A flash of light sparking off the angelic sword in his hand distracted me for an instant.

He reached for me, and like a frightened child I cowered back from his grasp. He let me.

"I'll chain you in the deepest cave I can find, use your body until it withers on your bones, and then feed your shriveled carcass to my minions," Rifion said. "You'll birth females for me until your insides tear out. And from those daughters will more of my seed beget more children, until I have an army strong enough to storm the very throne of God."

"Emma!" My gaze snapped to Dan, his gun training on Rifion, fire exploding from the barrel, though where the bullets hit I couldn't tell. The Fallen angel before me showed no signs of having been hit.

I looked to the single nephilim standing at the center of the room, her partner sprawled on the floor, bleeding from a gunshot to his side. Dan had let my situation distract him from what I'd asked him to do.

"Dan, no. Stop her. Stop the other nephilim," I said, needing Dan to take on the only semi-human threat in the room.

Officer Wysocki knew what he was doing, ducking behind the desks, avoiding Imad's wild shots, popping up to fire off a few of his own. The moment I barked the order, Dan gave three more rapid-fire shots at Imad, each one hitting the mark, then sprinted up and across the cluster of desks he'd been using for cover. Three steps and he dove at the lone nephilim, his body crushing against hers, sending them both tumbling across the floor.

As though he'd done it a million times, his cuffs were out before they'd come to a stop, and he had her hands painfully twisted behind her and ready. Impressive. But Imad had already recovered, his sights unwavering on Dan. The demon raised his gun.

Determination pulsed through my veins. I had to get to Imad before he got lucky with the spray of bullets he was throwing at Dan. I scrambled to my hands and knees, trying to get my feet under me so I could cut off the demon before it was too late.

But Rifion's iron hand gripped my left bicep, sending a stab of blinding pain searing through my body. I could feel the bullet boring deeper beneath his touch, forcing the red hot metal through meat and muscle with the power of his angelic mind. My mouth opened on a scream that stuck in my throat. I couldn't breathe for the agony of it, and my knees turned to jelly. Rifion yanked me to my feet, determined to have me or kill me.

Crap. I couldn't go out like this. I couldn't let these people pay for what I was. My jaw clenched, determination steeling my spine. I pushed the pain from my thoughts and threw my weight, trying to break his grip. I had to get to Dan, to the other cops who sat at their desks like rubber ducks in a shooting gallery, their brains sluggishly coming back under their control.

My gaze snapped to Imad, and what I saw nearly stopped my heart.

"No. You can't interfere. Rifion! Rifion, he starts the war," Imad wailed.

"Eli, no!" I said, and Rifion turned in time to see Eli's sword slice through the demon's neck with a lightning-fast, fluid grace.

Eli turned, his glacier-blue eyes fixed on Rifion, his gleaming sword in his hand. His black jacket fluttered around his calves, his midnight curls shifting against his stiff white collar in the current of his blazing power.

Behind him, translucent wings, even more brilliant than Rifion's, stretched at least nine feet wide on either side of him. The tips brushed the floor; the top arches touched the ceiling. The brilliant light they emitted haloed around his body from head to toe like a translucent neon outline.

"Mind yourself, angel. You'd start the war for this?" Rifion said, giving my wounded arm a hard shake.

Eli's gaze flicked to me. *Finish him,* he said to my mind. I didn't need to be told twice.

"No," I said, and Rifion turned his attention to me. "He's not starting a war. He's just here to watch me fight one."

I opened my gift to him, pushed my will hard and fast into his mind, like a red-hot pick through ice. Shock loosened his hold on my arm, and I spun from his grip. He staggered back, raising his sword just as I mirrored the move, sword up, ready to attack or parry.

"You'd battle an angel?" he said. "You're a fool."

"You're not an angel," I said. "You're an escaped con, and I'm Heaven's bounty hunter."

Rage gouged deep lines in his face, his eyes darkening until they were black as pitch. His snarl bared his teeth, and he let loose an unearthly growl. The sound rumbled across the floor, vibrating through my chest, and a splash of cold fear froze my heart.

I clenched my jaw. *Screw that.* "I was born for this."

Rifion advanced. He was fast, damn fast, faster than I was, but not so fast I couldn't track him. The gleam of his sword sparked in my vision as it hurtled toward my neck. I shifted, swung, and blocked, the impact rattling down my arms like a million jolts of electricity.

The fallen angel let his momentum carry him around, so I had to spin to keep him in front of me. In a whirl of golden cloth and shimmering hair, he struck again, and so did I. Our blades clashed, sparks showering between us. I twisted my wrists, turning my blade, circling his sword so his strike was deflected, pulling his arms with it. For a brief instant, his midsection was bare to me.

I spun. Thrust. And drove my sword deep, deep into his gut. Rifion doubled over, his hand grabbing the small section of my blade still outside of his body. White smoke steamed from his palm, stinking of brimstone, the sound of flesh sizzling like bacon on a griddle hissing between us. His black eyes met mine, shocked. But too quickly, his beautiful mouth slowly closed as his expression hardened into resolve, his brows knotted, his lips curling again, baring teeth. He stood, clenching his jaw against the burning flesh and yanking my blade, pulling it halfway out.

"Stupid woman," he said. "This won't kill me. It just pisses me off." He jerked again, and the full length of my sword slipped free, wet and sloppy, from his body.

The hole I'd made was already healing, the palm of his hand burned black from holding my sword. It was more than enough. "I wasn't trying to kill you, Fallen. I just wanted you to stand still for a second."

I raised the hilt to my shoulder. Power swelled inside me, humming through my veins, glowing white hot along the blade of my sword. Energy pulsed up from somewhere deep inside me, filling my mind with words that weren't my own but somehow familiar, as though buried there since my conception. "Rifion, hallowed angel fallen from grace. By the power of God, I sentence you to the abyss until the end of days."

I swung faster than human, demon, or Fallen angel could track. My sword sliced through the air, making a faint whistle as it sailed toward Rifion's neck.

The edge of my blade made contact with what was once his flesh and bone, triggering a brilliant burst of light, filling the room like a small nuclear explosion and sending me careening backward onto my butt. Fluorescent lights overhead popped and hissed, a hazy cloud billowing along the ceiling. Wind swirled from the outer edges of the room, gathering everything that had been blown outward toward the center again, forming a tornado-like funnel in the very spot Rifion had stood.

"Emma, watch out!" Dan was suddenly beside me, tucking me against him, using his body to shield mine. The air sucked from the room, drawn into the vortex. I turned my face into Dan's chest, shielding my eyes from the spinning debris, and he tucked his head against my back, both of us trying to breathe. Pressure built in my ears. My eyes hurt like my brain was swelling in my head. The inescapable energy reached critical mass a half second before the whole room shook with a deafening sonic boom.

Seconds ticked by. A strange absence of sound pulsated through the room as shredded papers, bits of carpet, and random debris floated to the floor. Everything settled.

Nothing of Rifion remained. It was over.

I straightened, Officer Wysocki still holding me close. Muscles along my shoulders eased, tension flooding out of my body like an unplugged sink. I closed my eyes, willing my heart to slow, then collapsed, boneless, into Dan's arms, fighting to catch my breath.

"Rot in Hell, Rifion."

CHAPTER TWENTY-TWO

"The suspects in yesterday's shooting, in which one police officer was killed and another seriously wounded, will be arraigned today. The shooters, Noah Caster and Grace Bookmen, deny any responsibility, despite the security footage graphically depicting their rampage."

The anchorwoman on Channel Six's news had used too much hairspray again today. I grabbed the TV remote from my nightstand but waited to see if she'd get anything right about what'd happened at the police station yesterday.

"Mr. Caster, originally from Fairfield, Iowa, and Miss Bookmen, from San Francisco, California, had come to Pittsburgh with their church, Faith Harvest, to participate in the annual revival at the David Lawrence Convention center. Both claim to have no recollection of the shooting and insist they'd come to the station to speak with police regarding the various minor arrests made during the weeklong revival."

A spike of doubt tripped my heartbeat and drained the blood from my face. After the charges against me were dropped, Dan had promised my name wouldn't be released to the press. I was an illorum, Heaven's bounty hunter, but I still had my day job to worry about.

Reputation takes forever to build and a second to destroy, and no one wants a tarot card reading from an ex-con. At least not at the rates I charge. Plus, I seriously did not want to have to explain to my mother why I'd been arrested for waving a sword around at a religious convention. She didn't like when I sent food back at a restaurant. She thought *that* was making a scene.

"Channel Six contacted Faith Harvest Church for a comment, but our calls were never returned," the anchorwoman said. "However, minutes before airing, we received a fax stating that Richard Hubert, a recognizable figure in the controversial church, has left on sabbatical with no word when he'll return."

Can you call a trip to Hell a sabbatical? I jabbed the power button with my thumb and tossed the remote onto my unmade bed. Thanks to Rifion's nephilim mind trick, the officers who were in the room with us didn't remember much after Grace and Noah took control of them.

They looked to Dan and me to fill in the blanks. Dan went along with my version of events, mostly because he wasn't sure he knew what'd happened either. Rigging the security tape to match our story was Eli's handiwork. Of course, now I had to explain it all to Dan. But I didn't really mind. It'd be nice having someone normal— not to mention cute—to talk to about all the craziness in my life.

My gaze drifted to the world map I'd snagged from Tommy's apartment and my heart gave a sad tug. Would I ever stop missing him? I'd tacked his map on my wall just like he had, and I'd managed to keep all the strings and pictures connected. I probably wouldn't keep track of my kindred like he had, but looking at it reminded me of him, helped ease the lonely spot he'd left inside me. Seeing how many people out there were just like me helped too. It really was a kind of comfort. I sighed, my gaze flicking to the neon-green numbers on my alarm clock.

It was already 6:25, and Dan would be around to pick me up any minute. I checked myself in the mirror. I was going for a casual *this isn't a date, but don't you wish it was* look. The stretchy mauve top clung to my curves, making me look good, but not like I was trying. I'd add my black cotton bolero jacket before we left. My good jeans, the ones that hugged my butt without flattening too much, plus my black, pointy-toed boots gave me just enough dress-up without the fuss.

The doorbell rang, and I wasted another second or two fluffing my hair, checked the small amount of makeup I'd put on, and adjusted the little dangly heart earrings I'd picked out. After I centered the matching silver heart necklace, I jogged downstairs to open the door.

"Eli."

Resting a shoulder against the doorjamb, he gave a small bow. Very old-world, very sexy. "Emma Jane."

"Why'd you ring? I've invited you in before."

"Yes. But I know how you treasure the illusion of privacy."

"Right." I gave him a sarcastic wink and one thumbs-up. "Thanks. You're a prince."

His gaze traveled the length of me and back. "You're going out for the evening?"

"Yeah." I shrugged. "Dan Wysocki's picking me up."

"The police officer?"

"Yeah."

"The *nephilim* police officer?"

"That's the one."

He raised a questioning brow.

"What?"

"You'll bring him into the fold tonight?"

"Hell, no." I walked into my office. Eli followed, closing the front door behind him. "This isn't even an official date. I'm not sure I'll kiss him, let alone screw up his whole life."

"What is it, if not a date?" Eli asked.

"An exchange," I said. "I'm going to tell him what I know about my angelic sperm donor, and he's going to use his connections to help me get a lead on him."

"Romantic."

"You bet." I hiked a shoulder. "Besides, the ink's still too fresh on Dan's divorce papers. Anyone he dates now is either revenge or a replacement, and that ain't me."

"And in exchange for his help?" Eli asked.

"I fill him in on all the fun demon-hunting, sword-fighting, acidy-brimstone details that go with being the spawn of a fallen angel."

"You know if you allow him to be marked, I can help explain everything? It's what I do," he said.

"Dan's already doing his part for humanity by being a cop. He's got kids, Eli. I'm not going to be the one to take him away from them. Besides, if you had recognized the picture of my dad, I wouldn't need to ask Dan for help."

"Yes. It's unfortunate the picture from your aunt's scrapbook wasn't clearer." Eli glanced away, a strange look haunting his expression before he banished it. "As for Officer Wysocki, not everyone resents the call to duty. Some find it a noble and satisfying use of God's gift."

"Oh yeah? Bet they don't date much." I snagged my purse from the couch and brought it over to the desk, where I could transfer the basic necessities into the tiny black clutch. The little purse went great with my jacket and boots. Not that it mattered, 'cause this wasn't a *date* date. *Riiiggght.*

"Thomas never complained about such petty things."

I turned, mouth agape. "Petty? Sex is not petty. Sex is…sex is… *SEX.* It's like eating and sleeping, it's what makes life worth all the crap you have to go through. Hell, it's what makes life possible." This was pointless. Look who I was telling.

He glanced away. "I thought this wasn't an official date."

My mouth snapped shut. I sighed, deflating a little. "That's beside the point. Anyway, just because Tommy didn't complain doesn't mean he didn't think about it. Trust me."

Memories of our kiss flickered through my mind, warmed my heart, and made my throat tight. *Crap.* I didn't want to cry. I turned and went back to figuring out how to make my six-inch wallet fit into my four-inch clutch.

"He's in a better place, Emma Jane," Eli said. I could feel him close behind me. We weren't touching, but then, we didn't have to. His power pulsed around him like an electric force field. I could feel the warmth of it tingling up my back. The smell of sunshine and fresh summer breezes swirled through me, and I closed my eyes, sneaking a quick, indulging breath.

His hands warmed my shoulders, his touch instantly easing the ache in my heart, the tension in my muscles. He was getting better at comforting me without turning me on, but the line was razor thin, and too often I held my breath wondering if he'd cross it—secretly hoping that he would. He didn't. But the wondering, the anticipation, was just as arousing.

I licked my lips, cleared my throat, and tried to focus my

thoughts. "Have you seen him?"

"Seen who?" Eli questioned, and I could hear the soft rasp of his voice. I wasn't the only one feeling the tempting heat between us.

"Tommy. Have you seen him since…You know, seen him up there?" I gestured with a quick twist of my wrist, though I knew Heaven wasn't so much up as not where we were.

"Emma Jane, I…" His hands dropped away, and I turned to face him.

"What?" He looked stricken, heartbroken even, his eyes downcast, his mouth a thin drooping line. *Shit*. "He's not there, is he? I knew it. He's not in Heaven."

My gut pinched, turned to ice. This was exactly what I was afraid of. No matter what we did, no matter how hard we tried, we'd never be forgiven. We were paying for a sin that wasn't ours. How can anyone make up for that?

I felt sick, not wanting to think about it, but not able to stop. Where had Tommy's soul been sent? What does God do with a product of sin? I really didn't want to think about it, but my brain was stuck.

Eli closed the small distance between us, his hands coming up to cup my cheeks. Our eyes locked. "Emma Jane, I'm sure Thomas has received his reward. I'm sure," he said. "I haven't seen him, because I'm not allowed."

"Why?"

His thumbs caressed my cheeks, the soft sensation so comforting my thoughts went fuzzy at the edges. "Because of my closeness to humans, to you and the other illorum I train, and the toll it takes on me to leave you."

I leaned back, freeing my face from the frame of his hands. It was just too hard to think with him touching me. "I don't understand."

"Leaving Paradise is not an easy thing, Emma Jane," he said. "Leaving those so dear to me is a near-impossible feat. Going back and forth between the two realms, witnessing such profound beauty and serenity, would be an unnecessary distraction for my existence here."

"Wait. How long has it been since you've gone…home?"

He glanced away, thinking, then back, his hands slipping into the pockets of his slacks. "I don't know exactly, but not since after Jeannette was taken from me. I returned to my brothers for a time and was nearly unable to force myself to come back to Earth. After that, my brothers thought it best that I stay here until my duty is complete."

"You can't go home until *all* the Fallen are chained in the abyss?" And I thought the illorum got a raw deal.

He blinked at my expression, and a smile blossomed across his face as laughter bubbled out of him. "Don't look so sorry for me, Emma Jane. I don't mind. My duty is my life, the reason I exist. Besides, I like it here, and the company's not so bad."

Heat washed through my cheeks, and I glanced away, feeling my smile tugging the corners of my mouth. Thoughts of Tommy tempered my mood again. "So what you're saying is, you don't know for sure if Tommy was accepted into Paradise."

"Life is the gift," he said. "Heaven is the reward for a life well lived. Tommy lived well. Toward the end he lived better than most, using the gift of life he'd been given to serve God. He received his reward."

I nodded, forced a smile, though the muscles that held it trembled with the effort. I sighed and tried to take comfort in Eli's certainty. The truth was, he didn't know much more than the rest of us. "Faith, right?"

He smiled. "Exactly."

Must be nice. I sighed and tried with all my will to push the worry from my mind. Turning back to my two purses, I opened my wallet, looking for essentials. "Right. At least all the rest of Tommy's siblings are free to lead normal lives."

"Yes," Eli said. "Although if any of Rifion's biological children were among those whose power he triggered prematurely, the release from the burden of his sin may not have the same effect."

I looked over my shoulder at him. "You mean they might still have their nephilim powers?"

"I don't know, but it's definitely something we need to address," he said. "If their angelic halves had been left dormant or at least activated like a regular illorum, they'd have lost the power and gone back to a normal life the instant you sent their angelic father to the abyss. With this new turn of events, the outcome is uncertain. It's our duty to determine what's become of all those Rifion corrupted."

"Okay. Sure," I said, turning back to my purse. "But not tonight. Tonight, it's just nice to have an evening without worrying some crazy demon will show up and try to hack my head off."

"But you're taking your sword, nonetheless," Eli said.

"Why? The only Fallen that knew about me is cooling his heels in the abyss now," I said, pulling out my license, my only credit card, and the twelve bucks I had in my wallet and stuffing them into my clutch.

"That doesn't mean he was the only Fallen in the area, or that his were the only demons watching."

I snapped the clutch closed and turned. "Right." Pleasant thought, that. "Speaking of watching. Are they? I mean, the Council, are they still watching you? I haven't seen any angels hanging around on roof tops."

"Neither have I, but that only means the Council watchers don't wish to be seen," he said. "Whatever made them begin their scrutiny of me, their interest is not likely to wane for some time."

"Right. 'Cause time isn't really an issue for you guys," I said, forcing a happy smile I didn't really feel at the moment. "Any fallout from you lending your sword to the fight yesterday?"

"There's been no word on the matter," he said.

"They're still deciding what to do?"

"There's been no word at all. No discussion. No mention of the incident. It didn't happen."

A cover-up? Sheesh, these guys were more like humans than I thought. "Good thing there's nobody left to say differently. Glad I'm on your side."

"It was my fault," Eli said. "I allowed myself to become distracted. Many of the events yesterday caught me ill prepared. I did not expect Rifion to so willingly expose himself to humans, simply to kill an illorum."

"You were surprised, too?" I said with no small amount of sarcasm. "'Cause someone assured me that wouldn't happen."

Eli shrugged. "Fallen are unpredictable. He must've sensed something about you that heightened his paranoia."

"It's only paranoia if they're not really out to get you."

"Very true." Eli acquiesced with another sexy old-world bow. "And a mind constantly on guard against an unseen threat doesn't often follow a logical course."

"Ah, the old catch twenty-two. They're only after you because you're crazy. But them constantly coming after you, y'know, makes you crazy," I said, collecting my house keys. "And Rifion was crazy's daddy. He wanted me on his side, or dead."

"I'm glad you were able to resist," Eli said. "Not everyone can.

Succumbing to their passions seems to make the Fallen particularly gifted at temptation. It's quite remarkable that you not only possess the strength of will to resist them, but something about you seems to be a temptation they themselves cannot resist."

The doorbell rang, and I hooked the thin strap of my clutch over my shoulder, pride stretching my smile from ear to ear. "Hellsbane. It's not just my name," I said. "It's what I am."

Acknowledgments

Thanks to Ashley and Katie for all your support. Thank you to the ladies of Entangled Publishing for your bravery, your ability to see outside the box, and your courage to make yours and my dreams a reality. And thank you to Stacy for her amazing editing and firefighting skills. Who knew there were so many fires to put out in publishing? You rock!

BONUS MATERIAL

Keep reading for a scene in Eli's point of view!

CHAPTER NINE

Part II

Eli sets the world at Emma's feet.

My chest squeezed, memories threatening to consume me. I'd lost sweet Jeannette more than five hundred years ago and still the thought of her could bring me to my knees. A flaw I knew could likely be the end of me one day. But not today. Today I worried for another young mortal woman struggling with the heavy weight of her birthright and all the blessings and horrors it bestowed.

"Joan of Arc died, Eli. I don't want to end up the same way." Emma Jane's voice trembled with fear, despite the effort she always took to hide it. "This may come as a shock to you, but I don't want to have my head hacked off or be burned at the stake or have my arms and legs tied to four horses while they run in opposite directions."

"I don't want you to die either, Emma Jane." I rose, ignoring the sorrow still weighing heavily inside me. The night air was warm and the cool breeze that washed up the hillside to the overlook helped to clear my head.

"Right," she said. "That might go over better if I didn't know most illorum die under your watch."

Emma Jane was bright, and braver than she gave herself credit for. She reminded me so much of my Jeannette. Too much. "You're fighting creatures stronger and more cunning than anything on earth. Their desperation makes them driven, not stupid. Naturally, there's some risk."

"Yeah, I'm picking up on that." She forced a smile.

"You were born for this," I said, wishing she could see the power and strength…and the beauty with which she'd been blessed. "I'll practice with you. Help you develop your angelic gifts."

"Why? So I can die with skill? No thanks."

The comment struck at me like a white-hot knife, searing me straight through to my heart. I'd given Jeannette every advantage of my knowledge; trained her to be a living, breathing weapon; and for all of it, she was struck down nonetheless. Standing by while Jeannette suffered as she had, dying slowly as the flames ate at her flesh, had nearly ended me. The mere thought that I might be forced to stand witness as Emma Jane endured even half that would surely send me to the very gates of the abyss.

It was a risk I'd known full well when I'd taken on her training. So why had I accepted this intimate connection with her and foolishly bargained my eternal spirit to prepare for a battle that might end us both?

I didn't know.

But when I'd first watched her in the parking lot of Saint Anthony's Chapel, blond hair speckled with demon blood, blue eyes wide and defiant as she'd stared into the face of evil, something inside me awakened. Something that was never meant to stir within the spirit of angels was born in that moment. I knew it then as I know it now—and have resisted it, denied it, every second since.

"I want to go home," she said.

"Emma Jane, don't you know how lucky you are? How special?" I bit back my words, raw emotion recklessly revealing more than I should.

She snorted. "Right. Lucky me."

Such a stubborn woman. Yet I couldn't deny how she amused me. "Come." Tempering my smile, I held out a hand to her. "I have something to show you."

She didn't move at first. I could sense her body's response to me, heartbeat racing, desire moistening deep within her.

"I'm outta here," she finally said, and turned from me.

With an easy thought, I moved into her path, too quickly for her to see, too quickly even for her to stop before she crushed her face into my chest. Her scent engulfed me: raspberry shampoo, baby powder, and a hint of vanilla in her fragrant perfume. My body tightened and I closed my eyes for a moment, gathering restraint.

She bounced back, rubbing her nose. "Hey. That's not cool."

"Perhaps you've mistaken my statement for a request." I forced a smile. "It wasn't."

"Ah. So it's like that, is it?"

I reached for her before my brain could think better of it, looping an arm around her waist, tugging her hard against me. Her soft feminine body molded to mine, her breath escaping in a small gasp. She braced her hands on my chest and I swallowed down a dangerous surge of desire.

"Yes," I said. "It's like that."

I could move us at the speed of thought, but Emma Jane's human brain would instinctively struggle to match the quick slip of time and space. For her, I transported us at a more sedate pace, though it was still faster than any mere human could track. In an instant the world around us vanished and we plunged into the cool, eternal stillness of space.

All around, distant stars twinkled in the vast emptiness and my mind went quiet. This far from the earth below, the constant din of human thought that always echoed through my mind faded to a soft whisper. I relished this escape, often seeking out the muffling comfort of space. Though I'd never appreciated it more than since meeting Emma Jane. Perhaps that was the true reason I chose to bring her to my silent sanctuary—it was where my mind was unhampered by earthly influences and my thoughts often turned to her.

Her fear lanced through me, her arms clamping around my neck bringing us cheek to cheek. I closed my eyes, the warmth of her skin like the brush of heaven on my face. "You're safe in my arms, Emma Jane. Always," I said, and felt her body shudder against me.

She leaned back enough to look at me, her blue eyes wide. Blink by blink, trust replaced fear and a smile hinted at the very corners of her mouth. Carefully, I withdrew the invisible shield of my power surrounding her, and her smile vanished. Her gaze unfocused, brows creasing as her mind worked hard to follow the fold in time we'd created in order to travel so quickly.

She held a hand to her forehead. "What was that?"

It was as I'd feared. I'd transported us too swiftly. "Your mind is struggling to match speed with your body. May I help?"

She'd told me once that she didn't want me to use my power to ease the burdens of her new duties, but she couldn't truly comprehend how instinctive the urge to care for her was. Like raising your hands to stop a fall or closing your eyes during a sneeze, it could not be helped. But for her, because she'd requested it of me, I tried.

She nodded and I pressed my hand to hers, sending my power into her, calming the spin of her mind, stilling its struggle—then took my hand away.

"I hoped moving slower would help lessen the shock, but it seems the effect allowed your vision too much time to try and compensate." Guilt squeezed my chest that I had caused her even a moment's discomfort.

"We moved at angelic speed?" she asked.

"No. I am able to travel at the speed of thought. We moved an increment slower."

"Um, thanks," she said, distracted by the scene—or lack of scene—around us. She squirmed against me, as though trying to get her footing. She couldn't, of course; there was nothing to stand on. We were adrift in space.

She looked at her feet and terror stiffened her to stone.

I gathered her close again, using my body to give her a sense of stability.

"Where are we?" she asked.

"Look behind you."

She glanced over her shoulder. "Is that…"

"Earth," I finished for her.

Finally, as though the reality of who she was and what she could do had overcome her fear, she turned. Like a kitten in the center of an ocean scrambling for a scrap of dry land, Emma Jane placed her small feet on top of mine, comforted by the only solid footing to be had, and balanced in my embrace to see the beauty of her world below.

I kept my hands on her hips, her back pressed snuggly to my

chest, and told myself it was only to make her feel safe.

"This can't be real. How?" she asked.

Her awe, her humility in the face of Father's work — in the face of her own potential — weakened me. I couldn't resist the temptation to pull her close. My arms around her waist, I whispered in her ear. "In the arms of an angel, Emma Jane, all things are possible."

Her body relaxed against mine.

"Behold what your birthright has brought you, Emma Jane," I said. "No mortal human could claim as much."

"It's amazing, Eli. Thank you."

"This is only the beginning," I said softly and took a secret pleasure in feeling her tremble at the sound of my voice. "You have been chosen to battle creatures far more powerful than mere mortals. You are not like other humans; you cannot be. Your task requires much of you, and for it, much has been given. Time and space unravel for you to traverse with the same intrinsic understanding as those you hunt. The world is quite literally at your feet."

Holding her near enough so my power protected her like an impenetrable shield, I transported us back to Earth to begin the next step in her training. I set her beside me and, when I knew she was balanced, released her from my protection. For me it was an easy progression, one thing done before the next. But to Emma Jane, it would seem as though one moment we were floating above the world and the next she was staring out over a large valley and the ocean beyond. She blinked at a waking cityscape miles below with large water inlets and busy harbors.

A fast wind tugged at her hair, the blond strands battering against her face, catching at the corners of her mouth. She held back the wild strands with one hand and yelled, "Where are we?"

We couldn't converse this way. That was the only reason I

reached out and pulled her to me, tucking her under my arm, extending my power to protect her again. Her hair settled, and the wind no longer touched us.

"Brazil." I pointed at the cityscape below us. "Rio de Janeiro."

"It's beautiful," she said.

I watched as she took in her surroundings, utterly unaware of how her nearness tempted the very core of my spirit. Her small hand grabbed the lapel of my jacket and she leaned over. "No way. Christ the Redeemer? Seriously?"

We were on the arm of the enormous statue, his white stone face looming like a small mountain to our left. "Remarkable, isn't it? And yet it pales in comparison to the miracle that is you and those like you."

Emma Jane tipped her chin at the milling crowds and the long procession of humans still climbing the mountain below. "They don't see us?"

"As in everything, humans only see what they wish to see, what is easily explainable—what is normal." Emma Jane still struggled to accept that human limitations no longer held sway over her. Not unusual for new illorum. Inevitably, however, I knew they must accept it as fact. "You could reach this spot on your own. It's within your abilities."

"Really? How?"

"Speed of movement is the key. If not for the physiology of humans, illorum could travel from place to place instantaneously like their fathers," I said. "But even moving faster than light, there are few places in the world you cannot reach."

"Sweet." She smiled and my chest tightened. "What do I do? Is there a magic word or something?"

"Put the image of where you would like to go in your mind,"

I said. "Allow your desire to stand in that exact spot fill you. Then take a step."

I touched her thoughts, reading the quick succession of her decision-making. She wanted to be sitting on the stone railing that edged the base of the statue far below. When she closed her eyes, I teleported to the spot she'd brought to her mind.

Unfortunately, she over-aimed and went careening into the low stone wall. Much as I should have, I couldn't allow her to injure herself further, so, lightning fast, I scooped an arm around her waist, steadying her.

Still, she'd done well for her first try. Very well. I sensed she was actually far more powerful than any other illorum I'd trained. There was a reason for her unusual strength—I was certain of it—but I wasn't ready to worry about that yet. Watching her discover her emerging abilities was the one pleasure I was permitted. Nothing would have me forfeit this time with her.

Emma Jane turned and sat on the railing next to me. I leaned close to her. "Don't aim into solid objects; you'll hit them."

"Thanks for the warning."

"I thought it went without saying."

"You thought wrong."

"Obviously," I said, pushing to my feet, needing to regain the space between us—needing to rein in my control. "Would you like to try again?"

She cleaned off her hands. "Where to? Some place soft?"

"The choice is yours," I said. "I will know it when the image enters your mind."

"Okay. We've been to Christ the Redeemer," she said. "Let's not play favorites. Ready?"

I agreed by way of a bow an instant before I touched her mind.

Her destination was clear, like a neon sign flashing in her mind—the eighty-eight-foot Buddha statue atop Elephant Rock in Kurunegala.

The instant the thought entered my mind, I was there, waiting for Emma Jane, smug with my superior speed. My thoughts petrified, however, the moment the determined woman appeared, stumbling across the folded lap of the Buddha like a freight train off its tracks.

Naturally, I caught her, her feminine body colliding into mine, her warm cheek pressing against my neck, her sweet flowery scent exploding around me like a puff of smoke. I breathed her in, battling its decimating effect on my resolve.

This was such folly. I knew it—yet I ignored it.

My palms held the feminine curves of her hips as she braced her hands on my arms, pushing up to look me in the eyes.

"You beat me here," she said as I quickly set her on her feet, sparing myself any further torment.

But my hands still tingled with the feel of her, and a dangerous part of me wanted to take hold of her again. I rubbed the sensation away, one thumb against the other palm. The effort was useless, so my traitorous hands cupped behind my back instead.

"My angelic speed is faster," I said, pointedly steering my thoughts away from desire. "The Fallen travel an increment slower, but still faster than any illorum I've known. Most demons move slower than light, but far faster than anything humans can visibly track."

She nodded in understanding—so bright, so beautiful…so dangerous. My body warmed, face suddenly hot. What was I doing? Why was I courting this disaster? There were hundreds of magisters capable of taking up her training—hundreds who would not feel the soul-deep lure of her as I did. But it was that strange attraction, that inexplicable connection, that had pushed me to interfere with her destiny at the Church in Pittsburgh, and that left me no choice but to take on her training. It was the same serendipitous attraction that made turning from her now a pointlessly painful act.

I was meant to be this woman's magister, just as volcanoes are meant to erupt and tsunamis are meant to wash across land — inevitable, unstoppable, and most often deadly.

I swallowed hard, accepting my fate and at the same time knowing I must struggle to resist it. "This time," I said, and waited for her to turn back from enjoying the view, "you follow me."

"Where are you going?"

"See it in my thoughts."

"Of course. Um, how?"

I smiled, though my hands trembled at the thought of what I was suggesting. I clasped my hands in front of me. "I'm not shielding. Simply find me in your mind and my thoughts will open to you."

"Right." She sighed, closing her eyes.

The touch of her thoughts to mine was distinctly feminine, feather light at first and then stronger with each passing second, like the sensual squeeze of her hand. Her mind slipped through mine, finding my love for her, a love not so unlike the love I felt for all illorum — and yet nothing like it at all. She couldn't know that, though, and so I relaxed, allowed her to push further.

Her body trembled and warmed with mine when she sensed her effect on me, the way the feel of her still haunted over my skin and stirred deep at my core. An easy nudge turned her from the embarrassing truth and pointed her toward the destination I held in wait for her.

Emma Jane's skill at traversing another's mind was beyond the norm. She'd had access to the gift most of her life, though she'd only just barely scratched the surface of her abilities until now. I could show her how to truly flex the power she'd been born with, and I realized her strength was even greater than I'd imagined.

Follow me to the Shiva. Bangalore, I said in a rush, amidst the erotic caress of her mental touch, and then escaped. I moved to the spot in India I'd shown her the instant it crystallized in her mind.

Far quicker than I'd anticipated, she walked across the black stone floor to me. I held my position, leaning against the guardrail at the base of the Hindu deity's statue and trying hard to appear unimpressed.

Her abilities were staggering. Far more than I'd ever seen. I didn't know what it meant, the triumph or peril it might herald. But I couldn't let her see my concern. If Emma Jane were to have any chance at all of being a force of good, she must believe to the very base of her soul that she was good. We all must.

Emma Jane's smile stretched with pride as she glanced up into the face of the four-armed statue.

"Remarkable, isn't it?" I asked when she was near enough. It wasn't as large as the Buddha, but the stone man still towered high over her.

"Pretty sweet. A little effeminate. Whatever. Could do without the snakes." She looked back to me. "So how'd you like the entrance? No slamming into things or stumbling. Smoooooth as glass. Pretty slick, huh?"

I cleared my throat, stiffening, wanting to test how truly powerful she might one day be. "Indeed. With each flex of your angelic abilities, your control sharpens. Shall we go again? Follow me, Emma Jane."

I turned and walked toward a canvas awning, where a crowd of tourists stood in line. For the briefest of moments I held in my thoughts the image of rocky cliffs and the towering water of Angel

Falls, then I left her. A moment later she stood next to me in the dim early morning light, a warm breeze ruffling through her hair. Pride and trepidation filled my chest and tempered my smile.

"Wow. How far down is it?" she asked.

We both leaned forward. The mist from Angel Falls cooled the air and flavored the breeze with the earthy tastes of the forest.

"Over nine hundred meters," I said. "More than three thousand feet."

"Cool. Angel Falls. Venezuela, right?"

"Yes."

"Nice they named it after you guys."

"Fitting, I think." I met her eyes, deciding at that moment to push the test even further. Without warning, I chose our next destination. I knew by the look on her face she understood the direction of my thoughts and instantly felt her mental touch igniting a warm shiver through my body. I ran from the unsettling temptation under the guise of our game.

A heartbeat and a half later—even quicker than before—she walked across the wide head of the Sphinx where I waited and stopped next to me. I could feel the soft brush of her mind on mine, the sensation quickly becoming a guilty addiction. She was already open to me, ready for the next test.

A dry desert wind pulled at the edges of my jacket and knotted the blond strands of her hair. I blinked up at the sky and the afternoon sun. As strong as she was, this was only the beginning. How much more powerful might she be?

You must move faster, Emma Jane. Reason quicker; open your mind to your prey on reflex. I knew she was listening. I could feel her there in my mind. And I liked it.

"I'm trying," she said.

I fixed my gaze on hers. "There's one more thing I wish to show you."

"Lucky me." There was a hint of irritation in her voice, but she asked, "What is it?"

Only this. Capri, Italy. Walk with me in Augusto's gardens. I spoke directly to her mind. It was different than waiting for her to search my thoughts and find my words. This time I placed my voice inside her head, knew the effect my voice had on her.

Father, help me.

I closed my eyes and vanished.

I waited for her on the wide terracotta-tiled terrace, leaning against the high stone wall that lined the edge of a cliff. Far below, the Mediterranean Sea crashed over large boulders, the water so clear I could see the underwater vegetation swaying in the current. It was a beautiful day on the Italian island, and my heart raced, anticipating Emma Jane's arrival.

Tour groups marched by, following guides as they recited practiced scripts, relaying dry antidotes about the gardens and Augusto's time here. I smiled, hearing the watered-down history and pretending I wasn't near breathless for Emma Jane's arrival. Never had I been so aware of time, each passing second practically an audible tick in my ear.

It was taking too long. I straightened, restless to go find her, to have her there. She'd proven herself a quick study—more than capable, and yet I struggled to remain the objective observer as never I had before.

Just when I'd nearly reached the limits of my restraint, I saw her. She raced with blinding speed, seeming to appear out of thin air. None of the humans mulling through the gardens noticed as she stepped up beside them, her bright eyes scanning the crowd...

searching for me.

She didn't see me, her view blocked by others each time her gaze swung my way. I took a moment to watch her, the grace of her movements, the power glowing under her skin. *Amazing.* But I'd waited long enough.

I pushed from the railing and stepped around a young family of four, the parents eager to point out the beauty and history that surrounded their children. She didn't turn until I spoke. "Well done, Emma Jane."

Her surprise at finally seeing me jolted through my heart an instant before her desire slipped like hot lava straight down to my center. I banished the maddening sensation and allowed pride to stretch my smile.

"Eli. Y'think? You know, I've never been here before. I didn't even know Capri was an island. I almost didn't make it."

I gave a shallow bow. "That was the point. To force you to think on your feet, to use your instincts, your innate abilities to track and hunt."

"Yeah? Well, here's some news. Apparently I speak Italian now," she said.

"You are able to understand all languages," I said. "Some are more difficult to speak. It's a simple matter of training the tongue."

"Nifty." She shrugged. "So, where to next?"

I reached for her hand, my power reflexively spreading out to envelop her. The next moment I transported us deeper into the gardens, past the terracotta-tiled grounds, giving way to a lava stone path. Water babbled in a small fountain in front of us, and the path we stood on traced in a circle around it. Trees and flowerbeds filled the rolling landscape, the grass meticulously cut and lusciously green, the air fragrant and sweet on my tongue.

Emma Jane's wide blue eyes darted from one flowering plant to the next, quickly taking in her new surroundings. A small twinge of guilt pinched at the back of my neck. I should not take such pleasure in her company. But watching her childlike awe and the quick working of her mind was such a joy—and such a danger.

Suddenly her enthusiasm shifted, pain lancing across her milky white face. She flinched and stared at the illorum mark on her wrist. Her skin burned like fire, and I felt her pain sizzle through me. It was a signal, a warning, to let her know a Fallen was near.

I searched the garden. He should be very near to trigger her mark. Then I saw him, and anger exploded through my chest. John of Lancaster, first duke of Bedford.

The bastard who'd killed Jeannette.

It was hard to breathe. I'd end him before I let him near Emma Jane. "Stay here."

In less than an instant I'd moved across the gardens to where his horde of demons, masquerading as human beings, followed a very human tour guide. I stopped behind the last in line—ten demons plus the duke in all. I didn't know the Fallen's given name. In truth it was our rule not to acknowledge a Fallen's existence at all. But rules seemed less dogmatic where Emma Jane was concerned. So I called him by the only name left to me. "John of Lancaster."

The tall man in the center of the group stopped and turned. He looked much as he had the last time I'd seen him more than five hundred years before. A middle-aged man, athletic, with corn-silk blond hair, cut short and feathered to the side. Although back then he'd worn loose cotton shirts and thick leather vests, chainmail, and armor, now he presented himself as a modern man, responsible-looking, with a short-sleeved blue shirt untucked from his beige cargo shorts.

It was all a lie.

"Elizal, you deign to speak to me?" he said, his demon minions parting around him, leaving the two of us to face each other. "You risk war, brother."

"We are not brothers," I said. "And I risk nothing but the purity of my own spirit."

He snorted, looking away and back again. "What do you want?"

I glanced at Emma Jane. She was strong, an extraordinarily quick learner, but she was still so new to this reality, to this fight. She'd never survive against a horde this large—not to mention a Fallen as old as John of Lancaster.

"Ah…" he said, noticing the direction of my glance. "We have a warrior in our midst." His demons behind him had already picked up her scent—raising their human noses, sniffing the air. Brimstone wafted up from their skin, excitement electrifying among them.

"Again, Elizal?" He *tsk*ed. "The last time we spoke, you begged mercy for your female illorum. And when I refused, you stood by while the flames ate away her flesh. Would you sacrifice another of your warriors to maintain peace in a war the Council created?"

Anger jolted through me, but I would not let him pull me into the ancient argument. "Please. She is no danger to you. Her power has only just been awakened."

His smile was wicked. "What better time to strike her down?"

"I will not permit it." Until that moment I hadn't known what lengths I would go to protect Emma Jane. I knew now—there was no limit, no line I wouldn't cross. I was doomed and I couldn't care.

"No?" The Fallen raised a brow at me, his smile fading. "And yet you refused to do half as much for young Jeannette. I was certain you loved her, but this one…this one heralds your fall. What's her name?"

I blinked at the question, but answered. "Emma Jane. Emma Jane Hellsbane."

He looked back to her. "Hellsbane…"

"Yes, but—"

"I won't stay my forces." He looked back to me, his face stone cold and serious. "Understood? You have less than no time to take her before our hands are forced and the war begun."

It was a contradiction, of course. His demons should've already set upon Emma Jane as we spoke. They hadn't. He'd given me the sliver of time I needed to save her and with it a way to walk the razors edge of our treaty with the Fallen. I was forbidden from interfering between illorum and their battles with demons and the Fallen. I could, however, end our training early—coincidentally, moments before a demon horde took notice of her and attacked. A thin excuse at best, but I'd take it.

I was at Emma Jane's side at the same instant the desire to be there occurred in my mind. "We have to go."

"Why? Who is that?" Her gaze shifted past me to the Fallen. "Oh shit."

"Exactly." I took her hand.

"No. Wait," she said. "That was a Fallen."

"Yes."

"You know him. Who is he?" she asked, too clever sometimes for her own good.

"The Duke of Bedford."

"The Fallen who killed Joan of Arc?"

"Yes."

Her gaze shifted back to the seething wickedness behind me and I could hear her mind working through the contradiction of what they were and their innocuous appearance.

We were running out of time we didn't have. "You must let me take you from this place."

"Those are demons, aren't they?" she asked.

"Yes."

"You're interfering?"

"No. I'm simply ending our training session and returning you to your home." The demon horde was twenty feet back, but I could feel them nearing, I could smell the brimstone thickening with their excitement.

Emma Jane met my eyes. "You're asking me to run from a fight?"

I glanced at the demons and then back to her. "Yes."

"Well…just this once…I'm okay with that."

My will asserted, transporting us to safety and despite my reasoning, in my heart I knew for the first time in my eons of existence I'd purposely defied my Father's wishes.